Island
Runaway

Alex Strong

Red Dahlia Publishing

Island Runaway

ISBN: 978-0-9913614-1-0

I dedicate this book to my husband for supporting me and for never losing faith in me, even when I sometimes lost it in myself.

One

THE NIGHT STARTED out pleasant enough, but quickly turned sour. Elana was working her usual Friday night shift at Bar Acuda, the wine and tapas bar in the small town of Hanalei on the island of Kauai. Her co-worker stepped out for a cigarette, and not wanting to leave anything on the hot plate for too long, Elana collected one of Janelle's orders. She added the bruschetta and flank steak skewers to the collection of small plates on a table surrounded by a boisterous group of guys.

"Elana Tanner?" said a man's voice from her left.

She looked for the speaker, wondering who could possibly know her, and gasped.

"It is you," he said through gritted teeth.

How many times had Elana imagined coming face to face with him and all the things she would say? Yet here it was and she could only stand there speechless, having never expected the opportunity to ever arise.

The tray in her clammy hand still had two glasses of wine on it for another table, but she didn't care. She thrust it into the hands of a nearby busboy and rushed to the back where she could think.

Her manager walked by, calling out to one of the chefs.

"Jack," she said quickly. "I'm not feeling well. I need to go home."

His brow furrowed in concern, but Elana's unwelcomed guest came barging into the kitchen before Jack could say anything.

"Hey!" said Kyle, pointing an accusing finger at her. His angular jaw clenched and his brown eyes locked with hers, causing her heart to race with fear. He wouldn't really hurt her here in front of everyone, would he?

"Excuse me, sir, but you aren't supposed to be back here," said Jack.

"Well, you should think twice about allowing people like her to work here. She's a god-damned murderer!"

"What?" Jack asked. He must have thought Kyle was just some raving lunatic.

"Not only is she a murderer," said Kyle, not taking his eyes off Elana, "but she's a coward as well."

Elana's hands flew to her hips. "How dare you!"

Jack placed a hand on her arm to silence her. "Sir, if you don't leave now, I'm going to have to call the authorities."

"Don't worry," Kyle said, narrowing his eyes at her. "I'm going. The last place I want to be is a place that is willing to hire her." He turned and stormed back out to the dining area.

Elana followed Jack to the door where they watched Kyle gather his friends, throw down a wad of cash, and shove his way through a crowd at the front door.

Jack turned to face her. "What the hell was that all about? Why did he call you a murderer? Do you *know* him?"

Elana closed her eyes and took a breath. It was all she could do not break down in tears right here in front of her boss. She did her best to regain her composure and re-opened them.

"I know *of* him. His name is Kyle, Kyle Barnett. Technically we've never been formally introduced."

"And the murder comment?"

Elana paused even longer this time. Maybe if she stood quiet long enough, the question would somehow disappear. The wrinkle in Jack's forehead deepened as he continued to stare at her.

She pursed her lips for a second and then said, "I'm not a convicted felon if that's what you're worried about."

Jack's jaw went slack. After a pause he said, "You're right. You should probably call it a night. Come in tomorrow before we open though so you and I can have a little chat."

Tears threatened to spill over again. Not trusting herself to speak, Elana nodded. She grabbed her things and made her way out to her piece-of-crap jeep.

Kyle climbed into the driver's seat of the Dodge Charger and impatiently waited for the rest of the crew to climb in.

"Seriously, man, what was that all about?" his friend Stephan said from the back seat.

"An ex-girlfriend," mumbled Kyle. "I don't want to talk about it right now."

Kyle could feel the anger rolling off of him in waves and no one dared to ask him any more stupid questions. His friends found a new topic, but he tuned them out with his thoughts drifting back to the scene at the restaurant.

He'd heard that she'd left Seattle and Kyle had said good riddance without giving her any more thought beyond that. But now here she was, ruining his vacation. Didn't employers run background checks anymore? Kyle imagined that jerk of a manager probably took one look at her thick brown hair and luscious red lips and decided that was enough. Or maybe she batted her blue eyes him and convinced him she had nothing to hide.

"You just missed the turn!"

Stephan's voice brought Kyle back into the present and he slammed the brakes to flip a U-turn on the two lane road, causing the Charger's tires to peel through gravel. An oncoming car blared its horn as it continued on its way.

"Jesus, Kyle," said Stephan. "You really shouldn't get this worked up over a girl."

Kyle took a deep breath. "You're right." He needed to forget about her. But there was just one more thing he needed to do.

Elana sat on the postage-stamp sized deck of her equally small cottage with a second glass of red wine, trying to decide what to do. Thoughts of running away again first thing in the morning popped into her head. Perhaps she could avoid the conversation with Jack altogether. But a simple internet search of her name and he would know everything she had tried so hard to forget the past several months. It was possible he would do it anyway before their meeting tomorrow if he was curious enough. If she didn't explain it face-to-face, it would just make it that much harder to get the next job. She polished off the last of her merlot and hoped Jack would be nice enough to give her a good reference. Hell, even no reference would be better than a negative one.

No, she decided, she wasn't letting Kyle and his family run her out of town again. She would just have to face Jack tomorrow and convince him that none of this was her fault.

The roosters started their daily crowing around half past six, rousing Elana from her sleep. She enjoyed nearly a whole minute's peace before the previous night's event ran through her mind. She groaned and pulled a pillow over her head, wishing it could keep the unpleasant memories out. When that didn't work, she threw on some denim shorts and a faded University of Washington shirt and made her way out across the yard of the main house, passing the plumeria tree with the intoxicating scent that Elana never tired of. At the end of the driveway, she darted across the two-lane highway and sunk her barefoot toes into the sandy shoreline of Wainiha Bay.

The coarse sand crunched beneath her feet and the salty breeze whipped her dark hair as she headed west along the sunny beach, reflecting on the past few months. It was hard to believe it had been almost a year since she'd come to Kauai. Almost a year since she'd done her best to leave the nightmare behind her. And just when she had started to feel comfortable with her new life, the past had to show up and smack her, no—punch her across the face. Elana chose Kauai because it was about as remote as she could get without having to apply for a visa. It was either this or Alaska, and she wasn't too keen on the colder weather.

Footsteps snuck up behind Elana and she jerked around to come face to face with a jogger who nodded as he ran by. Who did she expect it to be? There was no doubt Kyle's appearance on the island had her spooked.

Elana glanced at her watch and decided to head back. She never did eat dinner last night and her belly was starting to protest.

"Good morning, Mrs. Wilson," she said, approaching the main house.

"Oh! Good morning, Elana." Mrs. Wilson stopped sweeping and gave a cheerful wave. "You're out and about early."

"I couldn't sleep, so I thought I'd get in a walk."

"Is it that bed? Do you think it needs a new mattress?"

"No, no, Mrs. Wilson. The bed is fine." Loretta Wilson was already giving her a screaming deal on the cottage, and Elana didn't want to take advantage of her kindness.

"All right, you just let me know if you need anything."

"Will do," said Elana. "Have a good day."

"You too, dear!"

Elana went into her cottage and disrobed before heading out the back door with a towel. Her outdoor shower had a perfect view of the lush green jungle behind her cottage and fortunately not much else. Some days she missed having the privacy of an indoor shower or even a bath tub to soak in, but so far it hadn't been an issue and the view couldn't be beat. How many people got to enjoy the sight of blooming orchids during their daily bathing? Once she finally paid her parents back everything they had given up for her, she hoped to really start anew, and maybe even live in a proper house or apartment again. But she didn't see that happening anytime soon, so it was best not to dwell on those thoughts for too long.

Elana glanced at the clock on her dresser and

realized the market would be opening soon. The Hanalei Farmer's Market was opening in an hour and it had been a while since she had been up early enough to get there right when it opened. The Saturday market was popular with the locals as well as tourists, and the good produce went pretty quickly.

She opened the fridge, where there wasn't much to be discovered, so she decided to head into town and grab a coffee and wait for the market to open.

In Hanalei, Elana pulled into the Ching Young Village Shopping Center and parked her jeep. She ordered a caramel latte and plain bagel from the café she often frequented before work.

"You're up early," said the perky redhead behind the counter.

Elana smirked. "So I've heard."

She sipped her coffee, walking along the same two-lane highway she had crossed earlier that morning, down to the market, munching her bagel while she and the rest of the crowd waited patiently behind a rope for the market to open. Right at 9:30, a gentleman came out and dropped the rope, granting access to everyone. Here was where you could tell the tourists from the locals. The first tents past the rope were the artist vendors. But it was farther in and to the right where the locals bee-lined to get first dibs at the freshest fruits and vegetables. Elana followed this crowd and picked up a perfectly ripe mango for later that day, as well as a few under-ripe ones for later that week. She'd been craving guacamole, so she also snagged an avocado and some cilantro. Elana would have picked up more, but she didn't want to spend too much without knowing where her next paycheck was coming from. With her grocery shopping done, she perused the artist row to see what was new, and then hiked back to her car. Crowds were beginning to appear in town, and Elana took that as her cue to head home.

The Bar Acuda didn't open until five so it was only staff when Elana walked in just after four. Her heart pounded as she looked around for Jack. She hated this feeling of not knowing what the future held. Would she still have a job an hour from now? Would she be able to find work nearby if she didn't? She spotted Jack at the bar going over inventory and he nodded before leading her into the back office.

"So last night..." he trailed off.

"I know. Messed up right?" She couldn't help avoiding the inevitable.

"I sense that you're reluctant to talk about this."

No shit, Sherlock. Elana bit her lip to keep from saying it out loud.

"Let me ask this then," he said. "Is there anything I should be concerned about? Something that might damage the reputation of this restaurant."

"No, there is not," she answered. *As long as Kyle doesn't decide to come in and make another scene.*

"Then what was last night about?" he asked, shaking his head.

Elana sighed. "He thinks I'm responsible for his brother's death."

"Are you?" Jack blurted out.

She squirmed. "I happened to have been driving the car that struck him. But the jury found me not guilty," she quickly added.

Jack's jaw dropped. "Were you intoxicated?"

"What?! How can you ask me that? Do you think they'd have found me not guilty if I'd been drunk?"

"I don't know. The right lawyers these days can get anybody off with the right amount of money."

Elana rolled her eyes. She walked over to the laptop on the cramped desk, pulled up the Internet browser, and typed her name along with the name Barnett into the search engine.

"There." She tried to swallow the lump in her throat. "Knock yourself out."

Jack sat down at the desk and scanned the links to various websites, mostly Seattle news pages, before clicking on one. Elana chewed her thumbnail as she waited, shifting her weight from foot to foot.

"Oh," Jack said when he finished it. "Wow."

"So do I still have a job or not?" she asked point blank.

Jack closed the browser and looked up at her. "Were you worried I would fire you over this?"

"Yes."

"Elana, you have been nothing but reliable and a hard worker since you got here. You have never been late or missed a shift. While I imagine this is not something you would want to share with anyone, it is not grounds for dismissal. You said it yourself last night. You are not a convicted felon; you never lied on your employment application. Of course you still have a job here."

Elana let out the breath she hadn't realized she'd been holding.

"Thank you," she whispered.

"At your interview, I asked you why you had decided not to use your law degree and you said you'd felt burned out on the legal system. Is this why?" he asked, pointing at the computer.

She nodded.

"We will keep this incident between us. If that guy from last night returns, let me know and I'll deal with him.

She nodded again. "Thank you. You don't know how much I appreciate it."

"I know tonight's your night off, but Ryan called out sick again. Do you want his shift? It would make up for going home early last night."

"Absolutely," she answered. Elana always took any shift that was offered to her. She needed the money, and it wasn't like she had any life outside of work. "I just need to run home and change my clothes."

"Great. Be back in an hour."

"Will do." Elana left the office and walked back out to her jeep, feeling a little of the weight lifted from her shoulders.

Saturday night in the restaurant proved to be more uneventful, but it didn't stop Elana from looking over her shoulder every time someone walked in. She wondered how long it would take her to not be paranoid. She wished she knew how long Kyle Barnett was going to be on the island and whether or not he was going to tell anyone else. If the rest of his family knew where she had disappeared to, would they harass her, or were they trying to forget it all as well?

As usual, Elana was one of the last servers to leave. She was five feet from her jeep when she heard footsteps on the gravel behind her.

Elana gripped her keys and turned around to come face to face with Kyle. He didn't look as menacing as the night before, but he still looked angry, and seeing as how there was no one in the parking lot, she was terrified. The adrenaline began coursing through her body, but she did her best to appear calm.

"All I have to do is scream and someone will be out here in less than ten seconds," she warned, forcing the bravado in her voice.

Kyle snorted as he took a step closer. "Do you think I'm going to hurt you? I'm not like you. I'm not a murderer."

"Please stop calling me that," Elana begged.

Kyle continued to glare at her, not saying anything, so she spoke again.

"What do you want then?" she asked.

"I just wanted to ask you something," he said. "Something I've wanted to ask you since the trial."

"And what's that?"

"How do you sleep at night knowing you killed my brother?"

The truth was she didn't sleep well, but she wasn't prepared to give him that satisfaction.

"Hey!" someone shouted.

They both looked over and saw Jack coming out of the building.

"Is he bothering you?" Jack asked.

Kyle looked back at Elana to see what she would say.

"You asked your question," she told him. "Now leave me alone."

"But you didn't answer it."

"I never said I was going to answer it."

His nostrils started to flare.

"Elana?" Jack called out as he moved into a wide stance, planting his hands on his hips.

Kyle kicked some gravel in her direction. "I was just leaving," he said.

Elana took a deep breath when Kyle walked away. "I'm fine," she called out to her boss as she watched Kyle disappear around a corner.

Jack continued to keep an eye on her as she got in her jeep and tried to start it. On the third attempt, the engine finally turned over. The gears grinded a bit as she put it into reverse, and then first. The whole drive home Elana thought about what Kyle had said. The only thing he had ever wanted to know about her was how she slept at night, and for a split second, her heart ached for him. For the man who'd lost his brother because of her. She wiped away the tears with the back of her hand as visions of that night came back to her. She already felt guilty enough, but it would never be enough for the Barnett family.

Sunday was Elana's day off and she had promised Mrs. Wilson that she would run into Lihue and make a Costco run for her. When she was showered and dressed, she went next door to collect the list and money before heading out.

"Thank you, dear," Mrs. Wilson called out from the porch as Elana loaded an empty cooler into the back of her jeep.

"No problem," said Elana. "I'll see you later this afternoon."

It was only thirty-five miles into Lihue, home of the only Costco on the island, but it still took about an hour to make the trek along the mostly two-lane highway that ran the perimeter of the island.

Loretta Wilson hated making the drive, but Elana loved it. The jeep was topless and Awolnation was blaring from the speakers. The lush scenery still took Elana's breath away and she hoped the day never came when she stopped really seeing the green mountains capped in mist rising out of the heart of the island.

Elana's first stop in Lihue was the Kukui Grove Cinema where she caught a five-dollar matinee. She didn't have a TV in her cottage and that was perfectly okay with her, but every now and then she liked to catch a movie. Somehow it made her feel a little more connected to people on the mainland.

Elana took her time wandering Costco, making sure to stop at all the food sample stations, considering that her lunch. She waited patiently in line at the pharmacy to pick up Mrs. Wilson's prescriptions, then swung by the gas station before getting back on the road.

She was less than ten minutes from Princeville, the resort town just before Hanalei, when the engine started to make a clunking noise.

"No," she whined.

Then there was steam.

"Please, please, no!" She pulled over, killed the engine, and popped the hood. A giant cloud of steam escaped and Elana stepped back to avoid getting burned. When the steam cleared, she could see that the radiator hose was split. An easy enough fix if she could get her car to a shop. But she wasn't going to be able to drive it far without risk of the engine seizing from overheating. That meant she was going to need a tow. Which meant even more money.

"Dammit!" she said, kicking the front tire.

She was leaning against the front bumper with the hood still up, trying to decide what to do, when a car could be heard pulling in behind her. She peeked around and saw a shiny car that screamed "rental."

At first she smiled, thankful for the help. Because everyone had cell phones, most people never seemed to bother stopping to offer help anymore. But then Kyle stepped out.

"You've got to be kidding me," she muttered.

Two

"WELL, WELL, WELL. Look who it is," he said.

"Someone is on their way to help me," she lied, "so you can just go on ahead."

"That's okay. I'll wait. I want to revel in this hand that life has dealt you."

"You are a real piece of work, you know that?"

Kyle leaned against the hood of his car and watched her. She looked back down the road pretending to wait for her savior. Problem was, as long as Kyle stood there, no one else was likely to stop and help, and as usual, she had let her cell phone die. That's what happens when you don't use it very often. She really only had it to stay in touch with her parents from time to time.

As though to add salt to the wound, Kyle pulled out his own cell phone and texted or played a game or something. Elana didn't really care at this point; she just had to fight back the urge to ask him if she could borrow it. She glanced at the cooler in the back that was keeping Mrs. Wilson's insulin at the optimal temperature of not too warm, and worried how much longer she had to try and get it home. She would never forgive herself if Mrs. Wilson had to throw it out just because she couldn't afford a more reliable vehicle.

"Exactly how long do you intend to just sit there?" she asked.

"I don't know," he said. "How long are you going to be irritated?"

Elana rolled her eyes, but said nothing for fear of fueling him. Instead she grabbed the cooler from where it was sitting in direct sunlight and set it down in the shadow of her jeep. Hopefully that would buy her some time while she figured out how to handle her pest.

Kyle must have sensed her distress, because the sneer finally left his face and was replaced with concern.

"You don't have anyone coming, do you?"

She looked at him, but didn't answer.

"Fuck," he mumbled and pocketed his phone. "Let me give you a ride."

"No," she said. "I don't need your help."

"You're lying. You do need help. Your car is clearly not going anywhere, and I don't see a phone in your hand."

"I didn't say I don't need help. I just don't need *your* help."

He walked to the back of her jeep, grabbed the cooler, and walked back to his car.

"Hey," she shouted. "What the hell are you doing?"

"You've been eying this cooler. I'm guessing there's something important in it that you need to get home." He slid it into his back seat and then opened the passenger door. "Get in."

She scowled at him but didn't know what else to do. She grabbed the other box of items, put it in next to the cooler, and then went back for her purse and phone.

"You do have a phone," he said.

"The battery is dead," she growled.

"Your day just keeps getting better."

She crossed her arms. "You have no idea."

Kyle drove in the direction of Hanalei, assuming Elana would tell him where to go. He was second guessing his decision to help her, but he thought maybe it would be a chance to finally get some things off his chest. But now that he had her in a position where she couldn't run away, Kyle found himself chickening out.

"Exactly how long are you in town?" Elana asked, breaking the silence.

"Why do you want to know?" he asked, eying her suspiciously.

"Because I was thinking I would lock myself in my house until you were gone," she said, crossing her arms and looking out the passenger side window, "so I wouldn't have to worry about running into you anymore."

He smirked, reveling in the fact that his presence bothered her so much.

"I don't know," he said. "I might have to prolong my stay now that I know how much it annoys you."

"This is harassment, you know," she said, whipping her head around to face him.

"And I think you deserve it."

"Stop the car," she said. "I knew I shouldn't have agreed to let you help me."

"No. You killed my brother and then ran off to live the rest of your days in paradise. Why shouldn't I get to make your life a little harder?"

"First of all, your brother was the one who was severely intoxicated that night, *not* me!" she shouted at him. Kyle stole a glance at her. Man, her eyes got bright when she was angry. Good, he was glad she was pissed off.

"And did you not see the piece of crap I just left on the side of the road?" she continued. "You are sorely mistaken if you think I am living in paradise! I came out here to get as far away from your family as possible. I lost my job and boyfriend because they couldn't handle the media circus. All my friends stopped calling because they didn't know what to say, didn't know how to handle me. I left my parents! Their only child had to leave the continent because your family wouldn't leave me alone!"

"At least you can still talk to your parents," he shot back. "Jarod is dead. We will never see my brother again."

"I know that! I can't tell you how sorry I will forever be. But continuing to persecute me is not going to bring him back!"

Kyle stared straight ahead, gripping the wheel until his knuckles were white.

"I have played that night over and over in my head a million times," she said, facing the window again. "What if I had been able to react faster? What if I had left the office a minute later or a minute sooner?"

Kyle heard her sniff and suspected she was crying, but refused to look at her. Elana Tanner did not get to cry over *his* brother.

"His eyes still haunt me," she said.

"What do you mean?" he asked.

"I held his head in my lap while I waited for help. I prayed, begged for him to hold on just a little bit longer. I watched the life go out of Jarod's eyes before anyone else could get there."

"You stayed with him until the end?" That was not at all how Kyle had pictured it.

"Yes. What did you think I did?"

Out of the corner of his eye, he could see her turn to him again and allowed himself to meet her eye.

"I–I don't know," he said softly. "All I had heard was that he was pronounced dead at the scene. I guess in my head I imagined you standing on the sidelines."

"It's just past this bridge," she said, wiping her face with the back of her hand.

"What?" He looked back at the road where they were about to cross yet another single lane bridge.

"My place is just a couple driveways pass this bridge."

Kyle turned down her driveway, which served the four houses grouped together, and she directed him to the end on the right.

Kyle got out and grabbed the cooler while Elana got the box with the dry goods.

"I thought you said you weren't living in paradise," he said, looking up at Mrs. Wilson's four-bedroom home.

"Um, that would be the owner's house." She stepped to the side and nodded to her tiny little cottage at the back of the property. "That is where I live."

"Oh."

"Elana, you're back." Mrs. Wilson had stepped out of the laundry room that was on the ground level of the house. "You've brought a friend even."

Elana frowned at the word *friend*. "Mrs. Wilson, this is Kyle Barnett. Kyle, this is Loretta Wilson. She owns this property."

Kyle set down the cooler and offered his hand and in true Barnett fashion, turned on the charm. The same charm that convinced the DA to press charges. No wait—that was the Barnett money.

"Hello, Ms. Wilson," he said with a bright smile. "It's a pleasure to meet you."

Elana watched Loretta flush ever so slightly.

"Oh, the pleasure is mine. It's so nice to finally meet a friend of Elana's. She never brought anyone over before."

"He was just helping me get your stuff to you after my jeep broke down," Elana explained, trying to keep the irritation out of her voice.

Mrs. Wilson frowned. "Again?"

"Yeah. But I made it a whole two months this time without any issues." She threw on a fake smile.

"Well, let's get this stuff inside," said Mrs. Wilson.

Kyle picked up the cooler and followed Elana and Mrs. Wilson up the stairs to the main level of the house. They set the items down in the kitchen, and Elana pulled out the couple of things she had picked up for herself.

"I'm just going to run these over, and then Kyle can drop me off at Ricky's auto shop so I can get my jeep towed."

"Would you two like me to make you some dinner before you head out?" asked Mrs. Wilson.

Kyle and Elana looked at each other appalled.

"Thanks, Mrs. Wilson," said Elana, "but that won't be necessary."

They said good-bye to her landlady and Kyle waited at the car while Elana dropped her things off. The drive back in to Hanalei was uncomfortable and silent, until Elana had to direct him to the auto shop.

"Looks like today is your lucky day," Kyle said, when they pulled into the driveway.

"What?" She looked up from her purse where she had been digging for her keys and saw the closed sign Kyle was pointing at.

"Shit. I forgot it's Sunday." Elana was beginning to feel like this day would never end. And it had been off to such a good start this morning.

"Now what?" Kyle asked.

She sighed. "May I borrow your phone? Please."

He handed it to her and she dialed the shop number. After several rings, the voicemail picked up.

"Hey Ricky, it's your best customer. Looks like the radiator hose on my jeep busted, and I was hoping you could tow it in and take care of it. It's off the highway a couple miles past Princeville. Give me a call tomorrow and let me know what needs to be done. Thanks." She hung up.

"That's it?" asked Kyle. "You just call him and tell him where your jeep is?"

She shrugged. "He knows I'm good for it. I'm a regular here."

"Why don't you just buy a new car if you're always having to dump money into this one?"

She snorted. "That would require me to have enough money at one time."

"I realize I'm prying here, but that restaurant you work at seems pretty nice. Do they really pay you that little? I mean, the tips must be good."

Elana leaned back and took a good hard look at him. "You are something else, you know that?"

He frowned. "What's that supposed to mean?"

"You do realize that my wages are being garnished to pay off the settlement, don't you? You know, the settlement from your parent's wrongful death suit." *The bullshit lawsuit.*

"I guess I hadn't really thought of it."

"Of course not." She undid her seat belt and opened the door. "Well, thanks for all of your help and the conversation, but I think I can take it from here."

She got out and closed the door.

Kyle jumped out after her.

"Wait, where are you going?"

She turned around, walking backwards as she answered him. "I'm going home, Mr. Barnett. There's not much else I can do at this point." Elana turned her back to him.

He jogged up beside her. "You can't walk home. That road is too narrow and dangerous for pedestrians."

"Don't tell me what I can and can't do," she said, staring at the pavement in front of her. "Now if you don't mind, I think I've taken about as much of you as I can handle. Now go away."

"This is ridiculous," Kyle said, keeping step with her. "Let me drive you home."

She stopped walking and threw her hands up, making eye contact with him. "No, thank you! I don't want to seem ungrateful, because I do appreciate you helping me out today. But the sooner I can have you out of my life, again, the better. Besides, it's in the opposite direction for you if you're heading back to Princeville."

"How do you know I'm headed to Princeville?" he asked.

"Please," she said, rolling her eyes. "This is the third time I have seen you on this part of the island, and with your family's money, I'd be willing to wager that you're staying at the St. Regis resort there. If I had any money of my own that is."

"Who's making judgment calls now?" he said, narrowing his eyes at her.

Her hands landed on her hips. "You're right. I'm sorry. For all I know, you've rented one of the upscale vacation homes in the area."

Kyle's gaze bore into her and for the first time

she noticed tiny flecks of gold in his otherwise chocolate colored eyes. Shit colored, she revised. Because Kyle was full of shit.

"So tell me, Mr. Barnett. Where are you residing during your stay on our wonderful island?"

He didn't answer.

"I knew it. You're at the St. Regis."

She started to walk away again, but he grabbed her arm. "Fine. So maybe I am. Now let me give you a ride home."

She wrenched it away. "Don't touch me," she seethed.

"What is your problem?" he yelled.

"My problem is that I am stuck in a living hell because of you and your family. The night that your brother got wasted and stumbled in the path of my car flipped my world upside down. And if being responsible for a man's death, a man who I watched die in my arms, wasn't bad enough, your parents decided to bleed me dry of every penny I had ever earned, and then some. Never mind that your family didn't need it, not in the least bit." She took a deep breath before continuing with slightly less volume. "So please excuse me if the thought of having to accept help from anyone in your family makes me sick to my stomach."

They stood there, staring at each other. Kyle finally nodded and walked back to his car. Elana watched him get in and start the engine. She had been prepared for the argument to escalate, and was relieved when he finally let it go. She continued her walk to the rural highway and turned right to make her way home. It was still four miles to her driveway and the afternoon was slipping away, taking the sunlight with it. Fortunately hitchhiking was not only common, it was legal, so she stuck out her thumb as she walked and hoped someone found her before the darkness did. But it wasn't long before a neighbor stopped to pick her up.

"Thanks," Elana said as she climbed in.

"No problem," said the driver. "Saw your jeep a ways back. Wondered if I might pass you on the road."

Elana mustered a small smile.

Kyle dropped the car off at valet and made his way to the suite. His head was swimming with all the things that Elana had told him. At the door to the room, Kyle stopped and pulled his cell phone from his pocket and paced in front of the door while he waited for Linda, his attorney, to answer on the other end.

"What's up, Kyle?" she answered.

"Hey, Linda. Sorry for the odd hour, but I was hoping you could look into something for me."

"Lay it on me." Kyle was used to Linda's brisk tone. She was usually doing a million things at once, and doing them damn well.

"What can you tell me about the Tanner settlement?"

"The Tanner settlement? What exactly do you want to know?"

"Are we garnishing her wages?" Kyle asked.

There was a pause while Linda racked her brain. "I think so."

"Could you look it up for me?" he said.

"Now?"

"Yes, now," Kyle told her.

"May I ask why the sudden interest?"

"Call it curiosity. Just call me back when you have the numbers in front of you."

"Of course."

The line went dead, and Kyle finally walked

into the suite where his friends were sprawled out. He tried not to be so annoyed at how much they were enjoying his generosity. After all, he did invite, or rather begged, them to accompany him on this little break. He had needed to get away and it looked less suspicious if he had friends with him.

"You're back," Stephan called out from the couch. "What kind of car did you get?"

"I snagged a Jeep Cherokee," Kyle answered. "It should handle the rougher roads better than the Charger. I thought we were going to lose the muffler yesterday. Hey, where's the iPad?"

"Right here." Stephan held it up for a second and then returned to his game. Kyle walked over and took it from his hands. "Hey, I was just about to beat my best score!"

Kyle ignored him and walked over to the dining table.

"And what took you so long?" Stephan asked.

"Huh?"

"You were gone for over three hours. How long does it take to swap out a rental?"

"I had to wait for the jeep to be returned and detailed," he muttered. Kyle couldn't remember the last time he'd lied this much to his best friend.

Kyle sat down and opened the Safari app to do a search on Elana Tanner. He remembered seeing a lot of the headlines that popped up, but he hadn't read them then, and wasn't sure he wanted to read them now. Then he found a link to her Facebook page. He clicked on it. There hadn't been any activity on it for quite some time, but it did gave some basic info. The rest was locked, and he went back to the search page and found her again on LinkedIn. This one gave more info such as work and school history.

"Huh," he said aloud.

"What are you looking at?" Stephan asked, appearing next to him.

Kyle hit the home button on the iPad and everything disappeared.

Stephan gave him the stink eye. "Seriously?"

Kyle looked around the corner and made sure Amar and Tad were fully engrossed in whatever was on the television.

"Do you remember the girl at the restaurant the other night?" he asked.

Stephan cocked an eyebrow and grinned. "Which girl are you referring to?"

Kyle rolled his eyes. "The server from the Bar Acuda."

"Oh, yeah."

"That was Elana Tanner."

"Elana Tanner? Wait, the girl that killed your brother?"

Kyle flinched slightly. "Yes."

"I though you said she was an ex-girlfriend."

"Do you really think I have an ex-girlfriend that you don't know about?"

Stephan shrugged. "I don't know. Maybe I was drunk."

Kyle's phone started ringing.

"I have to take this," he said, picking up the phone along with the iPad. He moved up to the bedroom, where he would have more privacy.

"What did you find, Linda?"

"I have all the details here in front of me, Kyle. We are garnishing her wages. Was there anything else you wanted to know?"

"How much?" he asked.

"Sixty percent of her current salary."

"Sixty percent," he exclaimed. "Why so much?"

"It was her request. I'm guessing she wanted to pay it off sooner."

"How much does she still owe?" asked Kyle.

"About four-hundred and fifty-thousand," Linda answered. "Give or take."

"And how long until she has that paid off?"

"Let me grab a calculator."

Kyle could hear her punching keys in the background. "Based on the average salary she has earned the past several months, if she didn't have any increase in income, she's looking at about twenty-two years."

Kyle's jaw dropped.

"Anything else?" Linda asked when Kyle hadn't said anything.

"No. That's all I wanted to know. Thank you, Linda."

"Any time."

Kyle hung up the phone and decided to read some of the articles he'd been avoiding for so long.

It was almost noon when Elana woke to her phone ringing. She'd had trouble falling asleep and had consequently slept in even later than usual.

"Hey, Ricky," she answered.

"Morning, Elana. I've got your jeep here."

"Thank you so much." She sat up and ran a hand through her tangle of hair. "So what's the damage?"

"You were right about the radiator hose, but unfortunately it wasn't just that. There's a crack in the radiator as well."

Elana plopped back down on her pillow. "Shit. How much is that going to cost me?"

"About a grand."

Fuck. And she suspected he was already giving

her the friends and family discount.

"Know of any cars for sale for less than that? *Much* less than that." she asked.

"Not any that are worth driving. I'm really sorry, Elana. I wish there was something else I could do to bring the price down more, but—"

She cut him off. "Don't worry about it, Ricky. I appreciate everything you're doing for me. Is it all right if I pay you over the next couple weeks?" If she could pick up more shifts, then the tips would help her out big time.

"Of course."

"Then go ahead and get started. Give me a call when it's ready."

"It will probably take a week. I need to track down the right parts."

"Sure," she said. "Just let me know."

"Will do. Later."

"Bye." Elana hung up and pondered her situation. How was she supposed to pick up more shifts if she had no vehicle to get to work? Walking to work wouldn't be so bad, but the trek home at night would be downright deadly.

It was two hours until her shift started, and Elana was swallowing her pride as she walked up the stairs to Mrs. Wilson's house. She could see Loretta reading at the kitchen table, and she tapped on the screen door.

Loretta looked up and waved her in.

"Hey, Mrs. Wilson," Elana said.

"Have a seat," Mrs. Wilson instructed her. "Would you like some coffee?"

"Coffee sounds good. Thank you." Elana sat down at the table as Loretta stood up to get a mug.

"I have a favor to ask," Elana said, when

Loretta had joined her at the table.

"What's that, dear?"

"You know my jeep broke down yesterday." Loretta nodded. "Well, I talked to Ricky about it this morning, and it's going to take a week to fix it. I was wondering if I could maybe borrow your car to get to work until it's fixed. Only if you don't need it of course."

"Of course. You know me, I don't get out much." She paused to think. "Yeah, I don't think I have anything going on this week. We'll figure it out if something comes up."

"Thank you so much," said Elana. "If you need me to run any errands for you while I'm in town let me know. I owe you big time."

"No you don't."

Elana looked at her in surprise.

"I don't think you realize what a favor you have done for me by renting the cottage," Loretta explained.

"I know it's made it easier for you to not have to deal with the constant turnover of vacation renters."

"Yes, that's part of it," she said. "Jim always handled that. I didn't realize just how much it entailed until I tried to take it over after he passed. But you're more than just another renter, Elana. It's a comfort having someone I know close by." Her eyes started to tear up. "It was lonely after I lost Jim and all the family that came out for his funeral finally headed home. It's less lonely with you around." She patted Elana's hand. "So please don't be afraid to ask for help. I like feeling needed. And besides, you do help me all the time, even with little things like bringing the garbage bins in or picking up the mail."

Elana put her other hand over Loretta's. "I don't know what to say. Thank you."

"Thank you, dear."

Elana walked into work that night with her spirits slightly lifted. She still had to come up with the money to pay for her jeep, but she was confident she could scrape that together in time.

By Thursday, Elana was feeling pretty good when she pulled into Ricky's before going into work. The restaurant had been slammed the past couple days, and after setting aside the money she needed to pay the few bills she had, she was still left with three-hundred to give him already.

She walked into the garage and found Ricky just pulling out from under an older Ford truck.

His face broke into a grin when he saw her, and he got up to wipe his hands on a dirty rag.

"Hey, I was just about to call you," he said.

"Good news, I hope," said Elana.

"Great news. Your jeep should be ready by tomorrow."

"Really? That is great." She reached into her bag. "I even have my first payment."

Ricky's smile faltered. "Um, yeah, it's actually already been taken care of."

Elana frowned. "What do you mean?"

"I mean it's all paid for. You don't owe anything."

She pulled the envelope of cash out and tried to thrust it into his hands. "That's crazy, Ricky, you can't afford to not charge me."

"It wasn't me," he said, putting his hands up. "Someone else paid for it."

"Someone else," she said, frowning. "But who?"

"I'm not supposed to say."

"This is ridiculous, tell me who paid for my

jeep."

Ricky shook his head. "That was the deal; it was to be an anonymous donation. I promised I wouldn't tell."

Elana's arms slowly fell to her side. She thought of her conversation with Loretta just days earlier.

"Mrs. Wilson," she said softly.

Ricky looked at her. "My lips are sealed."

"It has to be Mrs. Wilson." She shoved the envelope back into her bag. "Fine, I'll just give this to her then. I'll be back tomorrow to pick up my jeep. Call me if anything changes."

"You got it."

She hugged him. "Thank you again for everything, Ricky."

He gave her a squeeze. "Anytime, Elana."

She pulled away and walked out the door. Elana suspected that Ricky had a slight crush on her. He was probably the closest thing she had to a real friend on the island it was Ricky who had helped her find the beat-up Jeep Wrangler and even introduced her to Mrs. Wilson. Once upon a time she may have been interested, but Elana didn't want to do anything to jeopardize their friendship. She also knew she was the last person to be in a relationship right now. After Benjamin had moved out during the trial, she was reluctant to entertain the thought of putting her heart in someone else's hands. Ever.

Elana had a hard time concentrating at work that night. Twice she had to go back to a table to have the customer repeat their order. There were just too many thoughts going through her head and she blamed it all on Kyle Barnett. All the memories she had been trying so hard to repress had been brought fresh to the surface with his arrival. She'd had enough to deal with without him stirring up trouble. Luckily she hadn't seen him since Sunday, and she hoped that he had finally headed home. Or at the very least, decided to back off.

Friday morning, Elana was back in Loretta's kitchen asking if she could give her a ride in to town to pick up her jeep, which of course Mrs. Wilson agreed to.

They pulled up and before Elana got out of the car, she dug into her bag and pulled out the envelope of cash that she had been able to add after last night's shift. She handed it to Mrs. Wilson.

"What's this for, dear?" Loretta asked.

"I know that you paid for my jeep and I intend to pay you back," said Elana. "Consider this a down payment."

Confusion was all over Loretta's face. "I don't understand. I didn't pay for your jeep."

"When I went to give Ricky some money yesterday, he said someone had already paid for everything anonymously. I know you didn't want me to know, but that's too much. I have to pay you back."

She handed the envelope back. "I promise you, it wasn't me, Elana. Are you sure Ricky didn't just decide to not charge you?"

"No, at least I don't think so. But if it wasn't you, then who?"

"I don't know, dear. It appears you might have a guardian angel."

Elana shook her head and shoved the envelope back into her bag yet again. "Well, thanks for the ride, Mrs. Wilson. See you soon."

Elana went inside to get the keys and found Ricky at his desk.

"It wasn't Mrs. Wilson."

Ricky looked up from his computer. "Huh?"

"It wasn't Mrs. Wilson," Elana repeated. "She isn't my anonymous benefactor."

Ricky leaned back in his chair. "I never said she was."

Elana opened her mouth, but then realized he was right. He hadn't denied it, but he hadn't confirmed it either.

"Well, then who was it?"

"I told you. My lips are sealed."

Elana played the only card she could think of. "I'll take you out to dinner if you tell me."

She saw his eyebrows go up just a bit, but then he shook his head. "I can't, Elana."

She sighed. "I tried."

Ricky got up and grabbed the clipboard with her keys and paperwork on it. She signed the completed work order, then flipped though the other sheets to see if there was any clue to who had paid for it.

"You won't find anything," said Ricky. "It was paid in cash."

Elana's lips pursed together as she tossed the clipboard across the desk.

"Well, I've got some errands to run before work tonight," she said. "You should come in and have a drink later."

"I just might. Take care, Elana."

Elana went back out to the parking lot and got in her jeep. She started it and swore it sounded better than it had in a while. The gears didn't even seem to stick as much.

Her first stop was to the bank in Princeville to get a money order, then on to the post office to send it by certified mail to her parents. They had been getting close to retirement when they had taken a second mortgage to help Elana pay for all the legal fees. She sent them money to help pay it off whenever she could.

As she stood in line, she tried to think more about who could have paid Ricky. Very few people knew about it. And she couldn't imagine any of them having that kind of cash on hand.

Someone at the counter turned around to leave and Elana caught the words 'St. Regis' embroidered on his polo. She suddenly realized there was only one person she knew who would have that kind of cash readily available.

Elana sent off the money order along with a note she had tucked in the envelope, and looked at her watch. She should have just enough time.

Three

ELANA PULLED INTO the parking lot of the St. Regis and immediately felt out of place. Walking into the beautiful and spacious lobby did nothing to boost her confidence. She had never entered the resort before and did her best not to gawk.

She walked up to the front desk and tried not to take it personally when the woman greeted her with a fake smile.

"Good afternoon," the blonde woman said. "What can I help you with today?"

Elana flashed her own best smile. "Hi. You have, or maybe had, a guest staying here, and I'm not sure if he is still here or not, but I was hoping I could get a message to him."

The women's smile faded. "I'm sorry, miss, but we don't give out guest information."

"Oh, I know. I just thought that if I left a note, you could get it to him."

"You have the guest's name then?"

"Yes. His name is Kyle Barnett." Elana saw the corner of the woman's mouth go up. She knew exactly who Elana was talking about and Elana resisted the urge to gag.

"You just need me to get a note to him?" the

blonde said.

"Yes, please."

"I think I can help you with that," the woman told her. "Do you have it ready?"

"No. Do you have a sheet of paper and pen I could borrow?"

"Of course."

"And perhaps an envelope." Elana wasn't sure she trusted the woman not to read what she wrote.

Blondie handed the items to Elana, and she found a chair and side table nearby to compose her letter. She tapped the pen on her chin trying to decide exactly what to write. A thank you note, an I.O.U? Or better yet, fuck off and mind your own business. She smiled at the thought.

"Elana?"

Looking up, she saw Kyle along with three other men just coming into the lobby. She was pretty sure they were the same guys that had been with him at the restaurant that first night.

She continued to stare at him as he made his way over to where she was sitting and swore under her breath. Once again, a face-to-face confrontation with Kyle was not what she had been expecting.

"What are you doing here?" he asked.

Kyle's 6'2 frame towered over her. It was intimidating so she stood, but it didn't help her much as he was still several inches taller than her.

"I wasn't sure if you had gone home yet, but I was trying to leave you a note." She nodded at the still blank piece of paper. "I know that you paid for the repair work on my jeep."

She watched that strong jaw of his go tight. "That was supposed to be confidential."

"It wasn't Ricky; he never betrayed you. But there aren't too many people who could have done it."

"I see. And so what was it you wanted to say to me?" he asked.

"I hadn't really figured it out yet." She rubbed her temple. "To be honest, I don't understand why. You've done nothing but berate me since you've seen me. Is this just something you hope to be able to hold over me? Because I intend to pay you back." She started digging through her bag.

"What? No!" Kyle shook his head. "That's why I did it anonymously; I didn't want you to think you owed anyone."

She pulled the envelope out and slapped it against his chest. "Well, I don't need your charity, Kyle. I've survived this long and I fully intend to keep surviving without it. I'll wire the rest to your attorneys when I have it."

Just then one of his friends called out. "Kyle, man, let's go. I'm starving!"

"Just give me a minute!" Kyle shot back. "Elana, I—" but she was already heading out the door by the time he turned around.

At work Elana did her best to not think about Kyle, but she wasn't having much success. He hadn't been wrong when he'd said she would feel like she owed him if he helped her. Ricky had been pretty tight lipped about it, and Kyle had even seemed mad when he thought that Ricky had spilled the beans. But then why would he help her like that? It didn't making sense to her.

To make matters worse, she found her envelope of cash dropped in the driver's seat when she got to her jeep that night. She'd never had such a hard time giving away money before. Kyle Barnett really knew how to piss her off.

Elana was up with the roosters the next morning, and after breakfast and a shower, she made the drive back to the resort in Princeville. She marched up to the front desk and was a little disconcerted to find Blondie manning her post again.

She slapped the now wrinkled envelope on the counter and scribbled Kyle's name on it.

"Good Morning," said Elana. "I need you to get this to Kyle Barnett."

"He said you would probably be in this morning," the attendant told her.

"I'm sorry," Elana stuttered. "He what?"

"He said that you would probably be in this morning and we were instructed not to accept anything from you."

Elana's jaw dropped.

The woman was enjoying Elana's reaction. "He also requested that we call him when you did show up." She picked up the phone while Elana just stood there, unable to speak.

"Good morning, Mr. Barnett," Blondie said in a sugary voice. "This is Mari from the front desk." She paused. "Yes, she is." Another pause, and then the blonde frowned. "I will let her know, sir." She hung up and directed her attention back to Elana. "He would like you to wait for him at Makana Terrace."

Elana finally managed to close her mouth and she wrinkled her brow.

"The restaurant." Blondie pointed Elana in the right direction. "He says he shouldn't be more than five minutes."

"Um, okay."

Elana walked out to the terrace and was greeted by the host.

"Aloha. How many this morning, miss?"

"Just one, wait, two I guess."

The host raised an eyebrow, but said nothing as he grabbed two menus, led her to a table, and pulled the chair out for her. A busboy came by to fill the water glasses and then she was left alone to wait for Kyle. She looked around at the crowd in the restaurant enjoying breakfast on the beautiful Saturday morning. There was one couple she remembered from work last night, but her flip flops and cut off shorts were a far cry from the black pants and white shirt she wore for her work uniform, and her hair was loose about her shoulders instead of in the bun she usually sported. It was doubtful they would recognize her.

A server came over and asked Elana if she would like anything else to drink while she waited.

"I'm fine with only water, thank you," Elana told her.

What am I doing here, she wondered. Just as Elana was debating whether to make a run for it, Kyle came striding with ease across the terrace and sat down across from Elana. He looked noticeably more relaxed than she had ever seen him.

"Good morning," he said.

"Morning," she replied cautiously.

"I half expected you to run off before I made it here."

"The thought crossed my mind."

"Then why didn't you?" he asked. "Running away is your forte, isn't it?"

"Because I thought maybe you were wanting to have a civil conversation." She started to get up. "But I can see I was wrong."

He stood up as well. "Wait. That was uncalled for. I'm sorry."

She looked at him with skepticism as she sat back down and he followed suit.

Their server returned and Kyle ordered an

omelet and looked at Elana.

"Oh, I'm fine thank you," she said.

"Why don't you bring a side of fruit and some toast just in case," Kyle told their server.

"Any preference on bread?" the server asked. They both looked at Elana who rolled her eyes.

"Fine. Sourdough."

Kyle smiled.

"So how did you know I would be back this morning," Elana asked when they were alone again.

"I wasn't sure. But after I left the money in your jeep, I realized that you probably weren't going to let it go."

"Got that right."

"Well then I guess we're at a stale mate," he said, "because I'm not going to accept any repayment from you."

Elana leaned forward. "See, now that's what I don't understand. Why this sudden need to help me out after everything your family has done to destroy me? 'To make me pay for the inconsolable grief I have brought upon this family'. I believe those were your mother's words during the wrongful death suit."

The smile faded from Kyle's eyes. "Yes. That does sound like my mother." He shifted in his seat. "It's possible," he said slowly, "that I became aware of how harshly I was judging you."

Elana leaned back in her chair and crossed her arms. "Oh, really."

"I hadn't realized that your wages were being garnished. Once the settlement was reached, I never really thought anymore about it. It's not like the money was going to me personally."

"No, I'm sure it just went into the trust fund with all the other millions of dollars."

Kyle glared at her. "Look, I'm trying to say that

maybe I was wrong."

Elana looked out over the bay, shaking her head. She wasn't sure she was buying it.

He continued. "I contacted my lawyer and she said that at your current salary, it will take almost twenty-two years to pay off the remainder of the settlement."

"Wow," said Elana, "Twenty-two years? Is that all? I'd never actually sat down to do the math."

Kyle just looked at her with apologetic eyes.

"And so you thought that paying my repair bill would help to ease your conscience; is that it then?"

"No."

"What is it then?"

"I just realized you could use a little good luck." He said. "But I also knew you would never accept any help from me. You made that very clear outside the auto shop last Sunday."

She smiled remembering the scene. "I did, didn't I?"

The conversation was interrupted by the arrival of one of Kyle's companions.

"There you are," said the newcomer.

Kyle looked up at him. "Here I am."

"I tried calling you on your cell but there was no answer."

"I was ignoring it," Kyle grumbled. He caught Elana's eye and gave her a little smile. "Elana, this is Stephan. Stephan, Elana."

Elana held out her hand and Stephen took it. "Nice to meet you," she said.

"Nice to meet *you*." Stephan said as he gave Kyle a look and Elana wondered if he knew who she really was. If he did, it clearly didn't bother him as he pulled up a chair and joined them.

"Hope I'm not interrupting anything," said

Stephan with a mischievous grin, and Elana noticed Kyle didn't look as relaxed anymore.

"Was there a reason you were trying to find me?" Kyle asked.

Stephan leaned back in his chair and clasped his hands behind his head. Elana was sure he had to sense his friend's discomfort, hell, the whole restaurant could probably sense it right now. But if anything, Stephan looked like he was enjoying the tense moment.

"I just wanted to let you know we've decided to go hike out to that waterfall on the Na Pali trail this morning."

"Right now?" Kyle asked.

The food arrived and Stephan stole a slice of Elana's toast before continuing.

"Soon. We're looking to get back before noon."

Elana looked at her watch. "You're joking, right?"

Stephan looked at her. "No, why?"

"Because it's after eight already. There is no way you can make it to the waterfall and back before noon." She looked down at his boat shoes. "Especially not in that footwear."

"Have you hiked it before?" he asked.

"Yes. Many times. I live just down the road from the trail head."

"Then what would you suggest?" Stephan asked.

"Well, something with socks and traction for starters. And there's a lot of red dirt that will stain anything it comes in contact with so don't wear anything that you don't want to get ruined."

"Are you saying we shouldn't go then?" Stephan wondered.

"Oh, no, you should absolutely go. It's just that

you're easily looking at a half-day excursion. The hike is treacherous, but beautiful and the waterfall is amazing to swim under."

"You should come with us," said Stephan.

Kyle almost choked on his water. "She should what?"

"She should come with us. Be our guide. We," Stephan indicated him and Kyle, "clearly don't know what we are doing. And it seems like you do."

Elana cocked her head. "I don't know...."

"I'm sure we could get you back in time for work," said Stephan.

"I don't have to be in tonight," she muttered.

"That settles it," Stephan told her. "You're going hiking with us."

"But what if I have other plans?" she protested.

"Do you?" Kyle asked.

Elana didn't answer.

"Great," Stephan announced. "Why don't you run home and grab whatever you need. Kyle and I will round up some proper attire for the group and meet you back at your place."

Elana looked at Kyle for help, but he just shrugged.

"I don't know," she said. "It's kind of a late start. Parking is probably already filling up."

"Is it *too* late though?" Stephan asked.

Elana looked at Stephan with his puppy dog eyes. It was quite pathetic really.

"Well, I mean it's never too late if there's enough daylight, I'm just saying don't expect to be back before noon."

Stephan's face lit up. "I can live with that. It's settled then. We'll see you soon."

Stephan got up and started texting as he slowly walked towards the door.

Kyle signaled for the check and Elana looked at him in horror.

"What just happened there?" she said. "I don't remember agreeing to go hiking with you."

"That's Stephan for you," said Kyle. "I'll tell him you're out. This is a bad idea."

Elana looked at Stephan who had stopped at the door to wait for Kyle and was laughing obnoxiously at something on his phone. They would go with or without her. And she could see Stephan doing something stupid as he shouted, "Hey, look at me." She didn't need another accidental death on her conscience.

"No," she said with a sigh. "I'll go. Someone needs to protect Stephan from himself." Elana saw the hint of a smirk on Kyle's face. She suspected she wasn't the first person to say that.

On the way home, Elana stopped at the Foodland and picked up a couple larger bottles of water as well as some trail mix and jerky for snacks. She was surprised when she pulled into her driveway and found Kyle and his friends already there.

Kyle looked confused. "Did I pass you without realizing it? You aren't having problems with your jeep again, are you?"

Elana shook her head. "I stopped at the store to pick up provisions." She handed the bag to him.

"I just need to change really fast. Give me five minutes."

She ran inside and grabbed her two-piece and a backpack. She put the swimsuit on, and then put her clothes back on over it, but left her flip-flops in the closet, replacing them with socks and hiking shoes. She tried to think of what else she might need, such as sunscreen, and threw them into the pack, leaving room for the water and snacks waiting with Kyle.

Once the cottage was locked up she walked over to the shiny black Jeep Cherokee.

"All ready," she announced.

"Guys, Elana," said Kyle. "Elana, this is Amar, and that's Tad over there." Amar shook her hand and Tad nodded at her.

"So we were planning on letting you sit in the front," Stephan said as he scratched his head, "but it turns out us three," he pointed to Tad, Amar, and himself, "won't fit in the back seat."

"Okay," Elana said slowly.

"So you get to pick which two of us you would like to be sandwiched between."

She looked at Kyle in alarm.

"Stephan, you're in front," Kyle barked.

"What? Why do I have to be in front?"

Elana shook her head. "I'm regretting this already."

They all piled in and Kyle started the engine.

Amar turned to her. "How long have you lived in Hawaii?"

"Um, only about a year now." She was desperate to keep the conversation off of her. "So what brings you all to Kauai?"

Stephan smirked at Kyle before answering. "Oh, just a guys' only excursion. You know how it is."

"I see," she said, sure that there was in fact something she was missing. "Have you done anything fun yet?"

"We went zip lining yesterday," said Tad from her right side.

"Oh yeah? How was that?" she asked.

"It was pretty awesome," he answered. "They took us up into some backcountry and we got to go down a bunch of different zip lines. Have you done it before?"

"No, but I hear people recommending it all the time. Maybe one of these days I'll get around to it."

"What do you do on the island?" Amar asked.

"I'm a server at Bar Acuda in Hanalei."

Tad's forehead scrunched as he put it all together.

"The Bar Acuda?" he said. "Isn't that—"

"My favorite part so far was the helicopter ride," said Kyle, cutting him off. "We even had the doors open for it."

Tad was easily distracted. "Yeah, that was something else. That's actually where we found out about this waterfall. We flew over it from the air, but couldn't really see much of it."

"No, you definitely have to hike in to really appreciate it. Plus the swim is the best part."

"So what all did you buy for us?" Stephan asked as he rummaged through the bag at his feet.

"Oh, yeah. If you hand those back here I can load them in the backpack."

Stephan did and she just managed to squish it all in.

When they got closer to the trailhead, Elana tried to get Kyle to turn into the first parking lot, but Kyle insisted on going up farther to see if there was an open space.

"I'm telling you, it's too late in the morning," she said. "You're just going to have to turn around and come back."

"Then we'll turn around and come back," he replied.

There was one space open when they got closer, but it was being guarded by two younger girls obviously awaiting another car.

Kyle pulled up beside them and leaned out the

window.

"Morning, ladies," he crooned.

They giggled. They *actually* giggled. Elana thought she felt a little vomit in the back of her throat.

"Good morning," said the one in a Hello Kitty tank top. Elana wondered if these two were even legal.

Kyle pulled off his aviators and flashed his best Barnett smile.

"I don't suppose this space is available by any chance?"

They looked at each other.

"Well....We were supposed to be saving it for our friend," the second one said. This one's cut-offs were so short, Elana was sure she would be able to see her butt cheeks if she turned around.

"But she's really late, so maybe we could let you have it," Hello Kitty offered.

Kyle put a hand to his heart. "That would really make my day if you did."

They looked at each other and giggled again.

"Oh, okay," said Hello Kitty. They stepped aside and even went so far as to help Kyle back into it.

"My god, does anyone know how to say no to you," Elana muttered.

"Not if they know what's good for them," he answered.

Amar narrowed his eyes. "How exactly do you two know each other?"

This was exactly what Elana had been afraid of, but before she could say anything, Kyle came to the rescue.

"She was an intern back at the same firm as me back in the day. I recognized her when I ran into her here on the island."

"Intern?" asked Stephan. "How did you go from architecture to waitressing?"

"I decided that I wanted to live in Paradise instead," she said, echoing Kyle's earlier words.

They climbed out of the vehicle, and Kyle professed his undying appreciation to the ladies yet again for letting him have their spot. They blushed and then shot Elana a dirty look as the group moved past. Oh, look, there were Shortie's butt cheeks.

She checked her watch. "Almost nine-thirty. Not too bad. Anyone have to go to the bathroom before we leave?"

They all looked at each other and shook their heads.

"Lead the way," said Kyle.

Elana was at the head of the group and Kyle let the other guys go ahead between them. He was silently cursing Stephan for insisting she come along. So far it had been easy to dodge the personal questions Tad and Amar had asked, as well as Stephan who was just being a prick. Hopefully it stayed that way.

"Crap," Tad cursed as he just about tripped on some of the low rocks they were clambering over. "Is the whole trail this way?" he asked.

An audible sigh escaped Elana. "No, not the *whole* trail, but I warned you it could be treacherous. This is nothing compared to what we will find closer to the waterfall." A hand went to her hip as Kyle was learning it was prone to do when she was irritated. "If this is too much for you already, then maybe you should turn around right now and go wait for us in the car."

"No, I'm good," Tad muttered.

Kyle stifled a chuckle. He hoped she wasn't tired of Tad complaining already because the day was just getting started. He watched as Elana's small frame expertly maneuvered over the rough terrain far better than any of them. She was right though, it wasn't long before they were hiking on more dirt and less rocks.

At the first vista point, Tad pulled out his camera and asked Elana to get a picture of them with the sparking blue ocean at their backs, and she obliged.

"Do you want one with you in the shot?" Tad asked when she handed the camera back, but Elana quickly shook her head.

"Oh no," she said, "I'm not one for having my picture taken. I'm perfectly content to just be the photographer."

Kyle was relieved. He didn't need any pictures of him and Elana surfacing back home. As it was, he was going to have to figure out the most tactful way to ask the guys not to mention her. To anyone.

The pack marched on. An hour and several photo stops later, they were nearing the beach when they spotted a few surfers out on the water.

"I thought you couldn't drive out to this beach," said Amar.

"You can't," Elana answered.

"But I see surfers out there. I can't imagine them hiking with their boards."

Elana laughed and Kyle was struck by the sound of it. "They don't," she replied. "They boat in. See?" She pointed down between some trees and Kyle moved closer to see where she was indicating. As he stood next to her, he caught a hint of warm vanilla mingled with her perspiration. It was strangely arousing and he had to take a step back.

"You'd have to be a real die-hard to carry your board on this trail." She laughed again and Kyle gave her a quizzical look.

"What?" she asked.

"I just realized I've never seen you laugh before," he said. "I mean really laugh."

Her smile started to fade.

"You should do it more often," Kyle told her.

And it was gone completely.

"Yeah, well there was a time when I used to laugh a lot more often. You should have seen me back then." She turned around and continued their march down into the river valley.

Kyle tried to shake his guilt as he followed her.

Down at the beach they sat on the rocks for a water and snack break.

"Good call on the jerky," Stephan said as he bit off a chunk from his piece, putting a smile on Elana's face.

On the west end of the short beach there was a small cave that the guys wanted to check out before they continued out along the river valley to the waterfall.

"Just be careful of the riptides and currents," Elana warned them. "People drown here all the time."

"Thanks, mom," Stephan called over his shoulder as he ran off. This was exactly what she had been worried about.

"Is he always such a punk?" Elana asked Kyle who had hung back.

"Yes, he is," he answered.

Elana stuck a piece of jerky in her mouth and gnawed on it while she sat there watching the waves. They never failed to hypnotize her. She was surprised when she realized that Kyle was still standing on the beach near her.

"Aren't you going to go check out the cave?" she asked.

"Nah."

He continued to stand there staring out at the ocean as well. He had stripped out of his t-shirt when they got to the beach, and was now wearing only swim trunks. For the first time, Elana took full stock of him. He was dark, though she wasn't sure if it was from his time here on the island, or if he was naturally that bronze. Her guess was the latter. She was pretty sure that he worked out however, judging by his solid build. She found herself wondering what it would be like to touch his chest and quickly shook her head.

Where the hell did that come from?

"How did we get to this point?" she said aloud.

"Excuse me?" Kyle's eyes locked onto hers. She found it strangely intimidating, and moved her gaze back to the sparkling water.

"A week ago we were ready to rip each other's heads off."

Kyle sat down beside her. "I've been wondering the same thing."

"And?"

"And what?" he said.

"And what did you decide?"

He tilted his head to one side. "I'm thinking we may have passed judgment on each other too quickly."

"Speak for yourself," she said.

He gave her a light shove.

She laughed, but then said, "I'm serious. I still think you are a self-entitled rich boy." She gave him a sideways glance "But maybe you're not as evil as I originally thought. However the jury is still out so don't hold your breath just yet."

Kyle gave a warm, hearty laugh and Elana couldn't help but think that she liked this version of him much better than the cold, heartless Kyle Barnett she had built up in her mind. She didn't know if this was a good thing or not.

Amar, Stephan, and Tad rejoined them and they

continued their journey into the valley. It was almost another hour before they made it to the waterfall. And just as Elana had told them, the going got much tougher. She could see Tad getting ready to complain, but one look in his direction shut him up.

"Here we are gentleman," Elana announced as they stood at the edge of a small pool being fed by a waterfall originating from about one-hundred fifty feet above their heads tumbling down a sheer moss covered cliff.

"Wow," said Kyle. "You weren't kidding, this is amazing."

"Wait until you swim out under it. It will take your breath away. Literally. Between the cold, the exertion of getting out there, and the air being disturbed by the falling water, it's a bit hard to breathe."

"What do you mean cold?" Amar asked.

"I mean be prepared for the frigid temperatures. We're on the north shore of the island so this pool here never sees sunlight. "

Amar walked up to the water and stuck in his hand and immediately pulled it back out.

"Oh, hell no, I'm not getting in that!" he said.

"Don't be such a baby," Elana told him and the other guys snickered. "Why did you hike all this way if you weren't going to swim?"

"If I'd known it was going to be this cold I wouldn't have hiked here."

Elana rolled her eyes and then proceeded to strip down to her bikini. Everyone else but Amar removed their shoes and shirts.

The four of them inched along the rocks lining the edge of the pool.

"Shit! That is cold," Tad said.

"I promise you get used to it," Elana told him.

"Are you sure?" he asked.

"Sure. You eventually go numb and don't even notice the cold." She laughed at his reaction.

He got in to just past his knees before deciding he'd had enough and joined Amar on a dry rock where they started raiding Elana's backpack.

"Geez," Elana called out to them. "I had no idea I was surrounded by such chickens."

"You're not the one that has to worry about your balls shrinking up into your gut," Tad yelled back. "I would like them to see the light of day again someday."

Elana's head fell back in laughter.

Just then Stephan jumped all the way in, and let out a whoop when he came back up.

"Damn that is cold!" he said.

"Go swim out to the waterfall now," Elana said.

He started climbing out. "Nope. I jumped in. That's good enough for me."

Elana shook her head and looked at Kyle. "And then there was you."

He looked at her intensely and she fought the urge to look away again.

"And then there was me," he said.

They continued to stare at each other before Elana finally broke the trance.

"Well?" she asked. "Are you going to jump in?"

"I don't know," he answered. He moved a couple steps further and was now unable to take another step without plunging in completely, as the rocks simply provided a shelf around the pool. "It's pretty fucking cold."

"Wuss," she said with a sly smile.

"What about you? You haven't jumped in yet."

She carefully stepped down to the ledge next to him. "You don't think I'll jump?"

"No, I don't," he said. "You're shivering already, and you have goose bumps all over." He ran a hand down her arm, and Elana tried to ignore the sensation it sent through her body.

That was all the motivation she needed to dive in. When she came up, she was already a quarter of the way across the pool. She turned onto her back and faced them all.

"Chickens!" she called out.

There was a splash when Kyle jumped in, and Elana swam as quickly as she could towards the waterfall. She was a strong swimmer, but Kyle was faster, and she squealed when he gave a gentle tug on her ankle.

She splashed water in his direction, making him laugh that same warm sound.

"Sorry," he said, practically shouting over the roar of the waterfall. "I don't take lightly to being called a chicken."

"Duly noted," she replied.

Kyle swam past Elana under the curtain of water, and she followed him into the alcove that was carved out behind it.

"So what's up with your friends?" she asked.

"You called it earlier." He answered. "They're a bunch of pansies. But I keep them around because it makes me feel better about myself."

"Of course, you do," Elana laughed and Kyle smiled at her.

"You were right earlier," she said.

"I'm always right. Which time are you referring to?"

"You are unreal," she said, shaking her head. "I was referring to your comment about me laughing. I think I've laughed more today than I have in a long time."

Kyle swam closer to her until he was only inches from her face. Elana's first instinct was to pull back, but she forced herself to stay put.

"I think what I was trying to say earlier is that I'm sorry for what my family has put you through," he told her.

"Don't," she said, the smile disappearing from her face.

"Don't what?"

She rolled her eyes. "Please don't pity me."

"Pity—what? I'm not pitying you. I'm trying to apologize."

"But why? Why are you apologizing now, when only a week ago you wished nothing but the worst for me?"

"After we talked Sunday and I saw first-hand what you were dealing with—"

"And you took pity on me," she interrupted.

She could see him sighing even though she couldn't hear over the rushing water. "You're exasperating," he yelled at her.

Stephan appeared from the other side of the waterfall.

"What's going on back here?" he asked.

"Wow," Elana said, "you made it."

"Let's just say I drew the short straw. We were getting worried you guys had drowned or something."

"Sorry," said Kyle. "We should probably head back in."

Elana agreed and started swimming back to the rocks.

When she got back to the shore and climbed out, she turned to see that Stephan and Kyle were still treading water near the waterfall and deep in conversation. She couldn't make out anything they were saying.

"How do you all know each other?" Elana asked Amar and Tad.

"Tad and I met Kyle in college," Amar answered. "We were in the same fraternity."

She looked back over her shoulder. "And what about Stephan?"

"They go way back," said Tad. "At least high school, maybe even earlier than that."

Stephan and Kyle finally climbed out. The five of them sat on the rocks a bit longer to let Elana, Kyle, and Stephan dry off and rehydrate.

"Now that we're exhausted," Elana finally said, "we get to make the trek back."

For the return journey Elana let everyone else go ahead. Kyle started out in front of her and would periodically turn around to check on her pace.

When they came to a river crossing where they had to jump over the steam originating from the pool they had just left, he insisted on her going ahead of him, now putting her second to last among the pack. She was sure she could feel his eyes burning into the back of her neck. When she couldn't take it any longer, she turned around and he flashed a warm smile at her.

"You okay?" he asked.

She nodded and turned back around.

The trip back to the car took considerably longer than it did getting to the waterfall. Everyone was moving a lot slower, especially Tad, who had started to complain that his legs were getting tired. And that he was hungry. And thirsty. Elana finally thrust the backpack into his arms at one stop.

"Seriously, Tad, grow a pair."

Everyone but Tad laughed, especially Kyle,

which made her blush.

"Sorry," she muttered.

"Oh no, it's perfectly all right," said Stephan. "It's about time someone said it to his face."

Tad flipped him the bird and they continued on.

When they finally made it off the trail, Amar, Stephan, and Tad made for the bathroom.

"Do you need to go before we head back?" Kyle asked Elana.

"No, thank you," she said. "I've seen those restrooms. I can hold it until we get back to my place."

He chuckled and they walked back to the car. Kyle followed her to the passenger side of the vehicle that happened to be out of sight from the restrooms. She was about to grab the handle when Kyle grabbed her arm, spun her around, and gently pushed her back to the door as he pressed his mouth against hers. It didn't even occur to her to not let his tongue in. He never did put his shirt back on after the swim, and she now got her wish of wanting to know how his chest would feel beneath her hands. Warm, solid, strong. Kyle's own hands moved down her sides to grip her hips.

He slowly pulled away. Though the kiss had lasted only mere seconds, it left her breathless.

"I've been wanting to do that all day," he whispered.

Elana stared at him, wavering between wanting to slap him and wanting him to do it again. It was all so confusing. She turned clumsily and attempted to open the door. It was difficult with him still standing so close.

Kyle stepped back and helped her open it. When she had climbed in, he walked around to the driver's side and waited outside for the rest of their crew. Elana sat solitary in the car, fighting back the urge to cry, though she wasn't sure why. Wasn't Kyle supposed to be the enemy? Why did he kiss her? Why did it feel so damn good?

When the other three returned, they climbed in and made the trip back to Elana's cottage in silence. Everyone was too exhausted to make conversation. Just within her peripheral vision, Elana could see Kyle glancing at her in the rearview mirror, but she continued to stare straight ahead. They pulled into Elana's driveway and Amar got out to let Elana exit. She suspected Tad was still mad about her comment earlier.

"Thanks guys. It was…" She searched for the right word. "It was entertaining."

"You should join us for dinner," said Stephan.

"I don't think so," she replied.

Amar joined. "No, you should join us. We're going to the Dolphin Fish Market tonight. It's supposed to be really good."

"I've eaten there before," she said. "It is good; you guys'll enjoy it."

She could feel Kyle's gaze upon her, but he voiced no opinion either way.

"So thanks for the invite," she said, "but I'm exhausted. I'll probably be turning in early tonight."

"Have it your way," said Stephan. "Until next time."

Elana waved good-bye. "Until next time." She really doubted there would be a next time, however. She walked up the path to her cottage, and Kyle drove off.

"I call first dibs on the shower," Stephan shouted the second they walked into the hotel room.

Tad and Amar groaned while Kyle smirked and made his way up to his own shower.

The hot water felt good as it washed the grime of the hike off Kyle's body, and he found his thoughts drifting to Elana. He remembered the brightness of her eyes against her dark hair and olive skin and wondered if they had always been that blue. He thought back to the trial and could only picture her in subdued hues painted by his grief and anger.

But today he had seen her in full Technicolor vision. And not just the sight of her, but the sound of her laugh and her intoxicating scent. For a second Kyle thought he smelled warm vanilla again, and his body reacted.

"Dammit," he muttered and switched the water to cold.

Cleaned up and thoughts of Elana purged from his mind, Kyle came down the stairs to find Stephan and Amar showered, but neither looked dressed for dinner.

"What's going on?" he asked.

"I think I'm going to have to take a rain check on dinner," said Amar.

"You're kidding, right?"

"Dude, we are worn out," Stephan told him. "Room service is sounding pretty good right now."

"Bunch of wusses, that's what you all are," Kyle said.

Amar and Stephan just shrugged.

"Fine. Order whatever you want," he said as he grabbed the iPad. He made it halfway up the stairs before Stephan caught him.

"You should still go," said Stephan.

"And spend an evening one-on-one with Tad? No, thank you."

"Not Tad. He's out as well. I mean with Elana."

Kyle's head shook. "You heard her. She didn't want to go either."

"I'm sure if you showed up, she would change her mind."

Kyle looked down at Amar sprawled on the couch and Tad just coming out of the downstairs bathroom. His friends had always had a hard time keeping up with him, and he wasn't ready to put his feet up for the night just yet.

"I suppose dinner with Elana might not be so bad," he said.

After her shower, Elana put on the old track shorts and tank top she usually slept in. She picked up the library book she had been working on, turned on some music, and curled up on her bed. She was surprised when just after five there was a knock at her door. All she had to do was sit up to see who was standing on the other side through the thin white curtain that covered the glass-paned door. What the hell was Kyle doing on her front step?

Four

"WHAT ARE YOU doing here?" she asked upon opening the door.

The sight of her in pajamas seemed to catch him off guard. His eyes moved slowly down her body and back up again before he could form words and she cursed the current it sent through her.

"Well, hello to you, too," he said. "I came to see if you wanted to join me for dinner. I don't have your cell number so I had to come personally."

"What happened to your friends?" she asked, crossing her arms.

"Exhaustion overcame them. Room service is probably arriving as we speak."

"Well, as you can see," she said, "I'm not really dressed for going out."

"I'll wait while you change."

"I never said I was going to change."

"I've decided that you're having dinner with me tonight," said Kyle. "If you don't feel like changing, I'll be more than happy to pick up takeout and we'll eat here."

Elana could not believe the nerve of this man. "And what if I have decided that I am *not* having dinner with you tonight?" she said, planting a hand on her hip.

"Give me one good reason why not," he said.

She had a perfectly good reason, but she didn't dare voice it for fear of betraying herself.

"Have you eaten yet?" he asked.

"No." She reluctantly admitted. "Fine. I will go find something suitable to wear."

He grinned. "Damn. I was hoping you would decide to have dinner here."

"There isn't room to have dinner here," she said with an effort to brush off what he had just implied. She wasn't sure it was a good idea to be alone in her cottage with him.

"In fact," she continued, "you'll have to wait in the car while I get ready. It's just too cramped in here."

His face fell. "Are you serious?"

"Yes, I am. I'll be out in ten minutes." She closed the door before he could protest anymore.

She walked over to her closet and found a pale yellow sun dress that wasn't too wrinkled and a pair of sandals. She didn't own any 'date' clothes anymore, so she was just looking for something presentable. Not that this was a date, she reminded herself. In the bathroom she dusted a little powder on her face and applied a touch of lip gloss. She hadn't done anything with her hair after the shower, and now it had a wave to it. And not the sexy kind, but rather something that screamed, *I didn't run a comb through my hair*. She did so now and then worked it into a loose French-braid down the side to hide her lack of any real effort.

She opened her door and found Kyle not in the car as she had instructed, but sitting on her bottom step, playing on his phone.

"I didn't feel like sitting in the car," he said.

"Do you have any idea what a spoiled brat you are?"

He shrugged. "Let's go. I'm starving."

She followed him to the car, where he held the door open for her. It wasn't the first time that day that she wondered what the hell she was thinking.

"I'm surprised you're up for going out," she said as they made the drive into Hanalei. "I don't blame your friends for deciding to stay in tonight. I'm beat as well."

"It takes a lot to wear me down," he answered.

"Mmm….Well, don't be surprised if I'm not very good company."

"As long as you don't fall asleep at the table, I promise not to hold it against you," he said.

She feigned a yawn. "I don't know. That might be asking a lot of me."

Kyle laughed. "I'm sure I could find ways to keep you awake."

The Dolphin was just starting to fill up and they were able to get seated right away.

The hostess offered to take their drink orders and Kyle ordered the Kauai Golden Ale while Elana opted for the Mai Tai.

"A Mai Tai?" he said, raising an eyebrow.

"They're yummy, and I never get to have one," she said, leaning back and looking around at the other patrons. "It's not exactly the drink of choice when you're drinking by yourself…" she trailed off as she saw the concern spreading across his face.

"Not that I drink alone that often," she assured him. "A glass of wine now and then. I just mean that I don't have much opportunity to go out with anyone."

"That doesn't exactly make me feel any better," he said.

"It is what it is." She picked up her menu and looked it over.

"Any recommendations?" Kyle asked, opening his own menu.

"I only ate here once before with my parents when they came out just after I arrived on the island," she said. "I really liked the ahi. If they have the Mahi Mahi available, that's supposed to be good."

"I like ahi. I think I may have to order that tonight."

The server brought over the drinks and took their dinner orders before leaving them alone again.

Elana took a sip of her fruity cocktail and decided to ask something that been on her mind all day.

"Do your friends really not know who I am, or are they just being polite?"

"Stephan knows," said Kyle, "but Tad and Amar have no idea."

"And what does Stephan think of you and I—you and I spending time like this?"

"I don't know. I guess he finds it entertaining."

"Entertaining?" she asked. "How?"

"Just that he finds it amusing. As you have probably noticed, he can be a bit immature at times."

"He wouldn't do anything rash like tell your parents, would he?"

Kyle thought for minute. "Doubtful."

"Doubtful? That doesn't sound very reassuring," she said. "Aren't you worried about your mother finding out you're consorting with the enemy?"

"Well, being her son, I think she would eventually forgive me. And as for you, I don't think she could hate you anymore than she already does."

"Glad you find this so humorous. I knew this was a bad idea."

"Why?" he asked.

"Why? Why not? Why are you being nice to

me? Why are we spending time together?" She leaned in and lowered her voice. "Why the hell did you kiss me?"

Kyle smiled. Elana wondered if he was remembering the kiss and she felt herself flush as the memory of it went through her own mind.

"Answer me or take me home," she said.

"First I want to go back to your comment about me pitying you."

"Don't change the subject," she snapped.

"I'm not," he said, "I'm explaining myself. I'm not pitying you. I'm just seeing you. The real you."

"I don't understand."

"From the moment you came into our lives, I only ever knew you as the driver that killed my brother."

She opened her mouth to defend herself, but Kyle raised a hand to stop her.

"I'm just saying that's how I saw you at the time," he said, and for the first time, she met his intense gaze and felt no desire to look away. "I didn't know anything about you," he continued. "I didn't want to know anything about you. And of course my mother, being the lovely women that she is, did everything to encourage that sentiment. But then last Sunday you said some things that made me wonder if I wasn't seeing the whole picture. I told you that I called the lawyers after I got back to the hotel, but I also started looking up past articles on-line. Turns out that there was a lot of information in there. Personal information. About how you grew up in Redmond with your parents who work at Boeing. How you graduated valedictorian from Lake Washington High School. And apparently we not only both attended the University of Washington, but for two of those years, we were enrolled at the same time."

"Huh," she said. "I didn't know you were a Husky."

"I've begun to realize that my mother may have been misguided in her mission to seek justice for my brother's death."

Elana looked down at her hands as Kyle continued.

"I'm being nice to you because my family, mainly my mother, took their grief out on you, and now I'm trying to do the right thing. As for why I kissed you, that was simple."

She looked back up at him.

"Because you looked pretty damned adorable every time you mouthed off to Stephan."

His words made her blush. Again.

"Not to mention Tad," Kyle added. "He's still a little sore over you telling him to grow a pair."

Elana cocked her head to one side. "Yeah, I suspected."

"So what do you think, Elana Tanner?" he asked. "Can we be friends?"

"Friends seems a bit strong," she said, narrowing her eyes at him. "It's not like you'll be calling or emailing me after you leave."

"Fair enough. Can we at least call a truce? Maybe I can look you up the next time I'm in the neighborhood."

Elana pretended to contemplate his proposal. "I suppose I could accept your surrender."

"You just can't cut a guy a break, can you?" Kyle laughed.

She giggled.

"Are you giggling?" he teased.

She shook her head and then nodded. "Sorry, it's the Mai Tai."

"Don't apologize. It's cute."

She stopped and cleared her throat as the food arrived. They sat in silence for a moment tasting their selections.

"Good call on the ahi," said Kyle. "This is delicious."

"Here," she lifted her fork, "you should try a bite of my scallops."

Kyle took the bite and chewed.

"Not bad. If you ever find yourself in Key West though, there is this hole-in-the-wall restaurant called Blue Heaven that has the best scallop sauce in the world."

Elana smiled at his enthusiasm.

"I kid you not," he said. "A critic reportedly claimed that the sauce could make cardboard taste good, and I don't doubt it."

"Well, I'm glad I haven't had them yet then, because I think these taste quite delicious." She took another bite.

"I'm sorry; I wasn't trying to knock them. They are delicious. It just made me remember. I swear Blue Heaven has ruined me for scallops."

"And I have been to Key West before. But I don't think I've ever heard of Blue Heaven."

"When were you in Key West?"

"Benja—" She stopped herself. "My ex-boyfriend's father lived in Florida, so whenever we went to visit we tried to make a run down. Go do the Duval Crawl."

Kyle nodded. "I am familiar with that one. A lot of fun. Maybe too much fun."

Elana laughed with him. "Yeah, the hangover the next day was never quite as fun."

But then Elana's smile disappeared. "I don't think I could ever drink that much again."

Kyle's smile faded as well. There was a

moment of silence and Elana knew their thoughts were in the same place. And then came the words Elana never imagined she would hear from Kyle Barnett's lips.

"He could be a real asshole, you know."

"What?" she said. "How can you say that about your brother?"

"It's true," he said. "I loved him. He was my brother and I miss him. But he was an asshole."

Elana knew they must have reached a new level in their 'relationship' for him to be sharing this with her.

"You call me spoiled and self-entitled," he continued, "but you should have seen my brother. He didn't care about anyone but himself. My parents were always having to clean up after his messes. Did you know that he got two different girls pregnant?"

Elana gasped. "But there was never anything said about him having children."

"There's only one. He convinced the first girl to have an abortion. The second time he denied being the father. Of course she demanded a paternity test and, get this, Jarod bribed the tech to use his own DNA instead of his."

"That's horrible! What happened to the woman and child?" Elana asked.

"She was pissed, but there wasn't much she could do," said Kyle. "She didn't know how Jarod had done it, but I think she realized she could never win against him. She later married a guy who did well in construction, and last I heard he adopted the child as his own. It was a girl, by the way. And I guarantee she is better off, both of them, without Jarod in their lives."

"Wow," said Elana. "I had no idea."

"Of course not, my mother was determined to keep any of it from leaking to the press."

"But that doesn't make me feel any less guilty about what happened that night," she said.

Kyle gave a little smile. "That's because you're a good person."

"It's nice to hear that someone in your family thinks so," she mumbled, avoiding his gaze.

They continued to eat while Elana thought about Jarod's child.

"You seem to know a lot about what happened to that girl and her baby," she said.

Kyle squirmed. "Technically she was family."

"Having a baby can be expensive."

"I may have heard that."

"I'm not your first beneficiary, am I?" she asked.

Kyle said nothing and just continued eating his ahi, but his silence spoke volumes to Elana.

When the server left the bill, Kyle reached for it, but Elana beat him to it.

"Tonight is my treat," she said with a hand over it.

"You know I can't let you do that," he said, placing his hand firmly over hers. "Besides, I'm the one that dragged you out."

"I don't care." Elana ignored the heat of his hand on hers. "I want to thank you for helping with my jeep, since you won't let me pay for that either."

Kyle stared her down, but Elana held her ground.

"You either let me pay this check," she said without breaking eye contact, "or I wire the money for my jeep to your lawyers with explicit instruction to give you half and keep the other half for themselves. That way they will be less motivated to honor your request to send it back."

"You don't play fair, you know that?" he said, finally letting her go.

She giggled again as she pulled out some of the cash she had been carrying around for the past three days. She was pretty sure it wouldn't be handed back to her this time.

"In that case, thank you for dinner. And the company," he added.

"My pleasure."

Kyle stood up when Elana scooted her chair back and walked behind her with his hand on the small of her back. His warm touch through the thin cotton became the only thing she was aware of, and as they made their way to the exit, she nearly knocked over a woman standing by the hostess booth.

"I'm so sorry," she said to the dark-haired woman.

"It's all right," the women said.

"Elana?"

Elana looked at the gentleman standing next to the woman and did a double take.

"Benjamin?" she said. "What are you doing here?"

"I could ask you the same thing," he said. The woman put her arm around his waist. Benjamin looked down at her, and then back at Elana. "We're, uh, we're here on our honeymoon. Over in Kapa'a."

The color drained from Elana's face. "Your honeymoon," she whispered.

"What about you?" Benjamin asked with an awkward smile.

"I—" She couldn't think what to tell him. Just then Kyle threw his arm around Elana.

"We're just here on vacation. Isn't that right, honey?"

Elana looked up into his warm brown eyes and

mustered a smile before looking back at the happy newlyweds. "That's right," she said. "Just taking in the Aloha Spirit."

Kyle held out his hand. "I'm Kyle, by the way."

Benjamin took it hesitantly. Elana suspected he recognized Kyle, but fortunately couldn't quite place him. "I'm Benjamin. And this is my wife Robin."

Kyle took her hand and flashed his best Barnett smile. "It's nice to meet you. Congratulations on your recent nuptials."

Elana watched her succumb to his charm.

"My nup – oh yes. Why, thank you!"

"Well, we should get back to the room, honey," Kyle said to Elana as he kissed her forehead. "It's been a long day hiking the Na Pali coast and all."

"Are you guys here in Hanalei?" Benjamin asked.

"We're just up the road at the St. Regis," Kyle answered.

Benjamin's eyes went wide. "Oh, I hear that's nice."

Kyle smiled at Elana. "Yeah, we like it, don't we sweetie?"

She smiled back up at him trying not to giggle as he used words such as "sweetie" and "honey. Not to mention the thought of her and Kyle actually being a couple.

"Oh yes," she told Benjamin and Robin. "Breakfast on the terrace is absolutely gorgeous."

Kyle turned back to Benjamin and Robin. "Well, we will let you go enjoy your dinner. I hope you enjoy the rest of your honeymoon."

Kyle kept his arm around Elana as they walked out to the car.

"Thank you," Elana said when they were back on the road.

"I'm guessing that's the jerk that left you during the trial."

"But how did you—"

"You mentioned it during one of your rants," he told her. "You said that you'd lost your job and your boyfriend because they couldn't handle the media circus."

"Oh. Yes, that was him."

"Had you seen him since?"

"Briefly, when he came to collect the last of the stuff he had left behind," she said. "After things died down he tried to reach out as a friend, but I couldn't do it. It hurt too much."

Kyle reached over and took her hand.

"If he couldn't stick with you through that mess, then he didn't deserve you."

She slowly untangled her hand from his. She didn't trust these feelings that were stirring inside of her.

"Again, thank you for coming to my rescue tonight."

"It was my pleasure." He grinned at her.

"When do you go home?" she asked.

"Why? Are you really that eager to get rid of me?"

She shrugged and turned to the window to watch the dark shadows slipping by. "I'm just wondering."

"Tuesday. We head home Tuesday morning."

"Oh, that's coming up soon." She tried to keep the disappointment out of her voice. Because she wasn't disappointed. She couldn't wait to have him out of her life again.

They pulled into the driveway and Elana jumped out. Kyle killed the engine and got out as well.

"Thanks for dragging me out tonight," she told him. "It really was more fun than I thought it would be."

She watched him, hoping he would take that as his cue to leave, but he was looking up at the night sky.

"God, the stars are amazing out here," he said.

Elana smiled. "I guess."

"We should go see them from the beach."

"You should probably get back to your hotel," she said.

He grabbed her hand and pulled her in the direction of the shoreline. "C'mon, we won't be long."

Elana groaned. Now she really knew this wasn't a good idea.

They crossed the highway and found a log nearby to sit on. Kyle leaned back to take in as many stars as he could, while Elana looked down at the sand already sticking to her toes.

"This sand is going to be everywhere," she said.

"Stop being such a downer and enjoy the moment."

Elana shook her head and looked up. He was right. It was a relatively cloudless night and the stars were at their best.

"You forget just how many of the stars you are missing in the city," said Kyle.

"They are quite beautiful. And the waves crashing on the beach...it's like being in a dream."

They sat in silence for a minute just absorbing it all.

"I can understand why you chose to move here," Kyle said.

Elana snorted. "I didn't exactly have a choice."

He looked down at her with a raise eyebrow. "Nobody said you had to leave Seattle."

"Well, your family didn't make it easy for me to stay."

"Don't you think you're being a bit dramatic?" Kyle asked.

"I knew this was a mistake." Elana stood up. "This whole evening, this whole *day* was a mistake." She started to walk away, but Kyle jumped up and grabbed her arm.

"Hey—" But before she could say anything else, Kyle was pressing his mouth against hers and Elana lost her resolve. This kiss was different than the one at the trail head. It was much harder, more urgent, and Elana didn't want it to end. She grabbed his shirt and pulled him into her. Kyle responded by tightly wrapping his arms around her until they were one entity standing on the starlit beach.

Elana needed air, and she withdrew her lips from his.

A slow smile crept across Kyle's face. "I thought that might shut you up."

Elana pushed him back hard. "Unbelievable!"

"Wait! I didn't mean it like that!" But Elana was already crossing the highway and running back to her cottage. Kyle came after her.

"Go home, Kyle," she said when he caught up to her.

"I'm sorry. That came out wrong."

She ignored him and started to unlock her door. He grabbed her wrist and pulled her into him again.

Elana thought he was going to kiss her, but then his head shifted and his lips were now at her ear.

"You don't really think I'm going to let you say goodnight to me now, do you?"

She wanted to tell him to go away, but she

could feel the warmth spreading across her chest.

"What if I say no?" she whispered back. "Would you take me against my will?"

"Absolutely not." He nipped at her ear and she trembled. "But we both know you don't want to say no."

"How can you be so sure?" It was getting harder for her to focus as he placed his free hand on her hip.

"Because you didn't slap me when I kissed you at the trail."

"I wanted to," she interrupted.

"But you didn't." His lips grazed her neck. "And before I opened my big mouth, I'm pretty sure you were enjoying that kiss on the beach."

The hand on her hip slid down to the top of her thigh and began balling up the hem of her dress until his fingers made contact with her skin. How was she supposed to be rational when his touch felt so good?

"Open the door, Elana. Let's take this inside."

"No." It didn't come out with as much conviction as she had hoped. She was holding on to the last of her willpower with every ounce of strength she could muster. But it was fading fast.

Kyle removed his hand from her thigh and turned the key in the deadbolt. "Yes."

Elana hated how demanding he was. And she hated how right he was. She didn't want to say no. Would it really be so wrong to enjoy this one night? It had been so long since she had been this close to anyone. Just one night of guilty pleasure, and then he would go home and her life could go back to being less complicated.

She stepped back to open the door and they walked in. She didn't turn on any lights. The porch light would be plenty. She had forgotten to turn off her iPod earlier and now Ellie Goulding's seductive voice quietly drifted from the speakers.

Before Elana could turn around, Kyle was behind her kissing the back of her neck and shoulders, sending a chill she felt right down to her toes. Her dress was pulled up over her head and Kyle threw it in the corner. Elana could feel the goose bumps as he undid her bra and slowly slid the straps down her arms with gentle fingers. When he let it drop to the floor, she instinctively crossed her arms across her chest. He turned her around, and she stood before him in nothing but her underwear. She was shivering more from anticipation than anything else.

"Are you okay?" he asked softly.

She stared up into his beautiful eyes and felt confident that he meant no harm.

"Yes."

He removed his shirt and pulled Elana's hands from her chest to wrap them around his neck. Kyle leaned down to kiss her, and he wrapped his arms around her. He held her so tightly that Elana feared she might break, yet she still didn't feel close enough.

Their tongues danced slowly at first, but quickly gained tempo. She could feel his chest rising in quick succession as he became breathless, and her heart raced with it.

She suddenly realized that she didn't just want him right now, she *needed* him. If only for tonight.

Her fingers tugged on the waist band of his shorts, pulling him towards the bed. Elana gently pushed him onto her coverlet. Amusement danced in his eyes, and she grinned at his reaction.

Elana slid his shorts and underwear off, leaving him completely naked on her bed. He was mostly shadows in the minimal light, but she could make out the finer points of his physique. The ripped abs, tight thighs, even the erect penis demanding her attention. She climbed up onto the bed and straddled him, leaving only the thin cotton between her and his erection. Kyle moaned. She leaned forward and gently pressed her lips to the base of his throat while he reached behind her and pulled the hair tie from the end of her braid. Elana kissed a trail up to his right ear as he ran his hand through her hair, causing it to cascade over her face and onto his torso. She licked and gently bit him and Kyle sucked in a breath.

Elana felt his hips grinding into hers, but he wasn't going to get far with her underwear still on and he knew that. Kyle rolled her onto her back and kissed her hard before she even knew what was happening.

"My turn," he growled and began kissing down her chest. He flicked his tongue across her right nipple as he reached down to that damned last piece of clothing. Once it was on the floor where it belonged, Kyle moved his hand back to between her legs. Elana gasped as his fingers began to explore her. His mouth was on her throat and then he was kissing her mouth again.

His tongue, his fingers, his skin against her hands; it was all so intoxicating. But then his fingers were moving away, and she was disappointed until she felt something of more stature sliding into her, and she gave a little cry.

"God, you feel good, Elana," he muttered into her ear.

Even hearing him say her name was heady. She needed to take control again before she lost all of her senses. Keeping one leg straight, she pulled the other up and pushed on him.

"I want to be on top," she breathed.

Kyle placed an arm under her and carefully

rolled onto his back, keeping Elana against his chest.

Elana gripped his hands, pinning them on either side of his head, tugged on his lower lip with her teeth before thrusting her tongue into his mouth, all the while gently sliding along his shaft. When Elana released his hands, Kyle slid them down her back and gripped her hips. Elana sat up and grinded against him, enjoying the sensation it caused. She could feel the electricity starting to tingle through her body and she knew she was close. She began to move faster and lost awareness of everything else as the orgasm swept over her. She arched back and bit her lip to keep from screaming and dug her nails into Kyle's chest. She felt like her whole body was about to explode. The electricity subsided and Elana slowly opened her eyes. She had forgotten just how good it could feel. She tried to remember if it had *ever* felt that good.

Elana leaned forward and planted her hands on either side of Kyle's head. She needed a second. But Kyle gripped her hips and lifted her only a little before thrusting again. It was a quick short movement, but it was enough to steal her breath. He did it again and she sat back up sending him deeper into her. Kyle quickened his pace and Elana moved with him. She could feel the warmth spreading through her body, and Elana didn't believe it possible, but another orgasm rolled through her in waves. Screw the neighbors, she decided, letting out the most erotic scream as she rocked back and forth even harder, trying to prolong the sensation.

And they weren't done yet. Kyle pulled her down for a kiss and rolled her onto her back again. He hitched an arm under her right thigh and continued to pound into her.

For the third time that night, she felt herself back on the verge. As Kyle moved faster in and out of her, nearing his own climax, Elana started to come yet again. She scraped her nails down his back and gripped him hard, no doubt pushing Kyle over the edge. Elana watched as his beautiful face went rigid while he succumbed to the moment.

Kyle collapsed on the bed next to Elana who was just as breathless.

"I," Elana started, "I don't even know what to say."

Kyle laughed and rolled over to kiss her shoulder. Without any words of his own, he got up and went into the bathroom.

Elana continued to lie there and realized that she did know what to say. That it was intense, amazing even. But she preferred to keep those thoughts to herself.

Kyle washed his hands and took a curious look around Elana's insanely small bathroom. Something was missing.

"Elana?" he called out, poking his head around the corner.

She propped herself up on her elbows and Kyle could see a light sheen of perspiration still lingering across her chest. It almost made him forget what he was going to say.

"Do you not have a shower?" he asked.

She smiled. "It's outside."

"Outside?"

She stood up pulling the coverlet off the bed and around her. He didn't know why she was being so modest now, considering what they had just on top of that very blanket. Elana slid past him into the bathroom and walked out the back door. Kyle followed her onto the equally small back deck where there was a shower head coming out of the side of the house with low walls creating an enclosure around it.

"And you use it?"

She laughed. "Of course I use it. Outdoor showers are more common than you think in Hawaii."

In the light streaming through the bathroom window, Kyle could see that it was only jungle past the edge of her deck, and with the main house at the front of the property, you couldn't really see it from here.

Elana sat down in one of the iron wrought chairs.

"I realize it's probably not the luxe accommodations you're used to, but it's private and functional."

Kyle sat down in the chair opposite her, still completely naked. Elana's eyes locked on his and he suspected it was only to keep them from wandering south. She wasn't blushing though, so he gave her points for that. She was, however, looking sexy as hell with her hair still mussed from the bedroom.

"Are you saying you don't think I know how to rough it?" he asked.

She extended one shapely leg out from beneath the blanket and rested the ball of her foot on the edge of Kyle's seat. Right between his thighs.

"I don't know. Maybe you have roughed it before. But I know you've never *had* to rough it."

"True," he said, looking down at her foot. She wiggled her toes.

"You're playing with fire, Elana."

Her eyes went dark as a seductive smile crossed her face. She had no idea the restraint he was practicing at the moment. But his body was about to give him away any second now.

"How long have you lived here?" he asked. Why not torture her a bit longer?

"It will be a year next month," she said. Her

eyes finally glanced down briefly and he could see the look of triumph on her face.

"And what you made you decide on Hawaii?" Whoops. Kyle had clearly said the wrong thing because the smile disappeared and her foot fell to the floor with a thud.

"I'm sorry," he said "I didn't mean—" But she was already getting up from her chair. He reached out and pulled her onto his lap.

"Hey," he said, pushing the hair out of her face. "I was just making conversation. Please don't be so sensitive."

She looked at him without saying anything, but she wasn't fighting him either. He saw it as a good sign.

"I seem to have a knack for saying the wrong things at exactly the wrong time."

This time she started to smile. Just a little. He softly kissed her lips, and when they parted for him, he knew that all had been forgiven.

She slid off his lap, and for a split second, Kyle thought he had misread her signals. But then she let the coverlet drop to the ground and carefully climbed back onto his lap with her knees on either side of him. Making love in the chair wasn't the most comfortable position, but being outside with the jungle behind them and the moon above, it was definitely the most exciting.

When Elana came out of the bathroom after washing her face, she had expected Kyle to be gone, or at least dressed and ready to leave, not passed out in her bed. She knew she should send him home, but couldn't bring herself to wake him. Instead she slid under the sheet next to him. She did her best to keep some space between them until he rolled over and pulled her into him. She began to wonder how asleep he really was. She was reluctant to admit it, but his body against hers felt entirely too good. *It's only one night*, she reminded herself as she drifted off to sleep with Kyle softly breathing into her neck.

Kyle woke the next morning to find Elana curled up in the only chair in the cottage, clutching a cup of coffee and staring out the window.

"Hey," he said, rubbing the sleep from his eyes.

Her face was pensive as she looked at him.

"How long have you been up?" he asked.

"Not long," she answered. "You're a heavy sleeper."

A grin spread across his face. "Yeah, well, someone wore me out yesterday. What with the hiking and...other activities."

Without any reaction to his comment, she stood up and walked over to the counter.

"I made some coffee if you want any," she said. "It's not very good, but it does the job."

"Sure, I'll take a cup."

Kyle climbed out of bed and pulled his shorts on. He walked up behind Elana and placed his hands on her shoulders, kissing the back of her neck. She immediately turned around and forced the cup into his hands.

"There you go," she said without so much as a smile.

"Um, thanks," he said.

She refilled her cup and sat back in the chair.

"Aren't your friends wondering where you are?" she asked.

He took a sip.

"Wow, this really is bad. Do you have any creamer or anything?"

"There's some half and half in the fridge," she told him.

"Guess I can make do with that." He grabbed it from the fridge and poured it in the coffee. "And as for your question, I'm pretty sure they figured it out." He put the carton back in the fridge and sat on the foot of the bed, only inches from where Elana was sitting in her chair at the small table. "But if I don't make it back soon, they may worry."

She nodded.

Kyle set his cup on the table and touched her knee, causing her to flinch.

"Is everything all right?" he asked.

"I'm fine. Why?"

"Do you regret last night?"

She couldn't keep the little smile from appearing on her face.

"No," she answered. "Last night was definitely something I don't regret."

"Then what is it?"

She set her own cup down next to his.

"Kyle, we both know exactly how this is going to end."

"Oh? And how is that."

She smiled and touched his cheek. "In a couple of days you are going to go home to your posh life in Seattle, and I will be here trying to keep my head down, and plowing through as usual. Last night was fun, but let's not make this more awkward than it has to be."

He grabbed the hand she had placed on his cheek. "But what if it didn't have to be that way? At the very least, couldn't I see you again before I leave? Maybe see what happens."

She pulled her hand away. "I don't think that's a good idea."

"I see." Kyle sat up straight now. "I guess now would be a good time to take my leave then."

She said nothing so he stood up and grabbed his shirt, keys, and phone. He walked over and leaned down to kiss her on the cheek.

"If you change your mind," he said in her ear, "you know where to find me."

She nodded, but remained speechless as he walked out the door.

Kyle climbed into his jeep and started the engine. He pulled onto the highway and tried to shake the irritation coming over him. He could honestly say that he had never been kicked out of a bed the next morning. Hell, he could remember a couple times where he was begged to stay. Was Elana always this callous? That was usually his job.

Was it just his imagination, how amazing last night had been? He remembered Elana's little smile when he mentioned the previous night. No, it wasn't just him.

He remembered very little of the drive back. His mind kept drifting to the taste of her skin on his tongue, her vanilla scent. He wondered if it was her soap or perfume, or if she just naturally smelled that seductive.

By the time he handed the keys to the valet, he was trying to shake those thoughts from his head. He hated to admit it, but Elana had been right. Kyle knew he was just asking for trouble by being involved with her. Then why the hell couldn't he get her out of his mind?

Kyle walked into the room and wasn't surprised to find Tad and Amar crashed out on the couches. He went upstairs to his own bed and was only mildly surprised to find Stephan in it.

"Please tell me you aren't naked in my bed right now," Kyle said.

Stephan grumbled before answering. "Relax. Housekeeping will change the sheets later."

Kyle rolled his eyes and grabbed some clothes to take into the bathroom with him.

"So?" Stephan asked.

"So what?"

"Did you sleep with her?"

"What do you think?" Kyle snapped.

"Are you sure that's a good idea?"

"Mind your own business." Kyle went into the bathroom. But then he came right back out. "Don't forget that you're the one who invited her to go hiking." He paused. "And then when everyone bailed on me for dinner, you're the one who insisted I take her instead."

"Because I thought she was fun," Stephan said. "I never expected you to sleep with her."

Kyle ran a hand through his hair. "Do you think it was a mistake?"

"Do you really want me to answer?"

Kyle shook his head. "Just forget about it. Let's not mention it, got it? If the guys ask, I just got back really late. What time did they crash?"

"We all crashed pretty early last night," said Stephan. "I'm sure you're fine."

"Good." Kyle went back into the bathroom and took his shower.

Normally Elana would have been off the next night, but she had managed to pick up the extra shift and was grateful for the distraction, though she wondered how productive she had actually been. As far as she could tell, she managed to get everyone's orders in properly and serve them to the right table, but she couldn't really remember doing it. Her mind drifted between memories of the incredible night before to the look on his face this morning. She tried to remind herself that he was a Barnett; a charmer. Women were surely a dime a dozen to him, and he knew how to make each one feel special. He wouldn't miss her. And she was determined not to miss him.

The next night was very similar, but she found herself fantasizing about running over to his hotel after her shift. Just to say goodbye perhaps. She knew she just needed to get through this last night. Tomorrow morning he would be gone, and she could focus on work and paying off her debts again.

It was drawing near to closing time when Elana came out with her last order of the evening and found Kyle sitting at the bar. He tried to catch her eye, but she ignored him as she delivered the order. She picked up the check from her only other table and swiped the card before returning it to the customer. The whole time she could feel Kyle's presence in the room as he sipped something amber and probably expensive. When she couldn't find anything else to do, she finally went over to the bar and stood next to where he sat.

"What are you doing here?" she asked.

"Why else would I be here?" he replied. "To see you."

The words made Elana's heart skip a beat, but she disregarded it.

"I can't stop thinking about you, Elana," he said when she didn't respond.

Kyle was not making this easy for her.

"Sounds like a personal problem," she told him.

"You can't honestly say that you haven't been thinking about me."

She sighed. "That doesn't mean anything."

"I leave tomorrow."

"I know. I've been counting down the hours. Can't wait."

He frowned as he pulled her closer to him.

"Please spend tonight with me," he said quietly.

"I can't," she whispered back, unable to keep her voice from trembling.

"What are you afraid of?" he asked.

"I have to get back to work," she said, and pulled away. She went into the back to get started on her closing duties. When she came back out, Kyle was gone.

But he hadn't gone far. When she went out to her jeep, he was leaning against it.

Five

"YOU REALLY DON'T know how to take a hint," she said.

"You aren't exactly being subtle," he said, blocking the driver's side door.

"Then what are you still doing here?"

"You didn't answer my question," he said. "What are you afraid of?"

"I'm not afraid of anything," she said. "I'm being rational. One of us has to be. What do you really expect to happen here, Kyle?" she asked, swallowing hard. "You leave tomorrow. Even if you didn't, what then? We get to enjoy a couple more days where we risk someone getting their heart broken. And more than likely it would be me and I can't handle that!" Her hand went to her mouth in surprise when she finished. Elana hadn't meant to reveal that much about her feelings.

Kyle moved in and placed his hands on either side of her face and kissed her. She felt her reservations melt away as she kissed him back. She tried to remember how he felt, how he tasted. She wanted to commit it to memory.

When he released her, he pressed his forehead to hers.

"You're right," he said. "I'm sorry." He kissed the top of her forehead and then turned and walked away.

Elana's eyes started to tear up as she watched him go, but she blinked and fought them back as hard as she could. She was not going to let Kyle Barnett make her cry.

The next morning Elana woke up feeling beat. She had gone to bed shortly after getting home, but it took her a long time to fall into a fitful sleep. She looked at the clock and saw that it was already eleven. If Kyle hadn't left the island yet, he was surely at the airport by now.

Deciding that he had consumed enough of her time and thoughts, she climbed out of bed and threw on some clothes before making her way to the beach to enjoy another long walk along the shore. During the walk she decided that she was going to get a second job. Even though she been so blasé about it to Kyle, the truth was that knowing it was going to take more than twenty years to pay off the settlement felt rather daunting.

After a shower and some breakfast, Elana headed into Hanalei to stop at the Kalypso Bar and Grill down the street from Bar Acuda, and see if they were looking for any part-time help during the days. Their schedule was currently full, but the manager thought he might need someone soon so he had her fill out an application.

Elana was doing her best not to think about Kyle at work that night, but it was harder than she expected. She had told him to leave her alone and he did. So why was she so melancholy over it? Maybe because deep down she had been hoping he wouldn't listen to her. That maybe he would be determined to prove her wrong. But she had been doing the right thing, and in the end they both realized it.

About halfway through her shift, the hostess brought an envelope over to her.

"A gentleman told me to give this to you," she said. "I offered to get you so he could hand it over personally, but he declined."

Elana frowned as she opened the envelope. It was a note from Kyle.

I couldn't get on that plane today. Meet me on the terrace after your shift.

She stuffed the envelope in her pocket. Damn him and his demanding ways.

She spent the rest of her shift going back and forth on whether or not she should go. In the end she decided she would. She needed to get it through that thick skull of his that he had to go home and forget about her.

Elana drove up to the St. Regis and pulled her key from the ignition. She was shaking as she entered and made her way across the lobby towards the terrace. She told herself it was nerves, not excitement at the idea of seeing Kyle again.

The restaurant was closed, but Kyle was sitting at one of the tables, reading a magazine while he waited for her. Her footsteps caught his attention, and a huge grin broke across his face. It was enough to make her heart flutter.

"You came," he said as he stood up.

She sat in the chair across from him and he sat back down.

"I almost didn't," she told him.

"But you did."

"Why didn't you get on that plane, Kyle?" she sighed.

"Because I wasn't ready to say good-bye to you."

She rolled her eyes. "And what happens when you're ready to say good-bye tomorrow, or next week."

"I don't know. Maybe I'll drag you back to Seattle with me."

"Well that's never going to happen."

He sat back to consider her statement, but then leaned forward again.

"Last night you admitted that you're afraid I might break your heart. Did it ever occur to you that you're breaking mine?"

"I have trouble believing that," she said. "What could you possibly see in me?"

Kyle pulled his chair around so that he was sitting next to her. "Obviously a lot more than you see in yourself. I see someone who is incredibly strong and sexy. No matter what gets thrown at you, you keep doing whatever you need to survive. You are not afraid to speak your mind to anyone, least of all to me. Not many people are that brave."

Elana smiled at the last comment, and Kyle ran his finger across her cheek.

"And when you let yourself relax, you laugh quite easily," he continued. "It's a beautiful thing."

He softly kissed her lips.

"I know that you must feel something for me as well," he said as he pulled away, "or you wouldn't be afraid of me breaking your heart."

Elana continued to sit in silence. She felt more exposed before him now than she did when they had been naked together in her bed.

"What if this is the start of something wonderful and we just walk away?" he asked. "Do you really want to spend the rest of your life wondering what if?"

"I'm so scared," she whispered.

"To be honest, so am I. But I feel like I've spent too much time playing it safe, and it hasn't worked out real well for me. I'm willing to take a chance if you are."

A debate raged in Elana's mind. Was she willing to take the risk? Was he worth the risk? Could she even trust him?

Kyle grew impatient of her lack of response and kissed her much harder this time. She felt his tongue slip past hers lips and search for her own tongue, which greeted it enthusiastically. All the doubts were pushed to the far corner of her mind as she leaned into him and grabbed his shirt.

"Is that a yes?" Kyle asked when they parted.

"It's not a no," she said. "Yet."

He stood up. "Let's get out of here."

He took her hand tightly in his as though he were afraid she might run away. The thought did cross Elana's mind, but she knew she didn't have the courage to bolt right now. Curiosity was getting the better of her, and she wanted to see where this would lead.

Kyle led her through the resort towards the elevators. Elana thought her heart was going to burst, it was racing so fast. She couldn't deny it. The idea of spending the night in Kyle's arms again was exhilarating.

They entered the elevator and found themselves alone as it made its journey to the eleventh floor. Kyle kissed the hand he had been clutching and asked if she was all right.

She smiled and nodded.

The elevator door opened and he pulled her

with him. It was only a couple of doors down to his room. He swiped the key and held the door open for her. She stepped into a small foyer with a table, complete with a vase of fresh flowers. The door closed behind them and Kyle placed his wallet and cell phone on the table. From there they entered into the main area that included the bed at one end and a large seating area including a table and two chairs at the opposite end.

"I decided to downgrade with the guys gone," Kyle said, while Elana tried to take it all in.

"Downgrade," she exclaimed. "This place is bigger than my cottage."

"No offense, but that isn't hard to do."

"True."

"You should see the bathroom, though."

She followed him into the marbled bathroom that boasted a double sink vanity and jetted tub beneath a window looking out over the bay. She pretended to get misty eyed.

"Do you know how long it's been since I've even seen a tub, let alone sat in one?" she said.

Kyle sat on the edge of the tub and placed a hand on the handle.

"Would you like to take one?"

"Now?"

"Why not?" He turned the water on without waiting for her to answer, and she giggled.

He stood up and pulled her close. "Look at that, I can make you giggle even without a Mai Tai." She giggled again.

His hands grabbed the bottom of her white t-shirt and pulled it up over her head. Kyle let it drop to the floor as he kissed her and slid his fingers under the straps of her bra, pulling them off her shoulders. His lips moved down her neck and chest, where he began tracing a line along the top of her bra with his tongue. She moaned softly.

"Sorry. I got distracted," he said as he stood upright again. He reached around and undid the clasp on her bra and pulled it off her arms completely. It joined the shirt on the floor.

Elana lifted her now free arms and wrapped them around Kyle's neck. He kissed her, but only for a moment.

"We aren't done yet," he said, and unwrapped her arms from his neck. "You can't get in the bath tub with your pants still on."

Elana wondered if Kyle realized how much he was torturing her. *He has to*, she thought as he got on his knees and removed her shoes and socks and then slid her pants down. She leaned back on the counter with both hands for support while he helped her step out of them.

A shiver went through her when he ran his left hand up the inside of her left leg. Without letting go of her leg, he reached around and shut off the water and it was suddenly quiet in the bathroom, making her aware of how heavy her breathing had become.

Kyle turned his attention back to her, starting with small kisses just above her knee, both hands now free to gently glide their way up and down the outside of her thighs. His kisses continued their journey north, and she almost cried in disappointment when they passed the apex of her thighs and landed on her stomach below the navel. But while one hand had migrated around to cup her left butt cheek, the other had worked its way forward and was gently caressing her now. She was like butter in his hands and knew there was nothing she would deny him…if only he would finish what he had started.

As though in answer to her silent prayer his

mouth veered south, and she urgently lifted her hips in an effort to meet him halfway. Kyle lifted her left leg over his shoulder and he began to lick her with his warm tongue. Elana gripped the edge of the counter and arched back as he began to suck harder. She ran her fingers through his hair and her grip tightened as she was pushed closer to the edge.

She suddenly screamed out, thrusting against his mouth, but Kyle quickly stood up and undid his pants to slide into her. Keeping the one hand on the edge of the counter for support, she wrapped the other one around him. He gripped her thighs, slamming into her, and Elana knew it wouldn't be long before she was coming again. She dug her nails into her back and as he sped up, she cried out once more as he lost it with her.

Kyle's right hand dropped her thigh and pressed against the mirror behind her.

"Wow," she panted. It had been quick, but talk about intense.

He slowly raised his head to look at her. "God, you're beautiful," he said.

"I think that's the sex talking," she replied with a smile.

A devilish smile appeared and he kissed her. "Are you ready for that bath?"

"Mmm, I'd forgotten all about that," she purred.

Kyle stepped back and pulled his pants back up before helping her get off the counter. "Go ahead and climb in, I'll go and pour you some wine."

When he had walked out, Elana turned around to splash some cool water on her face. This was certainly not what she had been expecting when she woke up this morning.

She turned on the jets and then carefully slid in.

She'd forgotten how good a bath could feel, and sank down until only her chin was above the water.

Kyle came in carrying two plush robes, monogrammed with the resort's logo, and a glass of chilled white wine.

"Are you going to join me?" she asked.

"Do you want me to?"

"Yes."

He stripped, slid in behind her, and handed her the glass. The cold liquid felt good sliding down her throat. Kyle put his hand around hers holding the glass and took a sip as well.

"You know, if you had come with me last night when I first asked, you would have saved us a lot of time."

"I thought I was doing the right thing, sending you away," she replied. "I still think it was the right thing to do."

He kissed her ear. "But you're here now."

"You didn't exactly make it easy for me to say no."

He laughed. "Probably not. But are you regretting it?"

"No. At least not yet." She took another sip. "But I still want to know what happens when you have to go back to Seattle. Obviously you can't stay here forever."

"No. I have some work I can do from here for the next week, but then after that I do need to be back in the office to meet with people face to face."

"And then what?" she asked again.

"Well, we have a week to figure it out. Can't you just enjoy the moment?"

Elana sighed and sunk into his solid body. It felt so safe to her. This *was* really nice. "Fine. You win."

"Good. Now that we have the whole next week to ourselves, what would you like to do?"

She laughed. "You forget that *I* still have to work."

Kyle frowned.

"Not every day though, right?" he asked.

"I work tomorrow, but then I have Thursday and Friday off, since I switched with someone for Saturday."

"Two whole days off in a row. Hmm..."

"What are you thinking?" she asked.

"We should go island hopping. How about Maui or the Big Island?"

Now Elana frowned. She couldn't afford to go island hopping and he knew that. He intended to pay her way, and she couldn't accept that.

"Let's just stay here," she said. "We can hole up in your hotel room and order room service."

He buried his face in her hair. "I like how you think," he said as his lips caressed the curvature of her neck.

Elana took the last swig of wine and reached over the tub to set the glass on the floor.

"I think it's time to get out," she said, "I'm feeling plenty warm."

Kyle agreed and climbed out first. He grabbed one of the robes he had brought in and held it out for Elana as she climbed out. When it was wrapped around her, he tied it loosely.

"I'm sure this won't be on for long," he grinned.

Before she could respond, Kyle's cell phone began ringing from the other room and he frowned.

"Sorry, I have to go grab that." He pulled his own robe on and walked out to answer it.

Elana faced the vanity and looked over the

toiletries. She found a moisturizer and decided to put some on her legs.

"Hello."

Kyle had pulled the door close, but it hadn't latched and now Elana could hear his half of the conversation.

"And what did she have to say?"

Elana inched closer to the door. With Seattle three hours ahead of them, it seemed unlikely to be a business call at this hour.

"Yes, I decided to extend my trip another week."

The conversation seemed benign enough, but Elana thought she detected irritation in his voice.

"Yes, is that a problem?" Pause. *"I'm fine, Mother. I just decided to take some more R&R time. It might even be more relaxing without the guys around. Especially Stephan. You know how he can be."*

Elana bit her lip as she realized who he was talking to.

"Her? No, I haven't seen her since that first night. Kauai is a small island, but it's not that small."

Elana's eyes went big. Adelaide Barnett knew she was on the island and that Kyle had seen her.

"Of course. Tell Dad I said hi. Love you too."

Elana took a step back from the door. Leave it to mommy dearest to bring reality crashing in. Kyle just lied to his mother. They were both crazy to think that this could be anything other than just a fling.

The door opened and Kyle walked in. His face lit up at the sight of her, and her heart skipped a beat. It was only one week. What would it hurt to pretend for only one week?

"Everything all right?" she asked with a smile.

"Yeah, it's nothing. Are you hungry? We could order room service if you need."

She wrapped her arms around him.

"I'm fine. I ate at work."

Kyle's hands slid beneath her robe and around her waist.

"I guess that leaves us with more time for other activities then," he said.

"You mean for activities like talking?"

Kyle's face fell. "If that is what you really want to do, then yes, I supposed we could talk."

Elana giggled. "I'm only teasing. There will be plenty of time later for talking."

Kyle picked her up and carried her to bed.

The first thing Elana became aware of in the morning was the sound of chickens clucking. It was odd because it didn't sound anything like the roosters she usually heard outside her cottage. The next thing she noticed was Kyle's arm across her stomach. She looked over and saw his sleeping face snuggled into her shoulder.

"Kyle," she whispered. "Kyle, do you hear chickens?" It sounded electronic now that she was listening better. And it sounded like it was in the room.

"Hmm?"

"I think I hear chickens clucking or something," she said. "Don't you hear that?"

"It's my phone," he murmured. "It'll go to voicemail." And it did. The clucking had stopped.

"Why does your phone sound like chickens?" she asked.

"It's a ringtone. It's, um, it's Stephan." He pulled her even closer to him. "Now go back to sleep."

The room phone started ringing. Kyle grumbled as he rolled over to answer the one next to the bed.

"Hello," he mumbled. "I'm sorry, what?" Suddenly he was upright. "What?! She's here now?"

Elana panicked. Was Adelaide on the island?

"No!" Kyle shouted into the phone. "Wait." He pinched the bridge of his nose trying to think. "Dammit. Yes, you can tell her what room I'm in. Thanks for calling."

He slammed down the phone and jumped out of the bed.

"Shit! Victoria is here!" He ran into the bathroom and Elana slid out of bed. Kyle rushed out with all her clothes.

"Who is Victoria?" she asked him.

Kyle ignored the question. "Here, you need to get dressed quickly and get out of here."

Elana felt she was being pushed out like a common whore.

"Excuse me? Kyle, who the hell is Victoria?" she asked again.

He looked at her with a pained expression, but still wouldn't answer the question.

"I'm not leaving here until you tell me who she is," she said, planting both hands on her hips and refusing to accept the rumpled clothing from him.

His shoulders slumped. "She's my fiancée."

Six

ELANA WAS PRETTY sure someone had just punched her in the gut. How could he? How *dare* he?

She opened her mouth to speak, but none of the superlatives going through her head seemed to suffice.

"Elana, I can explain," Kyle said with obvious panic rising in his voice. "But not now. She's on her way. You can't be here when she gets here."

She ripped her clothes from his arms and marched back into the bathroom, locking the door behind her, and dressed as quickly as she could.

"Elana?" Kyle called from the other side of the door. "Please talk to me. Say something."

She yanked the door opened and pounded her finger into his chest.

"You don't get to tell me what to do. I knew you couldn't be trusted!"

She grabbed her bag and headed for the door.

"Please," he pleaded. "It's not what you think. I promise I can explain."

She grabbed the vase on the table in the foyer and threw it at him. It missed when he ducked and hit the desk behind him, shattering into millions of pieces that went sliding on to the floor.

"Stay away from me, Kyle!" she screamed.

She stormed out of the room and to the elevator. When the doors opened, a very familiar blonde about Elana's age stepped out and walked in the direction of Kyle's room. Elana had no doubt that it was Victoria, but she couldn't figure out where she knew her from. What did it matter anyway? She stifled a sob on the way down to the lobby. She wasn't going to cry here.

Kyle stood frozen among the shards of glass after Elana had stormed out. Remembering that Victoria was on her way, he quickly grabbed his pants from the bed. He had just finished zipping them up when there was a knock at the door. Kyle took a deep breath and braced for the inevitable storm.

There was a second knock by the time Kyle opened the door.

"Victoria!" Kyle made his best attempt at a smile, but he suspected it wasn't going well. "What are you doing here?"

She kissed his cheek as she breezed in, towing a carry-on.

"I'm here to see you, of course," she said, walking through the foyer and parking her suitcase at the foot of the bed. She spun back around to face Kyle, who had reluctantly followed her. "It's smaller than I thought it would be. I thought the Regis had larger suites."

"It was only me. I figured I didn't need so much space," Kyle said through gritted teeth.

She frowned and toed a chunk of vase on the floor with her Jimmy Choos. "What happened here?"

"I accidentally knocked the vase off the desk. What exactly are you doing here?" he asked again.

Victoria closed the distance between them and wrapped her arms around him. "I just thought it would be nice to have some alone time with you. You've been so distant lately and I wanted us to try and reconnect."

Kyle's hands slowly pulled Victoria's arms down to her side. "We need to talk."

Elana didn't remember much of the ride home, but she was pretty sure she had driven much faster than she should have. She barely made it in the door before she lost it and curled into a ball on her bed. It was a mixture of sadness and rage. There had been plenty of reasons for her to avoid Kyle, all reasonable. But she chose to ignore them, and now to find out that he hadn't even been available in the first place only angered her more. Had she been a game to him? Was this just a sadistic pastime of his?

Eventually Elana got up to try and take a shower. She still had to work that night. But when she saw the mess in the mirror, she knew she was in no condition. Plus the thought of even taking a shower just felt like too much. For the first time since she had started at the Bar Acuda, Elana Tanner was calling in sick. And it pissed her off that it was over something as petty as a broken heart.

It was almost dark, and Elana was still curled up in her bed wearing the same clothes from the night before when someone knocked at her door but she ignored it. There was no one that could possibly come to her door that she wanted to see right now. Except her mom. God, she missed her mom. She missed her dad as well, but she could really use her mom right now. Someone knocked again, and she looked at the clock, wondering if it would be too late to call her.

"Elana, I know you're in there."

Crap, it was Kyle.

"They said you called in sick to work and your jeep is in the driveway," he said.

"Go away!" she yelled.

"No. I need to talk to you."

"Well, that's too bad," she shouted back, "because I clearly need to not listen to you."

"Elana, I meant everything I said to you last night."

Elana got up and walked to the music player on top of the fridge and turned the music on loud. Anything Kyle had to say to her, she didn't want to hear it. She lay back on the bed with her head at the foot and waited for his shadow to disappear on the opposite side of it. When he did finally leave, she got up and put on some fresh pajamas, turned down the music, and crawled into bed. What a difference a day made.

The next morning Elana lay in bed and contemplated her day. She had the next two days off and no desire to get out of bed. She cursed the day Kyle came into her restaurant.

As she continued to lie there, she realized that she hadn't washed the sheets since Kyle had been in her bed. Today was a good day for that chore. She dragged herself out of bed and stripped it. While those were in the washer she finally got her shower in. Feeling somewhat more human, she turned the water off, wrapped a towel around her, and walked back into the bathroom. She stepped in front of the mirror and gasped. In the reflection was Kyle sitting in the chair just outside the bathroom.

"How did you get in?" she demanded.

"The front door was unlocked."

"That's trespassing."

"Are you going to call the cops?"

She glared at him through the mirror. "No, but you should leave."

"I promise I will as soon as you hear me out."

"Where's Victoria?" she asked.

"She's back at the hotel."

"Did she sleep in your bed last night?" Elana regretted saying the words out loud, but it was the most painful thought that had kept going through her head all last night.

"Yes."

Elana blanched.

"But I didn't."

"Is that supposed to make me feel better?" she asked.

"I'm trying to break it off with her, but she isn't taking it well. I slept on the couch last night. I plan to get a separate room for her later today."

"I'm not a home wrecker. Don't leave her over me. That would be pointless."

"Victoria and I were over a long time ago," said Kyle. "I've just been dragging out the inevitable." He sighed. "This trip was supposed to be about taking a step back and getting some perspective. And figuring out the best way to proceed."

"Do you live together?" Elana asked.

"Technically yes," he answered.

"What does that mean?"

"For the past month I have found any excuse not to go home at night. Business trip, spend the night at the office," he said. "Come here. When I did have to go home, I pretended to fall asleep on the couch watching TV."

"She must have noticed."

"I'm sure she did. But I think she felt that as long as she ignored it everything was fine."

Elana had been carrying this conversation

through the mirror as she still had her back to him, but now she turned and walked out to the edge of the bed and sat down, still wrapped in her towel.

"Then why kick me out of the room yesterday morning?"

"Because I didn't want her to think that was why I was breaking up with her. She needs to know that it's because her and I weren't working, not because of some outside factor." Kyle ran his hands through his hair. "Obviously I didn't plan on you and me happening. But you have to know that no matter what happened, I was ending it when I got home."

"Why did you stay an extra week though?" she asked.

"I honestly wasn't ready to say good-bye. And I knew that once I went home and did what I had to do, it was going to be a while before I could come back. I wanted to know if you were feeling what I was starting to feel."

"Why is she here now?"

"She wants us to work things out."

"And what did you say?"

"I told her no. But she refuses to accept it. She spent the whole night crying."

"Yeah, well she's not the only one." Again the words came out before she could stop herself.

Kyle took her hand. "Oh, Elana, I'm so sorry."

She pulled her hand away and stood up. "You promised to leave once I heard you out. Is that all you had to say?"

Kyle stood up with her. "That's it?"

"Yep. That's it."

"But what now?"

"Well, you go back to that poor girl and end it once and for all. Stop stringing her along. Then you go home and get on with your life." She walked over to the door and held it open.

"But what about you?" he asked.

"Oh, don't lose any sleep over me, Kyle Barnett," she said. "You said it yourself. I'm a survivor. I'll be fine." She forced a smile. "Now get out of my house."

He paused on his way out the door and tried to kiss her, but she turned her face away from him. Kyle's body hunched over as he made his way out to the jeep.

Elana got dressed and while she was blow drying her hair, she found herself mulling over everything he had said. Was any of it true? Did it make a difference if it was?

After Elana got the sheets in the dryer she proceeded to clean out her fridge. Unfortunately it didn't take long, since it wasn't like she needed to keep a lot of food in stock. She was trying to kill time until she thought her mom might be home from work, but she finally sent a text asking her to call when she had a chance.

Her phone rang fifteen minutes later.

"Hi, Mom," Elana answered.

"Hi sweetie. Is everything okay?"

Elana sat down on her bottom step and picked at a blade of grass. "Yeah. I just felt like talking to you."

"Anything in particular you want to talk about?" Renee asked.

"Just feeling homesick, I guess."

"You should come home for a visit soon."

"I can't—" Elana started to say she couldn't afford it. But she knew that if she did, her Mom would offer to pay for it. "I can't take time off from work for a while. It's the busy season," she lied.

"Oh, I see. Hey, I ran into Marge yesterday."

"Yeah? How is she?" Elana had always liked Benjamin's mother.

"She's good. But um….I guess Benjamin got married. Very recently, in fact."

"I know," said Elana.

"You do? How?"

"Turns out they are honeymooning here in Kauai." Elana remembered the night she and Kyle ran into them, and her heart started to ache.

"Did you see him?"

"Yes, I was out with a friend and we ran into them." She started to think about how Kyle had come to her rescue without her even asking. How he looked at her and held her hand. She remembered the feel of his hand on the small of her back, earlier in the evening.

Suddenly she let out an involuntary sob.

"Oh honey," her mother exclaimed over the phone, "I'm so sorry you had to see that. Please don't cry over him though. He's not worth it."

"That's not why I'm crying," she sobbed.

"It's not? But then what's wrong, Elana? Everything's not okay, is it?"

"It is, or it will be. My heart just kind of hurts right now."

"You mean from a guy?" asked Renee. "A guy not Benjamin?"

Elana sniffled. "Yes."

"Sweetie, I didn't even know you were dating someone. Why didn't you tell me? Who is he?"

"I wasn't dating anyone. Everything just kind of happened so fast. And then it fell apart even quicker." She groaned. "I'm such a fool."

"Are you going to tell me exactly what happened?" her mother asked.

"It's too complicated."

"I'm not going anywhere."

"Aren't you at work?"

"Yes, but there's nothing else on my agenda for today. So spill the beans, kiddo."

"This guy that I knew but didn't like showed up here on vacation. I don't even know how it happened, but we ended up hitting it off." Elana was trying not to give any of the physical details to her mother. Seeing as how she had lived with a guy for three years, her mother knew she wasn't a virgin. But still. "I tried to break it off, since I knew he had to go home. But then he extended his trip so we could get to know each other better."

"That's so romantic. What happened?"

"Um, his fiancée showed up."

"His what? His fiancée?" Renee exhaled into the phone. "Run, Elana. Run as far away from this boy as you can and don't give him another thought."

"I know. I tried. But then this morning he was at my door explaining how they've been on the outs for a while now. He says they haven't even slept in the same bed for over a month."

"I don't know, sweetie. That sounds like a line married men give to their mistresses."

"Now that I've said it out loud, it kind of does, doesn't it?"

"Who is this guy anyway?"

"Kyle Barnett," Elana said very quietly.

"Kyle who?" her mother asked.

"Barnett, Mother. It's Kyle Barnett,"

"Kyle Barnett? Adelaide Barnett's other son?"

"Yes, the one I didn't kill."

"That's not funny, Elana."

"Sorry."

"What are you even doing hanging out with

Kyle Barnett?"

"I told you, I don't even know how it happened. One minute we're yelling at each and the next we're..." Elana waved her hand around even though her mother couldn't see it.

"Did you sleep with him?"

"Yes," Elana answered in shame.

"Shit."

"Mother!"

"Sorry. But Elana, you need to stay away from that family. They are manipulative and vindictive. Who knows what this Kyle is trying to pull, but you need to stay away from him."

"I know. I always knew. I guess I just lost my head for a second."

Renee's voice was much softer when she spoke again to her daughter. "I think you're lonely, honey. You can't live with your head in the sand forever."

"I'm not living with my head in the sand," Elana told her.

"Yet you refuse to come home and you refuse to make friends out there."

"I can't come home."

"Why not? There's no court order saying you have to stay out of Washington."

"I just can't," Elana mumbled.

Renee sighed. "Fine. Well when you can, you know we can't wait to have you home again."

Elana could feel a lump forming in her throat. "I know." So much for her mom making her feel better. "Tell Dad I love him. I miss you guys."

"We miss you too sweetie. I love you."

"I love you, too," Elana choked out. The call disconnected and she sat on her front step and cried.

Elana spent the next two days scrubbing out her

cottage. When that was done, she solicited Mrs. Wilson for any errands or chores she needed help with. On Saturday she was back to work, ready for the distraction. She gave the customers her best smile and made great conversation. If she pretended to be happy, eventually she would be happy again.

She was setting an order on the table when the hostess came up to her.

"Elana, there's a girl here that wants to see you," she said.

Elana glanced up at the door and saw Victoria standing there. She frowned.

"Did she say what she wants?" she asked.

"No."

"But she asked for me by name?"

"Yes."

Elana could not figure out what the hell Victoria would want to see her for, or how she knew her name and where to find her. Did Kyle say something?

"Tell her I'll be out as soon as I have a minute."

She checked on her other tables then asked Janelle to cover her while she stepped outside for a few.

As Elana walked up to Victoria she couldn't shake the feeling that she had seen Victoria before. Then it hit her: Victoria had been at the trials with the family. But she couldn't remember what Victoria had been to the family. Had she and Kyle been together that long? Even though Elana had not known of the two, she still couldn't stop feeling guilty for the heartache this girl must be feeling.

Victoria gave Elana the once over and said, "You don't look like anything I should be worried about."

"Excuse me?"

"Don't play stupid with me," Victoria snapped. "I know exactly what you're playing at here."

"Follow me," Elana said as she grabbed Victoria's arm and dragged to the side, away from customers' view. "What exactly is it that you want?" she asked.

"I want you to stop sleeping with my fiancé," Victoria answered.

Elana had already resolved to do just that, but she didn't like Victoria's attitude.

"Don't you mean *ex*-fiancé?" she shot back.

"He'll come around. But not if you keep chasing after him."

"I am not the one chasing him," Elana said, folding he arms across her chest.

"Listen here you little slut. The Barnett family fortune is mine, so you need to back off if you know what's good for you!"

Elana's jaw dropped, and she did her best to not slap Victoria. "Do you think I'm after his fortune?"

"Of course you are! Why else would you be going after Kyle?"

"Wow, you are delusional! I'd never even met the Barnett family until Jarod stepped in front of my car that night, and Kyle is the one who found me! I came here to get away from your whole lot! How did you even know I was here? How did you know where I worked?"

Victoria inspected a manicured nail. "I have my sources."

It couldn't have been Kyle, Elana thought. Victoria would've surely named him. Adelaide knew about Elana, but only that she was on the island, Kyle wouldn't have told her they had slept together. Then who else....

"Stephan!" Elana cried out.

Victoria's eyes went wide for only a split second, but it was long enough to give Elana confirmation.

"That little shit," said Elana. "I knew he was going to stir up trouble."

A smirk appeared on Victoria's face. "Oh, I don't know. Stephan isn't all that bad."

"Are you sleeping with him?"

Victoria narrowed her eyes. "How dare you!"

"Oh my god, you are! Wow, wait until Kyle finds out."

"You will not tell him a thing, or I will ruin you," Victoria seethed.

"Honey, I can't get much lower. But you don't need to worry about me. I want nothing to do with you people and your fucked up mind games. Go away, Victoria, and let me mind my own business."

"So long as we agree that you are going to stay away from Kyle."

Elana rolled her eyes. "Fine. Just leave me alone."

Victoria turned to leave, but Elana decided she couldn't quite let her go that easily. "One more thing though."

"Oh? And what's that?"

"Stephan is the one who pushed Kyle and me together."

"That's ridiculous."

"He was the one who convinced me to go hiking with them, and he suggested Kyle have dinner with me when the other guys bailed."

"Why would he do something like that?" Victoria asked.

Elana shrugged. "I don't know. Maybe he's starting to feel guilty. You should ask him the next time you guys are in bed together."

Even in the poor lighting, Elana could see Victoria's face turning red.

"And to think I felt sorry for you," she added.

"Me?" Victoria said in disgust.

"Yeah. When Kyle explained how he had been wanting to call it off for so long, I felt bad that he had been stringing you along."

Elana could almost see the smoke coming from Victoria's ears as she tried to think of something to say, but when words failed her, she turned and stormed off.

Elana felt like her head was spinning from everything she had just discovered. A couple deep breaths and then she headed back inside. Now the question was, should she tell Kyle personally, or would he have to wait for his best friend's guilt to get the better of him? Would Victoria find a way to trap Kyle if no one said anything? Better yet, did Elana care?

On Sunday morning Elana had to run in to town for some groceries, so she decided to check on Loretta and see if she needed anything as well.

"Hey, Mrs. Wilson," Elana said, when Loretta waved her in.

"Good morning, dear. What are you up to this morning?"

"I was just headed to Big Save for a few things. Did you need me to pick up anything for you?"

"I do, actually. I was just thinking that I needed...um, what was it that I needed?" Loretta looked around the kitchen trying to jog her memory. "Coffee? I think I needed coffee." She got up and looked in the cupboard, where there was a half-full canister of coffee. "No, that wasn't it. Maybe it was sugar." Loretta checked the sugar canister. It was almost empty. "Yes, that's it. I need sugar."

Elana looked at Loretta with concern. "Are you feeling okay?"

Loretta waved her off. "Oh, I'm fine. My brain is just a little fuzzy lately. That's what happens when you get older."

"Okay," Elana said, but she made a mental note to keep a better eye on Mrs. Wilson. "Sugar. Anything else?"

"Go ahead and grab some milk. I can always use milk."

"I will pick up milk and sugar then. Be back soon."

Elana got in her jeep and found herself thinking back to the unusual conversation with Mrs. Wilson. She wondered if she needed to look up the symptoms of Alzheimer's. But then she shook her head. It was one time. She was sure there was nothing to worry about yet.

After getting a coffee, Elana picked up what she needed from the store, including Mrs. Wilson's milk and sugar, and was headed right back home. She was waiting to cross a single-lane bridge, the last one before her driveway, when she noticed the vehicle that had followed her from town. Glancing in the rearview mirror she saw that it was a black jeep and couldn't help stealing a peek at the driver.

"Shit," she muttered. Kyle was following her home.

The last car passed, and she made her way across the bridge and to her house.

Kyle pulled in right behind her and climbed out. Elana slammed the door shut and walked right up to him.

"Have you resorted to stalking now?"

"Funny," he said without a hint of humor in his

voice. "No, I came here to talk to you."

"Well, I don't have anything to say to you, so you wasted the gas." She started to walk away, but he grabbed her arm.

"I can't stop thinking about you, Elana."

She tried to pull her arm away, but without much effort and Kyle wouldn't let go of her.

"Don't," she said softly. "Please don't do this to me."

Kyle took a step closer. "Don't do what?"

"Don't tell me things like that. You just make it harder."

"I know you're hurting, Elana, and I wish I could take that back. But if you're hurting, it has to be because you feel something for me."

She stepped back and yanked her arm harder out of his grip, remembering her mother's words.

"If I feel anything for you, it's because I'm an idiot."

He shook his head. "I'm going home tomorrow."

"Good," she replied.

"I only stayed because of you."

She knew he was trying to get to her. It was working, but she couldn't let her guard down.

"Well, that was a waste of your time."

"I'll stay if you ask me to."

"I won't."

"I think you want to, but you're afraid."

"Damn right, I am afraid," she said, practically screaming. "I'm afraid that if I give in again, you will just find some other way to hurt me." She enunciated her next words. "I can't trust you, Kyle."

"You can! I never—" Kyle stopped. He was looking at something behind Elana. "What is that?"

Elana turned around, confused. The laundry

119

room door was ajar, which was odd. Then she saw what had caught Kyle's attention. A shoe in the doorway. Mrs. Wilson's shoe.

"Mrs. Wilson?" Elana called out as she rushed over.

Loretta was lying face down on the laundry room floor.

Seven

"OH MY GOD! Mrs. Wilson!" Elana bent down and started to turn her over.

"Don't move her," Kyle warned. "If she's broken anything, you don't want to make it worse." He pulled his cell phone out and dialed 911.

Elana put her face close to Loretta's and could see that the woman's eyes were open, but she didn't seem to be focusing on anything. There was a strange noise coming from her throat.

"I think she's having a stroke! We need help now!" Elana started to cry as she patted Loretta's shoulder. "It's all right, Mrs. Wilson. I'm here."

Someone must have picked up on the other end of Kyle's phone because she could hear him talking.

"I'm in Hanalei and someone is having a stroke in her home." He listened. "Yes, hold on." He held the phone up to Elana.

"They need the address."

Elana took the phone from him and gave the address. They kept her on the phone until the EMTs arrived fifteen minutes later. She never left Loretta's side and Kyle had to pull Elana out of the laundry room so the paramedics could tend to Mrs. Wilson.

Elana had been right; it was a stroke. They got

Mrs. Wilson onto a gurney and loaded her into the truck.

"Where are you taking her?" Elana asked.

"The closest hospital is Mahelona," the driver answered. "We need to get her there ASAP."

"Can I ride along?" she asked.

"Are you family?"

"No, but…"

The driver furrowed his brow, trying to decide if he should let her.

"I'll drive her," said Kyle.

"That would be better. Please don't try to follow us. Be sure you mind all posted speed limits."

"Of course."

The aid truck tore off, and Kyle and Elana jumped into his jeep and followed in their direction. Kyle didn't try to keep up with the truck. However, he didn't obey the speed limits. Elana's knuckles were white from gripping the door handle through the tight turns, but she said nothing about his speed. When they made it to Princeville where the road straightened out some, she buried her head in her hands.

Kyle reached over and squeezed her thigh. "It's going to be all right. We found her and she's being treated now."

"I knew something was wrong this morning," she said, lifting her head. "She seemed so confused. I never should have left her!"

"You can't blame yourself. You had no way of knowing."

Elana didn't answer. For the rest of the drive she just sat there with tears silently falling down her cheeks.

Kyle parked the car and as they walked into the hospital entrance, he took Elana's hand and squeezed it. She didn't let it go.

They approached the front desk, and Elana told her they were with the woman that had just been brought in with a stroke.

"They are treating her now, but there is some information I need from you."

"I can try to help."

"Are you family?" the receptionist asked.

"No. She's my landlady. I'm the one that found her."

"Do you know if she has any next of kin?"

"Yes, she has a son and a daughter," Elana answered. "They live on the mainland."

"The only person she had listed on the forms is her husband, but he's deceased, isn't he?"

"Yes, he is."

"Do you have the contact information for the son or daughter?"

"I don't. I'm guessing it's in the house somewhere. Probably on her cell phone."

The receptionist said nothing.

"You need me to get those numbers so you can call them, don't you?" asked Elana.

"That would be helpful, yes."

"But shouldn't I be here?" Elana asked. "Shouldn't someone be here for her? She has no one!" She was doing her best not to start crying again.

"I'll go get it," Kyle said.

"No, I can't ask you to do that," she protested.

"You should be here. I'm sure I can find what I need. Do you have your phone?"

Elana reached for her back pocket, but it was empty. "Shit, it's in my jeep. My bag is in my jeep. I forgot everything!"

"I'll get it, don't worry." He asked the receptionist for pen and paper and wrote down his cell number. "If you think of anything else you want me to grab, I'm sure the nice people here will let you use their phone." He flashed a smile at the receptionist, who of course smiled back and nodded.

"Thank you," Elana said as she pocketed his number.

He kissed her forehead. "Hang in there. I'll be back as soon as possible."

As soon as possible turned out to be two hours, and in that time a doctor managed to come out and talk to Elana.

"Are you family?" he asked and Elana immediately went on the defensive.

"No, but I'm all she has right now. We haven't been able to get a hold of anyone, and it will probably take a day for them to get here when we do!"

The doctor put his hand on her shoulder.

"It's all right. I just wanted to know."

"I'm sorry," she said.

He removed his hand. "We removed the clot and blood is flowing. We won't know just how bad it is for a while. The good news is she has survived. She is sleeping right now, and when she wakes, we can start assessing the damage and go from there in planning her rehabilitation."

"Can I go be with her?"

"Of course." The doctor directed her to Loretta's room and left.

That was where Kyle found her when he returned with her bag as well as a small suitcase that Elana didn't recognize.

"Did you find any numbers?" she asked.

"Yes. Her cell phone was sitting right on the counter and I found several numbers in there. I gave it to the lady up front and they are calling her son as we speak."

"What's in the suitcase?"

"I grabbed a few of her personal items that I thought she might want. Change of clothes, a couple pictures and books, things like that." He saw the look Elana was giving him and explained. "I remember when my grandmother was sick in the hospital a couple years ago. I'm sure you or one of her kids could grab whatever I forgot."

"Wow," she said.

"What?"

"I just—I don't know. I guess I'm shocked."

"Whatever," he shrugged.

"Thank you," she said.

"For what?"

"For everything. For driving me here. I could have just driven myself."

"I don't think you were in any condition to drive."

"You're probably right."

"Oh," he said, holding up Elana's possessions and a white paper bag. "Here's your bag and I picked up lunch on the way." He pulled hamburgers and fries from the paper bag. Elana didn't see herself being able to eat anytime soon, but she appreciated the gesture none-the-less.

"I don't know what to say," she told him.

He smiled. "Thank you will suffice."

His phone started clucking and the smile faded. Elana was sad to see it go. Kyle hit the ignore button and set it aside.

"Sorry," he said, sliding the phone into his back pocket.

"It's Victoria, isn't it?"

"Yes, but I have nothing to say to her."

"Is she still on the island?"

"Yes. We're both supposed to fly out

tomorrow. But I told her I was moving out as soon as we got home."

"She's been sleeping with someone else, Kyle."

"What? How would you know?"

"She came to see me last night at work."

"What? But how did she even know where to find you?"

"Stephan told her."

"Why would he tell her?"

"I don't know." Elana decided not to be the one to tell Kyle that his best friend was sleeping with his fiancée. Even if Kyle wasn't hurt over Victoria's betrayal, he would be by Stephan's.

Kyle shook his head and started to take a bite of his burger, but then stopped.

"Is it strange that I don't find it so hard to believe?" he said. "And to think that all this time I felt bad about hurting her feelings."

"That's because you're a good person."

Kyle looked at her. Those were his words to her, not so long ago.

"If you'll excuse me," he said, "I have to go make a couple calls." Kyle shoved his half-eaten burger back to into the bag and left the room.

Elana continued her vigil over Loretta. The receptionist came in and informed her that they had gotten ahold of the son, Daniel, and he was planning on flying in sometime tomorrow.

"Thank you for letting me know," Elana told her.

Soon after, Kyle returned with a smug look on his face.

"Everything okay?" Elana asked.

"It is now," he said, and sat in the chair next to Elana's. "I got Victoria's flight changed to tonight and then I called her and said if she wasn't on it, she would be responsible for her own airfare home and her own room at the St. Regis or wherever she decided to stay. I also told her she had better be out of the apartment by the time I got back, or I would be taking legal action."

"Damn," Elana said with big eyes. "I can only imagine how she reacted to that."

Kyle laughed. "Not well. She tried being all sweet and begging at first, but by the time I hung up she was screaming at me."

"Do you really think she can be moved out by the time you get home tomorrow?" Elana asked.

Kyle just shrugged.

"You're not going home tomorrow, are you?" She saw a hint of a smile on his lips.

"Probably not."

Elana sighed. "I just can't get rid of you, can I?"

Kyle leaned over and kissed her cheek. "No, you can't," he whispered, "so you should just stop trying."

Just then Loretta started to stir, and Elana stood up and moved next to her bed.

"Mrs. Wilson," she said. "Loretta?"

Loretta smiled ever so slightly at Elana and reached for her. Elana took her hand and received a squeeze.

"How are you feeling?" Elana asked.

Loretta blinked slowly and then nodded.

"I'm going to go grab a nurse," Elana told her.

"I got it." Kyle jumped up and went out into the hall.

He returned with a nurse and the doctor.

They looked over Mrs. Wilson, who still wasn't speaking.

"Can she talk?" Elana asked.

"It may be hard for her right now. It could also

be temporary. We will just have to wait and also see what the scans say. We are going to keep her here overnight, and then tomorrow she will be moved to Wilcox Memorial in Lihue for treatment, and that's where they will do the more extensive tests."

"Thank you," said Elana.

"Of course." The doctor made some notes in the chart and he and the nurse left.

Elana moved back to Loretta's side.

"Do you want to watch some television?" she asked.

Loretta smiled again and nodded. It pained Elana to see her this way.

There was a remote plugged into the bed, and Elana grabbed it to scan the channels until she found something she thought Loretta would enjoy. Elana pulled her chair closer to hold Loretta's hand, and Mrs. Wilson gave it a good squeeze. Elana wasn't going to let go of it until Loretta was ready. She could only imagine how scared she was right now.

She looked over at Kyle, who had sat back down and was frowning while typing something on his phone. Even his mad face was smoldering. It annoyed her.

"You can go," she told him.

"But how will you get home?" he asked, looking up.

"It's easy enough to get a taxi from here."

"I don't mind staying with you."

"But you don't need to," she said.

"But what if I want to?"

She smiled, but said, "Then you're a fool. Now go away."

"And what exactly am I supposed to go do?" he asked.

"I don't care. But anything has to be better than

hanging out here with us."

He stared into her eyes, contemplating what to do. Elana suddenly found herself wishing he would stay. But she didn't dare voice it.

His phone buzzed, and he frowned at it again.

"Fine. I need to go deal with something anyway."

She forced a smile. "Good."

He stood up to go. "Just promise me you will call me if you need anything. Including a ride home."

She was prepared to make a smart-ass comment, but his gaze was so penetrating that she simply said, "I promise." Was it possible that Kyle could really care about her?

He nodded and left.

Elana continued watching TV with Loretta who eventually fell asleep. Elana turned off the TV and just sat in the chair, trying to hash out her feelings for Kyle.

It had been several hours since Kyle had left her and the sun had set when Elana realized she was getting hungry. She was just about to bite into the now cold burger when Kyle walked in with yet another bag of food.

"What are you doing here?" she asked. "I didn't call you."

"Nice to see you, too," he said with a smile.

"Sorry," she said.

"I was hungry and bored and thought you may be hungry and bored as well. So I thought maybe we could help each other out."

"Well, maybe I'm hungry," she grumbled. "But I'm not sure I'm bored enough for your company."

"Ouch," Kyle said, pretending to look hurt. "Good thing I don't believe you."

Kyle scooted the other chair closer to Elana and

dug into the paper bag he had brought, filled with goodies from one of the hotel restaurants.

"How is she doing?" he asked as he handed her the boxed dinner.

"The same. The nurses have been in a couple times to take vitals. She still hasn't spoken."

"The doctor said it may take time," Kyle commented.

"I know, but I'm still worried."

"You're a really good friend, staying here by her side like this."

Elana nodded. She took the plastic fork and napkin from Kyle.

Kyle opened his box and was about to start eating when the sniffle escaped her.

"Elana, what's wrong?" he asked.

She wiped her eye with the back of her hand.

"It's your brother all over again."

"What do you mean?"

"The night when I hit him. All I could think was that he was dying in the arms of a stranger and there was no one around to tell him that they loved him. No one deserves that."

Kyle put his food down and wrapped his arms around her as she cried harder.

"I can't let Loretta wake up and not see a familiar face," she said as she pulled away from. She expected to see horror on Kyle's face from the tears streaming down her cheeks, but all she saw in his eyes was genuine concern.

"I'm so sorry I hit your brother," she said. "I'm so sorry he had to die like that. I wish more than anything I could bring him back!"

Kyle shook his head.

"It wasn't your fault. You know that."

Elana shook her head. "It doesn't change the

fact that I was responsible for his death. I can never forget that."

Kyle pulled her face into his shoulder and stroked her hair. "Oh, Elana. There's something I need to tell you," he said.

But then a nurse came in to take Loretta's vitals again, and Kyle backed off while Elana used the napkin to dry her face.

They had to wake Loretta, and Elana complained.

"Isn't there any way to check on her without waking her every half hour?" she said.

The nurse shook his head. "Sorry."

Elana held Loretta's hand until the nurse was finished. Just before he left, Elana thought she heard Loretta say something.

"What was that?" Elana asked her.

It was difficult to make out the words, but Elana was able to tell that she was asking for water. Relief washed over Elana as she poured the water and helped Mrs. Wilson drink it with a straw.

When she was done, Loretta asked to watch some television and Elana grabbed the remote.

"Do you want to do it, or do you want me to help?"

Mrs. Wilson smiled and reached for the remote. Elana handed it to her, feeling much more optimistic about Loretta's condition.

"Are you hungry, Loretta?" Elana pointed to the tray of food they had brought in since the last time she had been awake.

She looked at it, but then frowned and shook her head. She looked over and saw Kyle. She waved and rasped out a hello. Kyle smiled and waved back.

"You remember Kyle, don't you?"

Loretta nodded.

"Is it okay if he is here?" Elana asked.

"It's fine, dear." She turned her attention to the television, and Elana sat back down and picked up her box of food.

"So what is on the menu tonight?" she quietly asked Kyle.

"Tonight we have cumin and coriander crusted ahi steak with grilled veggies."

She took a bite and swooned.

"This is the best take out, ever," she gushed.

"I'm glad you like it." Kyle took a bite of his own food. They ate in silence and watched TV with Loretta. The nurse came in yet again, and Loretta fell asleep soon after.

Kyle gathered their empty containers and tossed them in the trash.

"Thank you," said Elana, leaning back in her chair. "For everything. When did you get so amazing?"

"I thought I always was amazing."

She rolled her eyes and Kyle sat back down next to her.

"Have you really been holding on to this guilt the whole time?" he asked.

"Yeah, I guess. I mean, wouldn't you?"

"Why are you here, Elana?" he asked.

"What do you mean?"

"Why did you leave Seattle? Why do you have to be here instead of back there?"

"Because there was nothing left for me there."

"I think that's bullshit."

"Excuse me?" she said.

"I think you're running away," he said softly.

"Well, I didn't ask for your opinion." She pulled her knees up into the chair and rested her chin on them.

"Don't you miss your parents?" he asked.

"Of course I do."

"And I bet they miss you."

Elana thought of her mom on the phone the other day, wishing she would come home. She could feel the tears threatening to spill over again.

Kyle leaned in even closer. "Why are you so afraid to be around people who care about you?"

Elana remembered seeing the strain on her parent's faces as they stood by her side after the accident. She knew they had postponed retirement and taken a second mortgage to help pay her legal fees. And then she saw Benjamin pulling out of their driveway one last time. If she wasn't hurting people, they were hurting her.

"I don't know what you're talking about," she told Kyle.

He leaned back and sighed in exasperation. "Caring about someone doesn't make you weak."

"No, it just makes you vulnerable."

"True, but sometimes it's worth it." He placed a finger under her chin and forced her to look at him. "I've done nothing but put my heart on the line these past few days, and you keep trying to crush it. But I don't believe you. And I think if you would just let me, I could make you happy."

She looked into those brown eyes that always made her feel at ease and wondered if he might be right.

"For a second there you started to lower your defenses. I think you liked it."

Elana narrowed her eyes. "But then your fiancée showed up the next morning and it kind of killed the mood."

"You're right. I wish that I had handled that much differently, but I've explained the situation and she's gone. So what's stopping you now?"

Elana racked her brain for the best excuse that she could come up with. Surely there were plenty. But before she had a chance to answer, Kyle kissed her. It was slow and warm and as always, pushed all excuses from her mind.

When he was done, he pressed his forehead against hers.

"I should get you home so you can get some rest," he said.

"I told you I'm not leaving her side."

He looked around the room. "You can't sleep here."

"I don't want her to wake up alone."

"How about this," he offered, "the next time they wake her, we let her know that you are headed home to get at least a couple hours sleep. Then you can come back."

Elana bit her lip as she considered it.

"Nothing's going to happen to her if you go home for a couple hours."

She was exhausted, and not to mention stiff from sitting in the chair all day.

"Agreed. But only a couple hours."

He nodded.

When they woke Loretta again, Elana took her hand and explained that she was heading home.

"Unless you want me to stay," Elana said. "I don't mind."

Loretta shook her head. "Go, I'll be fine."

"Are you sure?"

Loretta nodded.

"All right, then I'll be back in a couple hours. Call me if you need me sooner."

"Take your time, dear. Don't worry about me."

Elana was still hesitant, and Kyle had to gently tug her out the door.

"Take care, Mrs. Wilson," he called to her and she shooed them off.

Kyle walked Elana to the car and helped her in. The road was dark and Kyle took it nice and slow. The hum of the road put Elana to sleep before they even hit Princeville.

He pulled into the driveway and looked over at Elana who was propped against the window, her breath fogging up the glass as she slept. When Kyle first got the call about Jarod, he had been filled with a grief he'd never thought possible. And guilt for having not been with his brother that night. Why he'd even been out on that street in the first place, they would never know. And now to find out that Elana, the woman he'd been so angry with since learning she was the driver, had been swimming in her own grief and guilt made him regret everything his family had done to her. Kyle's father had even tried to warn them, had said that they should wait for things to cool down before taking any legal action, but his mother wouldn't hear of it, and Kyle had been more than happy to join the crusade.

And now here was Elana, filling him with another emotion he would never have thought possible. One thing was for sure though, he had to convince her to come back to Seattle with him.

Kyle leaned over to touch her cheek and her eyes slowly opened.

"I guess I was more tired than I thought," she said in a groggy voice.

"Let's get you inside," he said, smiling at her beautiful face.

"What's your plan for tomorrow?" he asked, walking her to the front door.

"I'll hang out at the hospital until her family

arrives, and then I have to work tomorrow," Elana said as they stepped onto the porch.

"Call me tomorrow if you need anything," Kyle told her and he kissed her cheek.

"I—will you," she lowered her gaze as she stumbled on the words. "Will you stay with me?"

Kyle grazed his fingers along her cheek. "If you want me to stay, then I will stay."

She took the hand from her cheek and pulled Kyle into the cottage with her. Elana threw her bag in the chair, and Kyle set his keys and wallet on the table next to it.

"I'm just going to wash my face real quick," she said, and went into the bathroom.

When Elana came out, Kyle's shorts and t-shirt were lying across her bag in the chair, and he was in her bed with his eyes closed. He was propped up on the pillow with one arm behind his head, the other gripping the sheet that was pulled up to his hips and despite her exhaustion, felt a stirring upon seeing the trail of hair leading beneath the covers. Elana resisted the urge to run her tongue along his hard abs as she climbed in next to him. He opened his eyes and smiled, wrapping an arm around her and pulling her head onto his chest.

"Are you tired?" she asked him.

"I think I'm more mentally exhausted than anything," he answered. "It's been a long day."

"Yes, it has."

She closed her eyes and listened to Kyle's steady heartbeat while he ran his fingers along her back. It was so easy to ignore not only her mother's warnings, but her own reservations, as she lay there warm and secure in his arms. Was it so wrong to want this?

"Elana?"

"Hmm?"

"I'm in love with you."

Elana's eyes flew open, but she didn't move or say anything.

"Elana?"

She propped herself on his chest and looked into his face. "I don't know how to respond to that, Kyle. I can't say it."

"I know." He ran his fingers through her hair. "But I wanted you to know. No matter what happens, I wanted you to know that I'm in love with you."

Elana frowned, searching his face. "Is everything okay?"

He shook his head, but said, "Everything's fine. Now close your eyes and get some sleep."

She laid her head back down. "Does this mean you're not going to ravage me?"

"Oh, trust me," he said. "There is nothing I would rather do right now than have my way with you. But you need to get some rest."

She yawned. "I demand a rain check then."

"Just promise me you will cash it in," he murmured.

Elana smiled as she closed her eyes and was about to succumb to sleep when she remembered something. "What was it you needed to tell me earlier?"

"Hmm?"

"At the hospital you said you had something you needed to tell me, but then the nurse came in."

A long sigh escaped Kyle. "I'm sure it could wait."

But now Elana was concerned. She sat up and looked him squarely in the face. "Don't keep any more surprises from me Kyle."

"You're right."

There was a pause, and Elana tried to be patient.

"My father was coordinating an intervention for Jarod," he finally said. "We had plans to check him into a rehab facility the following week after...after the accident."

Elana looked at him. Surely she had misheard him. Or at least misunderstood what he meant.

"What kind of rehab facility? You mean *alcohol* rehab."

Kyle slowly nodded, and she sat up even straighter. Her gaze drifted from his face to the wall behind him. She couldn't believe what was hearing.

"Say something," Kyle whispered.

"What do you want me to say?" she asked, focusing on him again. "Why are you telling me this?"

"When I realized you were still holding on to this guilt, I thought maybe this would help."

"Help me see that I wasn't really the one to blame?"

He nodded again.

"That part I already knew," she said with an edge to her voice, "regardless of how guilty I felt. But that's not what the lawyers argued."

"I know. I'm sorry. I'm not saying what we did was right. But please understand that we were upset. I think my mother was especially frustrated that had we acted a week earlier, Jarod might still be with us."

"I find it interesting that this information never made it into the courts."

"I'm sorry," he repeated.

"In fact," she said, trying to keep her voice down, "the only reason I settled was because the legal fees were draining me *and* my family dry. Your parents was never going to win the case. But they did a hell of a good job dragging it out."

"What do you want me to say?" Kyle asked. "Because I'll say whatever you want me to."

Elana looked at him lying there with regret in his eyes. She wanted to kick him out. Maybe. Truth was she wasn't sure what she wanted. Did this new information really change anything? It wasn't like Kyle had ever imagined they would be this intimate with each other. Neither of them could have ever dreamed it.

"I should probably get some sleep." Elana laid back down with her back to him and pulled the sheet up to her chin.

Kyle's arms wrapped around her from behind. "Please don't shut me out," he said into her ear.

"I'm not. I'm just too tired to think anymore."

"All right." He kissed her ear. "I love you, Elana."

But it was a long time before Elana was able to fall asleep.

Eight

IT WAS RAINING hard in downtown Seattle, and Elana was driving her Volvo along First Avenue when she heard a loud thump. She stopped and looked back to find a body in the road. She got out and ran back.

"Oh my God, sir, are you okay?" she cried out.

The man was trying to speak but couldn't get any words out. Elana knelt down and put her ear close to his mouth.

"Why did you leave me?" it croaked.

Elana sat up and looked to find that it was now Mrs. Wilson lying on the ground.

"Mrs. Wilson! What are you doing here?" she asked.

"I think the better question is why are you bleeding, dear?"

"What?"

Mrs. Wilson pointed at her abdomen. Elana saw a spot of blood on her blouse that was spreading across her torso. She reached under her shirt and found her hand covered in blood when she pulled it out. Elana heard laughter, and when she looked up, she saw Jarod Barnett and the rest of his family standing on the sidewalk and laughing at her. She stood up but found it difficult. Everyone laughed even harder. She started to run towards her car and tripped over something that sent her flying face first into the pavement....

Elana sat up in bed covered in sweat. A hand touched her arm, and she let out a little cry.

"Are you all right?"

It was only Kyle.

She nodded, too breathless to speak. Her heart was pounding in her chest.

Kyle sat up with her. "Was it a nightmare?"

"It's nothing," she said.

"Well 'nothing' seems to have you pretty worked up."

"It was just a dream," she replied. "I'll be fine."

"Do you have these 'dreams' a lot?" he asked.

"It's been a while. I'll be fine," she repeated.

"Then lay here with me and try to get some more sleep."

She looked out the window and saw the gray beginning to lighten the sky. The roosters would be crowing soon.

"No, I think I need a shower. I should get back to Loretta."

She got out of bed, leaving Kyle looking only slightly dejected and went into the bathroom. She disrobed, grabbed a towel, and stepped out onto the back porch and turned the water on. She yawned, waiting for the water to heat up and heard the bed creak as Kyle climbed out.

Elana stood under the water and let it wash down her face and body. And then Kyle's lips were upon her shoulder. She turned around and placed her hands on his chest.

"Hey," she said.

Kyle grabbed her shoulders and kissed her.

"Are you sure you're okay?" he asked.

She smiled at his concern. "I promise, I'm fine."

"About what I said last night…"

"Don't worry about it," Elana told him. "Like you said, your family was grieving. What's done is done."

He pulled her against his chest and let the warm water wash over them.

"I'm still sorry. And I love you."

Elana still couldn't bring herself to say the words, wasn't even one-hundred percent sure that love was what she was feeling. But she couldn't deny how good it felt to hear him say it to her.

They got dressed, and Kyle walked Elana out to her jeep.

"Are you sure you don't want me to just drive you?" he asked.

"You don't really want to spend all day at the hospital with me."

"I can think of several things I'd like to spend all day doing with you," he said as he pulled her face up to his.

She stood on her toes and kissed his mouth. "Another time perhaps. Why don't you go back and try and get some work done? I'll call you when I'm leaving the hospital."

"Do you know what time her son is supposed to get in?" he asked.

"I have no idea."

"How about if I bring you lunch later?"

"You don't have to. I'm not even sure what time they're transferring her to Lihue."

He frowned. "Well, if I don't see you before you have to work, then I will pick you up after your shift."

"I do have my own car," she said.

"I know, but the sooner I get to see your face the better."

"You're a fool. I'm leaving now. I'll see you soon."

Kyle kissed her one last time and climbed into his own vehicle, and they drove off.

The sun had risen completely by the time she arrived at the hospital. Mrs. Wilson was asleep, so Elana sat in the chair next to her bed and pulled a book from her bag. The four hours of sleep apparently weren't enough, because she was having trouble focusing on the words and found herself reading several passages more than once. She closed the book, propped her elbow on the arm of the chair, and attempted to rest her head in her hand.

A nurse came in to take more vitals, and Elana asked how Loretta had been overnight. The nurse informed her there had been no changes.

It wasn't long before Loretta's eyes started to open.

"Good morning, Mrs. Wilson," Elana said.

"Oh, hello, Elana." Her speech had improved, though it still sounded like it was taking some effort to get the words out. "You're here awfully early."

"I wanted to see you. Did they tell you that Daniel is coming today?"

Loretta nodded. "Yes, and my daughter Samantha called as well about an hour ago. She had forgotten about the time difference."

"That was good that you got to talk to her though," said Elana.

Loretta smiled. "Yes. She is planning on being out here in a couple of days. I told her she didn't need to come out, but she wouldn't listen." She looked around the room. "Where's your handsome friend?"

Elana blushed. "He's back at his hotel. He sends you his well wishes though."

Loretta smiled and patted Elana's hand. "He's such a sweet boy."

"Yes he is, Mrs. Wilson, yes he is."

It was only an hour after Elana's arrival that Mrs. Wilson's son Daniel showed up.

"Mom!" he exclaimed upon entering the room.

Mrs. Wilson took her son's face in both her hands and kissed his cheek.

"It's so good to see you, Danny!"

"I'm sorry I couldn't get here sooner, Mom."

"Oh, don't worry. I've had Elana here generously keeping me company."

Daniel finally took notice of Elana. He held out his hand to her.

"Hello, I'm Daniel."

Elana took his hand. "I'm Elana. Elana Tanner."

"Elana is the nice girl I've told you about living in the cottage behind the house," Mrs. Wilson explained.

"Ah, yes."

Daniel smiled, but Elana detected suspicion or mistrust in his eyes.

"She's the one who found me and called 911." Loretta patted her hand. "I don't know what I would have done without her."

Elana squeezed her hand but didn't say anything. She didn't want to think about where they might be if she hadn't found Loretta when she did.

The doctor came in, and Loretta introduced her son to him.

"I have good news," Dr. Rivers told them. "We

feel comfortable with moving you to Wilcox Memorial down in Lihue, probably within the next hour. We're just waiting for an available ambulance, and then we will get you on your way. As I explained to Ms. Tanner here yesterday, they will be able to do better testing there and help your family with the rehabilitation process."

They thanked the doctor, and he continued making his rounds.

Elana spotted the suitcase that had been shoved in a corner and went over and grabbed it.

"Don't forget this," she said.

"What's that, dear?"

"When Kyle had to run back for your cell phone, he packed this with some items he thought you might need."

"Who's Kyle?" Daniel snapped.

"Oh, he's this very sweet friend of Elana's," said Mrs. Wilson. "Very handsome, too." She winked at Elana who blushed again.

"And he was rifling through my mother's personal affects?"

"Yes. We needed to get your number, and he was nice enough to pick up other items." Elana suspected that Daniel was worried Kyle had swiped something, and it irked her. But she didn't want to call him on it in front of his mother. "If there is anything else you think you need, I'll be happy to swing it by."

"I'm sure we can handle it," said Daniel.

Elana was getting the vibe that her presence was not as welcome here with the addition of Daniel.

"I think I will let you and Daniel catch up." She grabbed the pad by the phone and wrote her cell number on it. "If you need me for anything, don't hesitate to call. Otherwise I will go see you tomorrow down in Lihue." She squeezed Loretta's hand.

"Thank you, dear, for everything. I don't know how to repay you."

"It's the least I could do," Elana said as she left.

Elana intended to go home and crawl back into bed, but as she neared the St. Regis, she decided there was somewhere else she'd rather be. Or at least someone she'd rather be with.

Elana hesitated at the room door. She realized that by being here, she was admitting that she wanted to be with him. But why shouldn't she have something she wanted?

It took a couple knocks and for a split second, Elana was worried that she was about to walk another mess. But relief washed over when he answered the door in boxer briefs and his eyes lit up at the sight of her.

"I wasn't expecting you back so soon," Kyle said as she walked into the room.

"Her son showed up earlier than I expected and did his best to make me feel unwelcomed."

"What's his problem?"

"I'm not entirely sure. Whatever, it doesn't matter. Loretta has family around now, so I can rest easier."

She looked at the messed bed and him in his underwear. "Were you sleeping?"

"I was tired." He pulled her into him. "And now that you are here, you can crawl into bed with me."

"That sounds like exactly what I need."

Elana undressed and they crawled back into much the same position they were in the night before. But this time Elana was feeling much more playful and remembered her desire last night to run her tongue across his abs. It was several hours until she was due at work, and sleep could be caught up on later….

Elana woke to the sound of the room door being opened and Kyle's voice.

"That's fine," he was whispering, "I'll take it from here. Thank you."

The door closed and Elana propped herself up on her elbows to watch as Kyle rolled in a room service cart.

"What's going on?" she asked him.

"Sorry, did I wake you?"

"No, it's fine," she looked around for a clock. "What time is it?"

"It's a little after two."

"Mmm...I should go home and get ready for work soon."

"Are you hungry? I ordered room service."

"I'm famished," she said as she grabbed the robe from the foot of the bed, and moved over to the table where Kyle was setting out the food.

"This smells great," she told him.

"I aim to please."

She gave him a devilish grin. "Well, you're doing a pretty good job of it."

He smiled as he dug into his salad. But the smile started to fade and Elana felt that he was mulling something over in that beautiful head of his.

"You okay?" she asked.

"I have to go home Wednesday morning," he said.

"Oh. That's only two more days."

"I pushed my return back as far as I could, but I risk losing clients if I don't get back soon."

"Of course. I knew your time here was limited." That didn't mean she wanted him to go.

147

"Elana, I want you to move back to Seattle."

She set her fork down. "I told you that was never going to happen."

Kyle set his own utensil down a little less gracefully. "But I don't understand. Why not?"

"I just can't. It's too hard. There are so many bad memories."

"Then come back for me, and we can make new memories."

Elana stared into his eyes that she loved so much. He made it sound so easy, so pleasant. But what if it blew up in her face? She wasn't sure she could handle that.

Instead of answering she simply lowered her gaze and continued to eat.

"Dammit, Elana!" Kyle yelled, causing her to jump. "Why do you have to be such a goddamned martyr?"

"A martyr?"

"Do you feel like you need to pay penance for my brother's death? Is that why you stay here, struggling to get by? Why are you still punishing yourself?"

Her appetite was officially gone. Elana wiped her mouth with the napkin and laid it on the table next to her half-eaten food.

"I think I should go."

As she stood up Kyle came out of his chair and stood in front of her.

"No, wait. I don't want you to go. I'm trying to understand you, Elana, but I can't if you don't let me in."

"I'm scared, Kyle, okay? I'm fucking scared! You promise me the world if I go back with you. But what happens when reality sets in and you realize I'm not the person you thought I was? Where does that leave me?"

Kyle opened his mouth, but the words struggled to come out.

"Can you honestly promise me," she continued, "that it will be happy ever after if go with you?"

"You're right," he said. "I can't. Nobody knows what the future holds. But I do know that I'm willing to risk it."

"That's easy for you to say. I'm the one taking all the risk."

He shook his head. "I can't believe you would think that. What about my family? What if *you* hurt *me*?"

It was then that Elana realized how selfish she'd had been. Did she really imagine it would be so simple for Kyle to go home with a woman that his family despised?

"I—I'm sorry," she said. "Perhaps you're right."

Kyle just continued to stare at her without responding. Elana took a step forward and placed her hands on his chest.

"Let me think about it, please?" she pleaded.

He wrapped his arms around her and pulled her into him. "That's all I ask."

After running home to change, Elana went into work with mixed feelings. Part of her was almost excited at the possibility of going home, while the other part was terrified. Question was, which part was stronger?

When her shift was done, Elana was only half surprised to find Kyle's rental waiting in the parking lot. She walked up the driver's side, where Kyle was leaning against the door.

"How long have you been out here?" Elana asked.

"About an hour."

She laughed. "You're pathetic. You know that, right?"

A lock of hair had come loose from her bun and he pushed it behind her ear. "I want to make sure I get to spend every minute possible with you before I leave."

"I can relate to that." She kissed him.

"Hop in," he said.

"What about my car?"

"I'm sure it will be safe. I'll get you back to it eventually."

She grinned and Kyle walked her around to the passenger side.

Kyle stopped before turning onto the highway and hit the right turn signal.

"Do you think we could go back to my place instead?" Elana asked.

"You sure?"

"I just feel more comfortable there."

"Works for me." He flipped the signal and turned left instead. "I like your bed better anyway."

"You do?" She couldn't imagine why anybody would like her lumpy bed over the plush hotel mattress.

"Yeah, it smells like you."

Elana blushed.

When Elana woke the next morning, she was relieved to have had a nightmare-free night. She looked over to Kyle, who was on his stomach and snoring softly. She rolled onto her side so that she could admire him better. She decided that he really was a beautiful creature and was flattered that it was she whom he wanted to be with. She found herself imagining what it would be like to wake up every morning next to him. It certainly wouldn't be bad, she concluded.

She also wondered what life would be like if she returned to Seattle. Of course her parents would be thrilled, and Elana did like the idea of being able to see them on a regular basis again. Did she want to go back into law, or would she continue waitressing? The truth was she didn't really enjoy being a server.

Kyle moaned and rolled over onto his back. Elana scooted closer to him and ran a finger along his jaw, feeling the stubble. His hand shot up and grabbed hers.

Without opening his eyes he said, "Are you trying to seduce me, Miss Tanner?"

She giggled.

He slowly opened his eyes. "God, I love it when you giggle."

"What happens when my giggle starts to annoy you?" she asked.

He rolled over and pinned her beneath him.

"I don't see that ever happening, but I'm willing to spend every day with you until I have the answer." Then he kissed her, and her body arched up in response.

They finally left the bed and migrated to the shower, where Kyle asked what was on the agenda for the day.

"I want to go check on Mrs. Wilson."

"Do you want me to come with you?"

Elana remembered her unpleasant interaction with Daniel. "Yes. If you don't mind."

"Of course I don't mind. My objective for the next twenty-four hours is to spend as much time with you as possible."

Her face fell. "Twenty-four hours? Is that really all we have?"

He pressed his forehead to hers. "Give or take. I'm afraid so. But I intend to come back as soon as I can get away again."

"How long do you think that will be?"

"Maybe a month. I won't be sure until I get home and look over the books."

"Wow. That's a long time."

"Enough time for you to get everything ready to go home. Have you given any more thought to it?"

"I'm still thinking on it," she said.

"Well, you're not giving me a flat-out no anymore, so I'll dare to be hopeful."

After getting dressed, they headed out to grab breakfast before paying Mrs. Wilson a visit. Elana was surprised when Daniel came out of the main house as they approached the jeep.

"Miss Tanner," he called out. "I was hoping to talk to you."

She forced a smile. "Yes. What can I do for you?"

He eyed Kyle. "Perhaps it would be better if we spoke in private."

Kyle raised an eyebrow.

"Really, it's fine," said Elana. "This is Kyle Barnett. He's the one who called 911 and collected the items for your mother."

"Ah," Daniel replied. "Well, I wanted to talk about your use of the cottage."

"Yes," Elana said, feeling confused. "What about it?"

"I don't think that my mother should be on her own anymore, so I will be bringing her home with me when she is released from the hospital."

"Oh. I understand. I'll be sad to see her go. What will you do with the house?"

"We are going to be putting it on the market as soon as possible."

"Sure. That makes sense."

"But I have more family coming in to help with my mother and to get the house ready for being listed. Unfortunately I am going to need the extra space of the cottage."

Kyle spoke up. "What exactly is that you are trying to say, Mr. Wilson?"

"I'm saying that I need Miss Tanner here to be out of the cottage by the end of the week. Preferably in the same condition as when she first occupied it."

Elana was stunned. Kyle was pissed.

"You can't kick her out like that. There is such a thing as tenant laws."

"Yes, he can, Kyle."

Kyle looked at Elana.

"Mrs. Wilson and I never had a renter's agreement," she said quietly. "It was all under the table."

Kyle's jaw dropped. "You're a law student. You know better."

"It made it simpler for both of us. I wasn't locked into a lease and Mrs. Wilson didn't have to report the income."

"So, you see, Mr. Barnett," said Daniel, "I am completely within my right to ask Miss Tanner to vacate the property."

"That doesn't mean you have to be a dick about," Kyle shot back.

"I think you should watch your language with me."

Kyle started to open his mouth, but Elana put a hand on him.

153

"Don't, Kyle. He's not worth it. I'll figure something out. I always do." She tugged on his arm and they walked in the direction of the car again.

"And one more thing," Daniel called to them. "If I discover that any of my mother's valuables are missing, don't think I won't go to the police."

Kyle's face went red, but he managed to keep his mouth shut. They got in the car and he peeled off.

"Can you believe that jerk?" he said. "He can't really kick you out like that, can he?"

Elana nodded. "I'm afraid so. Technically I was little more than a house guest. To be honest, I don't want to be there anyway if he's going to be there." She shivered. "He gives me the creeps."

Kyle looked at her and his eyes went big.

"What?" she asked.

"You're absolutely right. We need to get you out of that place by tonight!"

"What are you talking about?"

"Forget the end of the week; I don't want you staying there by yourself. We need to find something before I leave tomorrow."

Elana rolled her eyes. "You're being ridiculous. It's only a couple of days. I think I can handle it."

"You said it yourself; he gives you the creeps. We didn't even know he was at the house until he came out to talk to you. When did he get there? This morning? Last night?"

An uneasiness swept over Elana as she thought of their shower only moments ago. Was he around then?

"True," she said.

"Is any of the furniture in the cottage yours?" Kyle asked.

"No," she said. "Pretty much everything I own can fit into the two suitcases I came here with. Getting packed up won't take me long. I just need to figure out where to go."

"After we visit Mrs. Wilson, we'll go pack up your stuff and then you're getting on that plane with me tomorrow."

Elana's heart leapt at the thought of going home tomorrow. He was right; they could do it. And right then she knew what she really wanted. But then she remembered work.

"I can't go with you tomorrow,"

"And why the hell not?" he demanded.

She smiled at him. "Because I need to give my two weeks' notice at work. It's the right thing to do."

Kyle's jaw dropped. He'd been preparing for another argument.

"Really? You'll come back to Seattle?"

She grabbed his hand. "Yes, I'm ready to go back."

His face lit up like a kid on Christmas morning, and Elana loved that she was responsible for it.

"I could kiss you right now if I wasn't driving."

She squeezed his hand. "There will be plenty of time for that. I promise."

After breakfast they made the drive into Lihue, and Elana was delighted to discover Loretta sitting in a chair.

"Mrs. Wilson!" Elana exclaimed. "How are you doing?"

Loretta's face brightened at the sight of Elana.

"Oh, Elana dear! I'm doing much better. What are you doing here?"

Elana sat in the chair next to her. "I'm here to see you, of course. I'm glad to see you out of that bed."

"Yes, they've had me walking the halls this morning." Loretta frowned. "It's a little difficult. I had to use a walker and even with that it was hard."

"Still, it's progress, right?"

Loretta nodded.

"I ran into Daniel this morning. He told me that you will be going home with him."

"Yes. He has insisted that I go home with him to Arizona where he can look after me. He doesn't want me here alone." Loretta placed a hand on Elana's. "I tried to tell him that I wasn't alone. I had you with me. But he wouldn't hear of it."

"He's worried, just like any son would be. But it's for the best, because I'm moving back to Seattle."

"You are? I hope it isn't because of me. You're welcome to stay at the cottage until it sells. I'm sure that would give you time to find something else."

Elana pursed her lips. Clearly Daniel had not told his mother all of his plans.

"No, Mrs. Wilson. It's just time for me to go home. I'm ready to be close to my own parents again."

Loretta patted her hand. "And I'm sure they will be happy to have you back. I certainly enjoyed having you around."

"Thank you, Mrs. Wilson. I couldn't have asked for a better landlady. Scratch that. A better neighbor."

When they left, Elana promised to see Mrs. Wilson again before she headed home. In the hall they ran into Daniel.

"I wanted to let you know that I will be out of the cottage by tonight," Elana told him. "If you aren't home, where would you like me to leave the key?"

"You don't have to leave so early on my account," he replied.

Kyle snorted.

"No really, it's okay," she said. "I'd rather just get it over with."

"Yes, I think she will be more comfortable with me at the St. Regis anyways," Kyle added and Elana elbowed him.

"Oh, is that supposed to impress me?" Daniel asked.

"It's my subtle way of saying I'd rather have her safe with me than anywhere near a creep like you."

Daniel took a step towards Kyle, but Kyle didn't back down.

"You'd better watch your step," said Daniel.

"Or what?"

Daniel glared at him, but then backed down. "If you don't mind, I'm going to go check on my mother."

They watched him go and then continued to the car.

Kyle started the engine. "Let's go get you packed up."

Back at the cottage Elana had her two suitcases opened on the bed and a garbage bag on the floor nearby.

She set a stack of books on the counter by the door. "We should swing by the library on the way to the hotel so I can drop these off before I forget. Don't need to leave behind a trail of overdue book fines."

Kyle was folding the clothes that Elana piled onto the bed, putting them in one of the suitcases.

"That's easy enough," he said.

"You don't really have to help me pack," she told him. "I'm sure I can handle it."

"Well, I'm not going to just stand here and watch you work. And I'm not leaving your side until I have to either."

She looked at her watch. "And that's happening in three hours when I have to go into work. I don't think my manager would take kindly to you following me around the restaurant."

He wrapped his arms around her. "That doesn't mean it will stop me from trying."

"As sweet as that sounds, I think it might be a little creepy," she told him.

"You're probably right." He released her and they went back to packing.

"I'll talk to Janelle at work tonight," Elana said, "and see if she might let me crash on her couch until I leave."

"Why would you need to stay at her place?" Kyle asked.

Elana frowned. "Well where else would I say?"

"Stay at the hotel."

"I can't afford one night there, let alone two weeks!"

"Please, I wouldn't dream of letting you pay for it."

She put her hands on her hips. "Kyle, I won't be kept."

"Kept? What are you talking about?"

"I'm saying I can take care of myself. You don't need to take care of me."

He put his hands on her shoulders. "First of all, I want to take care of you. Because I love you. And I would feel better if I knew you were safe and sound at the hotel."

"I just don't know..." She chewed on her lip.

"Elana, I am paying for the room through the next two weeks. If you don't stay there, you will be throwing away my money."

It didn't exactly make her feel any better, but she conceded. "Fine. But know that I am doing so under duress."

"Yes, life's a bitch when you're forced to stay in a five-star hotel."

"Damn straight." But a smile crept across her face.

When it was time for work, Kyle drove Elana to the restaurant where her car was still parked.

"I'll take the bags and you can head over when you get off," he said.

"This feels strange," she said.

"What does?"

"Having you take care of me like this. I have to admit I feel a bit weak right now."

"Hey," he said, lifting her chin. "You are not weak. And it's time you let someone take care of you for once."

"I promise I will try."

He kissed her and she headed into work. At the door she ran into Janelle.

"Wow! Where did you find him?" she asked.

Elana smiled. "More like he found me. It's a long story, but I'm glad he did."

They walked in, and Elana immediately found Jack and asked to have a word with him. He led her into the office and shut the door.

"Is everything all right?" he asked.

"Yes. I just wanted—I—" Elana found herself faltering on the words. Her confidence was waning without Kyle there.

"Yes," Jack prompted.

What if she was making a mistake? What if she quit her job, and then Kyle gets home and decides *they* were a mistake? But then the last several days ran through her mind, and she remembered everything Kyle had done to prove himself to her. Didn't she owe him the same trust?

"I'm giving you my two week notice," she said, before she could second guess herself again.

"You're leaving?" he asked.

"I'm afraid so. I've decided to go home to Seattle."

"I'll be sad to see you go, but I'm sure you must be excited to go back."

"I am." It surprised Elana to realize that she really was.

"I will get the word out that we are looking to hire someone. I'm sure it won't take long to fill your shifts."

"I'm sure it won't either."

"Although I'll be hard-pressed to find as hard a worker as you were," he said.

"Thank you. I appreciate the compliment."

"It's the truth."

Elana was genuinely happy at work that night, and it was reflected in her tips, which she was doubly grateful for. Kyle wasn't letting her pay for the room, but she fully intended to buy her own ticket home. It was important that she get home on her own and not on Kyle's dime.

She finished her end of shift work in record time and raced to the hotel. It was her last night with Kyle, and she didn't want to waste a minute of it.

The door was opened within seconds of Elana knocking on it.

"It's about time," Kyle said, pulling her into his arms and pressing his mouth against hers as he kicked the door shut behind them.

They were both breathless in the post-coital glow as Elana positioned herself on his chest to face him.

"Just so you know," she explained, "that's how I expect to always be greeted when I show up on your doorstep."

He grinned. "I think I can live with that arrangement."

She wove her fingers into his.

"What happens if I get back to Seattle and you decide that I don't quite fit into your world?"

He pulled her hand to his mouth and sucked on one of her fingers. "Then I will move heaven and earth to make room for you." He released her hand and touched her face. "Are you really that worried?"

"I am. You live a privileged life that is completely foreign to me. What if I just come across as out of place?"

"You're referring to my wealth, aren't you?"

She shrugged. "Well, yeah."

"It doesn't define me, Elana. Granted, you will see me in a suit more often, but I'll still be the same person that I am here with you."

Her mouth went up at the thought of him so smartly dressed.

"I bet you look good in a suit," she said.

"I think I do."

She playfully pushed off of him. "You would."

"And you forget that I did my research on you. I know that your upbringing was not so impoverished. Redmond is not exactly the wrong side of the tracks."

"It has its neighborhoods just like any other city," she protested.

"And did you grow up in one of those neighborhoods?" he asked.

"Well, no."

"In fact, correct me if I'm wrong, but don't your parents live on Education Hill?"

She sat up. "Wait, how do you know where my parents live?"

"So it's not my proudest moment, but I looked

them up. I was prepared to show up on their doorstep and enlist their help if you didn't agree to move back to Seattle."

"That's sweet, but you do realize my parents hate you, right?"

"I figured as much," he said. "But I doubt they hate me enough to not want you to come home. Speaking of which, have you told them yet?"

She rolled onto her back. "No, not yet."

Kyle turned on his side and leaned on his elbow. "Why not? Are you having doubts?"

She looked up at him. "I just haven't had a chance yet. Today's been kind of crazy."

"But you are going to tell them, aren't you?"

"Of course."

"Good. Now let's order some food. I'm starving." Kyle slid out of bed and walked bare-assed naked to the desk where the room service menu was located. Elana couldn't keep the childish grin off her face.

"Any preference?" he asked.

"Hmm? Oh, no, I'm good with whatever you order."

Kyle placed the order and rejoined Elana in bed.

"What are we going to do about our families hating each other?" Elana asked him.

"Do you think your family hates me personally?"

"My mother was pretty livid when she found out I slept with you."

Kyle's eyes went big. "You told her we slept together?"

"It wasn't my intention, but yes. And then she warned me to get as far away from you as possible."

"Well I'm glad you didn't listen to her," he

said.

"I tried."

He leaned in closer. "But you found my charm just too irresistible to resist."

She rolled her eyes but then placed a hand on his chest. "That, and your heart."

Kyle grasped her hand and stared into her eyes. "I love you, Elana."

She held his stare and spoke softly. "I love you too, Kyle Barnett."

When Kyle's alarm went off early the next morning, Elana felt like she had just closed her eyes. They had both been reluctant to fall asleep. He insisted she go back to sleep, but Elana refused. She could sleep after he had left.

"Here's your key," Kyle reminded her. "Feel free to charge anything to the room. I told them you were authorized to make charges."

She raised her eyebrow at him.

"What?" he said. "You have to eat, don't you?"

"I think I can handle buying my own food."

"You're right. I'm sorry."

"It's fine. I really do appreciate that you want to take care of me."

She wrapped her arms around his middle and sighed.

"After all the times you said you were going home, I can't believe you're actually leaving today."

"I know," Kyle replied. "I wish you could come with me now. Are you sure you have to stay?"

"We talked about this. Yes, I have to stay. I will buy the ticket today and two weeks from now I will see you at Sea-Tac."

"I don't mind flying out and then flying back with you."

"Kyle, no."

He sighed. "Two weeks it is." He took her face in both his hand and kissed her. Elana balled his shirt in her fists and dreamed of never letting go. But he had to leave, and the kiss had to end.

"I'll call you as soon as I land."

She nodded.

"And don't forget to call your parents," he added, and she nodded again.

"I love you," she said.

"I love you too."

He gave her one last quick kiss and opened the door. Elana took his hand and he paused.

"I'll see you soon. Promise?"

"I promise," she answered.

His fingers slipped out of hers as he walked out the door rolling his suitcase behind him. Elana stood in the doorway and watched him walk to the elevator. When he was out of sight, she walked back into the room and slowly closed the door. Elana sat on the bed and pulled her knees up to her chin. The room felt so big and lonely without Kyle's presence in it. This was going to be a long two weeks.

The TV was still on when the alarm on Elana's cell phone went off. She had turned on the television for background noise and eventually fell asleep from exhaustion. She had to be at work in an hour, and she decided now would be a good time to call her parents.

She called the house, and her dad answered the phone.

"Elana, sweetie, how are you?"

"I'm good, Dad. How are you?"

"It's so good to hear your voice." Her dad always said that when she called.

"Is Mom around?" Elana asked.

"No. She drove down to Portland for a meeting and is spending the night. She won't be back until tomorrow. What's up, kiddo?"

"I'll call her cell later, but I wanted to let you guys know that I'm coming home."

"For a visit or to stay?"

"To stay, Dad, I'm coming home to stay."

"That's great!" Hearing his excitement put Elana on the brink of tears.

"Do you know when you are coming back yet?" he asked.

"In two weeks. I'm going on-line tonight to buy the tickets. I don't have the exact day yet, but the plan is for two weeks."

"Two weeks! Oh honey, that's so wonderful. Your mom is going to be excited. We've missed you so much!"

"I've missed you guys, too!" There was no fighting back the tears now. But they were tears of happiness, and Elana couldn't remember the last time she had cried those.

"You should go call your mom and tell her the good news," he said.

"I will. I love you, Dad, and I'll see you soon!"

"Love you too, sweetie!"

Elana hung up and dialed her mother's cell phone.

"Hi Mom," Elana said when Renee answered.

"Is everything okay, sweetie?"

"Yes. In fact, it's better than okay. I've decided to come home!" The more she said it, the more it seemed real, and the more excited Elana got.

"Oh, Elana! It's about goddamned time!" Her mother was laughing when she said it and Elana laughed with her.

"You're right, it is," Elana said.

"Do you know when yet? Do you need us to come out and help with anything?"

"No, no, I've got everything covered. But my plan is to be out there in two weeks."

"Two weeks. Wow, that's so soon. Can I ask what changed between when I talked to you last week and now? You were so set against coming home when I asked you."

Elana started to finger the hem of the bed sheet. She was reluctant to answer the question. But she knew it was best to prepare her mother. Give her time to adjust.

The pause was too long for her mother.

"Sweetie?"

"I have something to tell you," said Elana, "and I'm pretty sure that you aren't going to like it."

"What is it?" Her mother sounded very concerned.

"Um, Kyle is the one who convinced me that I needed to go home."

"Kyle? As in Kyle Barnett? The same Kyle Barnett who didn't tell you he was engaged?"

"Yes," Elana squeaked.

"So you're still seeing him then, I take it."

"Well, not at the moment, since he left for Seattle this morning."

"And are you going to see him again when you get back to Seattle?"

"That is the plan, yes."

"Elana, what the hell are you thinking?"

"Mom, he makes me happy. Happier than I have been in a long time, and I am begging you now to trust me and give him a chance."

There was a long silence on the other end.

"Mom? Are you still there?"

"Yes, I'm here. I'm not making any promises,

but I suppose if he is the reason I get to have you at home again, then I should be grateful for that."

"Thank you. That's all I ask for. I have to get to work now, but I will talk to you soon. I love you!"

"I love you too, honey, and I can't wait to see you again."

"Me too. Bye!"

Elana tossed her phone on the table and jumped up to get dressed for work when it started ringing and she saw Kyle's name in the screen.

"I'm here and I'm already missing you like crazy," he told her.

"I know the feeling," she said. "I just got off the phone with my parents."

"I bet they're excited to hear the news."

"Ecstatic! Hold on." She pulled the phone away from her ear so she could change into her work t-shirt before continuing. "Although my mother was not excited to hear that I was involved with you."

"Do you think she'll come around though?"

"Maybe. She did say she was grateful that you convinced me to go back."

"It's a start. Have you bought your ticket yet?"

"No." She grabbed her bag and the hotel key and headed out the door. "I'm headed to work as we speak. I'll stop at the bank on the way to deposit my tips so I can get on one of the hotel computers tonight to purchase it."

"Just let me buy your ticket as soon as I get home."

"No. I've got it. You have done too much for me already."

"Fair enough. Text me the flight info as soon as you have it."

Elana stopped walking. "Are you worried I won't buy it?"

"No!" He paused. "Well, maybe a little. I'm scared you will change your mind without me around."

"I have nowhere to live and I've already given my notice at work. Kyle, I have nowhere left to go but home."

"I know. And I'll be waiting for you."

"I know. I love you."

"I love you too."

"Now go home and get some rest," she said. "I will talk to you tomorrow."

"I will. Take care of yourself."

She smiled. "I always do."

The line at the bank had been long and slow and Elana just barely made it to work on time. The restaurant was slammed that night, which she was grateful for. It helped to keep her mind off of the fact that she would be going back to an empty hotel room that night.

She had intended to use the hotel's business center computers when she got back there, but they were having issues, so she decided to just wait until morning and head over to the library.

As Elana swiped her key card in the door, she could hear soft music playing from inside her room. She cautiously wandered in to the living room and stopped dead when she saw who was sitting on the love seat.

"Hello, Miss Tanner," said Adelaide Barnett.

Nine

"I WAS BEGINNING to wonder when you would make it back."

Elana's heart pounded in her chest. It was hard to believe that a woman in a simple navy shift dress and string of pearls frightened her so much. Bit looks could be deceiving.

"Mrs. Barnett," Elana finally said.

Adelaide picked up the empty wine glass in front of her and walked over to the mini bar to refresh it.

"Would you like a glass?" Adelaide asked Elana, who just shook her head. She didn't know what to say. As she watched Adelaide refill her glass, Elana couldn't help notice how much Kyle looked like his mother. Adelaide's hair, at the moment pulled into a low chignon, was the same dark color. She also had the same brown eyes, but without the warmth of her son's.

"Imagine my distress," said Adelaide, "when my soon to be daughter-in-law calls me and informs me that my son has been sleeping with someone else. That was upsetting enough." Adelaide's delicate hand swirled the red liquid in her glass. "But then to find out it was the very same woman who killed his own brother? Well, that was just too much."

"Kyle ended it with Victoria," Elana said. "They were over a long time ago."

"You know how it is with men," Adelaide said, setting down the untouched wine and striding over to where Elana was still standing. "They always get nervous at the thought of commitment. They like to go out and have a little fun. It's nothing personal, dear."

Elana swallowed hard. "Kyle loves me."

Adelaide's head fell back with laughter.

"Oh, that's so cute," she said, scrunching her perfect nose. "And I suppose you believe him."

Elana's fists clenched at her side, but she said nothing.

"Yes. Well, Kyle was always a bit soft hearted," Adelaide told her. "Not like Jarod. *He* was much stronger."

"Kyle is ten times the man Jarod ever was," Elana said.

Adelaide slapped her and Elana gasped, feeling the sting spread across her cheek.

"Don't you dare talk about Jarod that way," Adelaide said, pointing a manicured finger at Elana, only inches from Elana's heart. "You have no right to make these accusations when you never even knew him. Not when you were the one responsible for his death!"

"I wasn't the one in a drunken stupor that night!"

There was a fire in Adelaide's eyes and Elana held her gaze, refusing to back down.

"Why are you here?" Elana asked with clenched teeth. "What exactly is it that you want?"

"It's simple. I want you to stay away from Kyle. Without you as a distraction, he will finally see that he and Victoria are meant to be together."

"Victoria has been cheating on him!"

Adelaide's face went sour. "Yes. I've had a talk with her regarding that and she has agreed to terminate her own indiscretions."

Elana could not believe what she was hearing. How could Kyle have sprung from this woman?

"And what if Kyle doesn't want to stay away from me?" Elana asked.

"Then I am prepared to cut him off from the family. That way I wouldn't have to worry about you getting your grubby little hands on our money."

Now Elana resisted her own urge to slap Adelaide. She would not stoop to her level.

"I'm not after your money. I could care less about it. Kyle is the one who pursued *me*."

Adelaide wrinkled her nose at the thought.

"You would really disown your own son," said Elana. "What kind of a mother are you?"

Adelaide narrowed her eyes at Elana. "The kind of mother who is willing to do anything to keep my son safe from the likes of you. Besides, I won't have to. Because if you really care for my son as you claim to do, you will leave him alone. So that he doesn't have to suffer."

"Kyle doesn't care about the money."

"I imagine that is something he would say, but that's only because he's never been without it," Adelaide explained. "I'm sure it would be cute at first living in a tiny apartment and eating noodles every night. But it would get old quickly. He is accustomed to a certain lifestyle. Nice clothes, fancy car, luxurious vacations such as this." She waved her hand around the room. "How long do you think it would take before he longed to have his old life back? The old life that you took away from him."

Elana wanted to believe that she was right, that Adelaide didn't know her son like she thought she did.

But there were doubts in the back of her mind. What if it was true and Kyle began to resent her? The truth was Elana had only known Kyle for two weeks; there was still obviously a lot to learn about each other.

"And what do you propose I do?" Elana asked her. "He is expecting me to show up in Seattle in a couple of weeks."

The corners of Adelaide's mouth curled up. "Good girl. I knew you weren't a complete idiot. You are to call him and tell him that you aren't going back to Seattle after all. You are staying right here and he is never to call you again."

A knife went through Elana's heart. Not only at the thought of telling that to Kyle, but of not going home and seeing her family.

"But I want to go home," she said. "I'm not staying here."

"My dear, you can go anywhere you want. But you are not to step foot in Seattle until Kyle and Victoria are back together and happily married."

The thought of Kyle marrying Victoria only twisted the knife deeper in Elana.

"Fine." Elana felt all the life go out of her as she said it. "I will call him tomorrow and do it."

"Oh no," laughed Adelaide. "I am not leaving here until you call him. Right here, right now."

"But it's almost three in the morning there!"

"I don't care. I need to be sure that you go through with it."

Elana stared at her in disbelief.

"You are a horrible woman."

"I do what I have to in order to protect my family. Now make the damn phone call, Miss Tanner."

There was a lump in her throat as Elana pulled the cell phone out of her bag. She was about to hit the send button when Adelaide grabbed her wrist.

"And don't you *dare* mention our little conversation, or you will regret it."

If there was one thing Elana had learned about Adelaide, it was that she was not someone to be messed with.

Elana completed the call and waited for Kyle to pick up. She hoped it went to voicemail so she didn't have to hear the hurt in his voice. But then she realized it would only be worse to break up with him through a message.

After the fourth ring, Kyle picked up.

"Elana? What is it? Is everything all right?"

Tears began to spill down her cheeks.

"I'm so sorry Kyle, but I—" she started.

"No!" he interrupted. "Don't do this, Elana!"

"I can't come home."

"Dammit, Elana, you promised!" He was shouting at her. "You promised me!"

"I know, but this was a mistake." She was sobbing. "We could never work."

"Christ! You can't keep doing this!"

"I'm so sorry," she repeated, "but you deserve better. You need someone who can make you happy."

When Kyle spoke again, he was no longer shouting.

"I want *you*, Elana. You do make me happy. Please come home."

The pleading in his voice was breaking Elana's heart. She looked at Adelaide, who appeared to be taking pleasure in this.

"I can't," Elana whispered.

"Please, Elana, don't do this. I love you!"

Adelaide took the phone from Elana's hand and ended the call.

"That's enough," she said, and tossed the phone on the bed behind Elana.

Elana stood rooted to the spot and buried her head in her hands. What did she do?

Adelaide made for the door.

"And Miss Tanner," she called over her shoulder. "I've informed the front desk that you will be checking out tomorrow. No more mooching off my son."

The door closed, and Elana fell to the floor, heaving uncontrollably.

Kyle sank back onto the bed and stared at the phone in his hand. He should have pushed harder for Elana to come home with him. This was exactly what he had been afraid of.

It was cold feet; it had to be. Just last night she had said she loved him. This morning she didn't want to let him go. Even this afternoon she had promised she was coming. Then he remembered that Elana told him she had no job and no place to live. Nowhere left to go but home. Then what the hell happened?

Kyle tried to call Elana again, but she wasn't answering.

He dialed another number, and just before voicemail could pick up, Victoria answered on the other end.

"Well, hello Kyle," she purred.

"What did you do?" he shouted.

"What the hell are you talking about?"

"Did you call my mother?" he asked.

"Oh, that."

Kyle could hear the amusement in her voice. Had he ever really known this woman he'd been about to marry?

"Yes, that," he seethed.

"I may have informed her of your extracurricular activities."

"Damn you, Victoria!" He ended the call without waiting for her response.

Adelaide wasn't picking up her phone, so Kyle tried the house phone at his parent's residence.

His father wasn't happy when he answered the phone, but Kyle didn't care.

"I need to speak to Mother," he demanded.

"She's not here, Kyle," answered Chuck. "Is something wrong?"

"Yes! I mean—no—it's fine. I just need to talk to her about something. Where is she?"

"I'm not sure. She said she had some business to attend to and called Rodney. She said she would be back in the morning."

"Dammit." If his mother had called the family pilot, she must have flown somewhere and he had a pretty good guess where.

"Kyle, what is going on? Are you sure you're not in any trouble?"

"No, I'm not in any trouble," said Kyle. "I can't explain right now. I just need to know where Mom is."

"I'm sorry, I don't know where exactly. She got a phone call at lunch that seemed to fluster her, and she left in a hurry. I assumed she would explain when she got home."

"Don't count on it," Kyle muttered. "Sorry for waking you, Dad. I'll talk to you soon."

Kyle hung up and started to work on a plan.

Light was streaming through the bedroom window when Elana woke up on the floor. She had pulled the comforter off of the bed at some point, and was now tangled up in it. Every joint in her body was stiff and sore, but she couldn't bring herself to move yet.

Last night's events ran through her mind like a horrible movie. Then she remembered Adelaide's parting words. She didn't know where she going to go, but she clearly couldn't stay here. Mustering all the strength she could, Elana freed herself from the comforter and stood up to go into the bathroom. She figured she'd better get a shower in while she still could in case she had to spend a few nights in her car.

Her phone had rung several times after Adelaide left, but Elana had ignored them all. Checking her phone she now saw several voicemails from Kyle. There was nothing he could say that would change anything, so she deleted each and every one of them. It would hurt too much to hear the pain in his voice. The pain that *she* had caused.

After her shower, Elana shoved the few items she had scattered around the room into one of the suitcases and rolled them both to the door. She took one last look around the room, and her eyes burned from the tears she was holding back. There was the bathtub they had shared, the bed where they had made love, the same bed where she had told Kyle she loved him for the first time only thirty-six hours ago.

She sniffed and wiped her eyes before grabbing the hotel key and walking out of the room. Blondie was working the front desk when she dropped off the key. Didn't that woman ever go home?

"Are we checking out, Miss…"

"It should be under the name Barnett," Elana told her.

"Ah yes," she replied. She took the key and processed the checkout. "Will you hold on one second?"

"Um, okay."

Blondie left and returned shortly with an envelope.

"This fax came in early this morning for you."

"For me?" Elana frowned as she peeked inside the envelope and started to cry. It was an e-ticket for her to Seattle. There was no name other than hers on the document, but she had no doubt who it was from.

"Are you all right, miss?" the receptionist asked.

Elana nodded and slid the envelope across the desk. "Will you throw this away for me please?"

"Are you sure?"

"Yes, please."

Blondie reluctantly took the envelope back, and Elana hiked out to her jeep with the suitcases. She tossed them into the back and then sat in her driver's seat and started bawling again. Thank goodness she was off that night, because Elana knew she was not in any condition to go in yet again.

When she was finally able to regain her composure, she decided to pay a visit to the closest thing she could call a friend on the island.

Ricky's shop had just opened when Elana pulled in.

Ricky walked out of the garage, eying the jeep.

"Don't tell me you're having car problems again. I thought I fixed her up pretty good—" He stopped when he caught sight of Elana. "Good god, Elana! Did someone die?"

She forced a smile. "Do I really look that bad?"

"You don't look so hot, that's for sure."

"It's been a rough night. But nothing I can't handle. I was hoping you could help me with something though."

"Of course. Anything."

"I don't know if you heard, but Mrs. Wilson had a stroke recently."

"I did," he replied. "I just went to see her last night. Brought her some flowers."

Elana smiled for real this time. "I'm sure she was thrilled to see you." She cleared her throat. "Well, her son is taking her home with him and they are selling her house and now I need a new place to live. I was hoping that since you hooked me up with the cottage, you might be able to help me find something similar."

Ricky scratched his head. "Nothing off the top of my head. But I could ask around. When do you need something by?"

"Um...today."

"Today! I don't understand."

"It's a long story," she sighed.

"But then what are you doing in the meantime?" he asked.

She shrugged. "I'll figure something out."

Ricky looked at her with such concern that she started to feel uncomfortable.

"Really," she assured him, "I'll be fine."

"I have an extra bed," he offered. "Why don't you stay at my place until you figure something out?"

"I can't do that," she said.

"That's ridiculous. You've already admitted you have nowhere to go. I'm hardly home so it's not like you would be in the way."

Elana stood there, contemplating his offer. She was hesitant to accept it. She did have the cash intended for the plane ticket, but she knew she was probably going to need a deposit on a new place, and hotels in the area weren't cheap. The only other option was sleeping in her car.

"I guess I could. But only if you're sure you're okay with it," she told him.

"I swear, it's no problem."

"And it's only until I find something more permanent. Which I promise will be soon," she added.

"Of course."

It wasn't the ideal situation, but Elana felt like some of the weight had been lifted from her shoulders.

"Thank you," she whispered.

He nodded. "I've got some work to do, but when I close the shop for lunch, I can run you over to my place and get you situated."

She looked at her watch. That was three hours from now.

"Sure. I've got some errands to run, but I'll be back before then. With lunch. My treat."

He smiled. "Sounds good."

Elana returned to her jeep and drove out to Tunnels Beach. She didn't really have any errands to take care of…save one. She needed to call her parents and let them know she wasn't coming home.

As expected, Tunnels Beach was busy with sun bathers and snorkelers. Elana strolled along the shoreline, past the crowd and around a bend where there were less people. Once she felt secluded enough, she pulled her phone out of her back pocket and sat down. She pulled up her mother's work number, but before she could hit send, she broke into tears. She rested her forehead on her knees and gave herself a minute before attempting to pull it together again. If she was going to make this believable, she couldn't fall apart.

Elana took a deep breath and placed the call.

"Hi, Honey!" her mother answered. Her excitement was breaking Elana's heart. "Did you buy your ticket yet?"

"No. I'm afraid I won't be coming home as planned."

"Why? What's going on? Is everything okay, Elana?"

"Everything's fine, Mom," Elana lied. "It's just that the staff at work is really shorthanded, so I agreed to stay a while longer so I could help out."

"How much longer?"

"I'm not entirely sure. It just depends on how long it takes to beef up the staff."

"But you are still planning on coming home, right?"

"I—I don't know," Elana said, fighting back tears. "I'll let you know when I have a time frame."

"All right. I have to run off to a meeting. But are you sure nothing is wrong?"

"Yes, Mom. Everything is fine. I can't wait to come home." At least the last part wasn't a lie. "I love you, and I'll talk to you soon."

"I love you too, honey."

The call ended, and Elana sat on the beach for a while longer. She looked at her watch and decided it was time to start making the trek back to her jeep. She stopped to pick up a pizza before heading back in to Ricky's shop.

He was just finishing up on a vehicle in the garage when she got there.

"Pull up a stool and open the box," he told her. "I should be done in about ten minutes." He grabbed a slice and practically inhaled it before rolling back under the truck.

Elana pulled out a slice and took a couple bites, but didn't really have the appetite to finish it.

"You know," Ricky called from under the truck, "I still can't believe Wilson is throwing you out of the cottage on such short notice. Even if they got the house on the market today, it would still be a while before the thing sells."

"She didn't. Her son did."

Ricky rolled out again. "Her son?"

"Yes. I don't think Mrs. Wilson realizes that he did it. Which is okay with me. I don't want to stir up any trouble within the family."

Ricky wiped his hands and stood up. He moved over to the sink to try and clean them properly. Not that a mechanics hands were ever really clean.

"Sorry you got the raw end of that deal," he said.

"It is what it is," she replied.

"Still." He dried his hands and threw the paper towel in the trash bin. "I'm gonna go call the owner real quick and then we'll head over to my place."

"No rush." She stood up and put the pizza box in the fridge. Ricky came out soon after.

"Why don't you follow me in your car?" he asked.

Elana nodded.

They arrived at Ricky's house, located off the highway between Hanalei and Princeville and Elana took one suitcase while Ricky took the other, even though she kept insisting she could handle it. When they entered, Elana had to admit it was cleaner than she was expecting. There were a few auto and sports magazines scattered on the coffee table and some dirty dishes in the sink, but it wasn't the carefree bachelor pad she had begun to envision on the drive there.

The house had two bedrooms and one bathroom. The bedroom Elana would be using had a twin bed with some boxes on it.

Ricky blushed as he picked them up and shoved them against a wall.

"Sorry about that," he said. "I don't use this

room that much and I forgot they were here. I'll get them out to the shed later so they aren't in your way."

"No, it's not a problem. I'm just grateful you are doing this for me."

He pulled some clean sheets out of the closet. "The sheets on the bed are clean, but they've been on there a while so I don't know if you want fresher ones. There's a washer and dryer in the kitchen if you want even fresher ones."

"Thank you," Elana said as she took them from Ricky. "I'm sure these will be fine."

"This used to be my brother's room," Ricky told her. "He lived here until he took a job over in Honolulu."

"I didn't know you had a brother."

"Yeah. I have a sister, too. She lives over in Kapa'a with her family."

Ricky checked the time. "Well, I should get back. That guy is coming to pick up his truck soon. Make yourself at home and call me if you have any questions."

Elana hugged him. "Thank you, Ricky. I can't tell you how much I appreciate this."

Ricky blushed again when she let go of him.

"No problem," he muttered.

After Ricky left, Elana changed out the sheets and put the older ones in the washer. She sat down in front of the television, but it had been so long since she'd spent much time in front of one that she couldn't find anything to hold her interest.

She switched it off and decided to do the dishes in the sink. It was the least she could do. But what started with the dishes turned into the whole kitchen, and as she stood back admiring her work, she hoped that Ricky didn't take it as an insult. She just didn't know what else to do with herself.

Ricky came home that night with sushi take out.

"I realized there wasn't much food at the house," he told her, "so I thought I would pick up some dinner. Hopefully you like sushi."

"It's perfect," she said.

Ricky did a double-take when he saw how shiny the kitchen was.

"I hope you don't mind," Elana explained, "I just had a lot of excess energy."

"No, it's fine. Who am I to complain if someone else wants to clean my kitchen?"

Elana mostly picked at her food and forced down a couple bites only so as not to be rude after Ricky went through the trouble of bringing it home.

"Did you ever figure out who helped you with your jeep?" Ricky asked.

Elana cocked her head. "Are you going to tell me if I don't know?"

Ricky smiled. "No, but I figure something like that probably doesn't stay secret for long."

"No, it doesn't. When you mentioned it was paid for with cash that narrowed the list to about one person."

"Damn. Guess I'm not as good at keeping my mouth shut as I thought."

"Don't worry about it," said Elana, "I'm pretty sure I still would have figured it out eventually."

"So how do you know this Kyle...Barton?"

"Barnett," Elana corrected. "And it's kind of complicated."

"Why would he pay for your jeep?"

"He felt somewhat responsible, I guess, and wanted to help me out. He has a big heart like that."

Now Ricky tilted his head. "Are you two an

item?"

"No. Not anymore at least."

Elana picked up her plate and washed it.

"It's been a long day," she said. "I think I'm going to turn in for the night."

"Okay. I'll see you tomorrow."

"Good night." And Elana went into her room to crawl into bed and cry herself to sleep.

When Elana woke early the next morning, she was surprised to find Ricky had already left. She knew the shop wouldn't be open for a couple hours, but she figured he was getting in some work beforehand.

The coffee pot put up a good fight, but Elana proved victorious and was enjoying her spoils at the kitchen table when Ricky pulled into the driveway.

Elana stood up and peeked out the window. Ricky climbed out of his truck wearing only board shorts and flip-flops. Elana smiled. She was sure Ricky would tell her they were slippers, as all the other natives referred to them.

She continued to watch as he lifted his surfboard out of the truck bed and carried it into the shed.

Elana rarely saw Ricky out of his coveralls and she had certainly never seen him shirtless.

She found herself wondering what if. What if she had shown more interest back in the beginning? Would they have started dating? Would she have been unavailable when Kyle showed up, thus eliminating the heartache she was now feeling? But she decided that whatever pain she was in right now, it was worth the brief time she had spent with Kyle. It had been so long since she had felt that alive, or had someone trying so hard to take such good care of her.

Her thoughts were interrupted when Ricky

opened the back door and walked in.

"Good morning," he said.

"Morning," she replied. "I had forgotten that you surf."

"Yeah, I try to get in every morning if I can."

"I've never understood the devotion to surfing. Maybe it's just because I grew up where surfing wasn't available." She took a sip. "I made some coffee, by the way."

"Thanks." He walked over to the pot and poured himself a cup. "So you're saying there's no hobby that you felt the need to devote as much time to as possible."

"No. Well, I guess I was a runner before I moved here. I use to go most mornings before work."

"Why'd you quit?" he asked.

She wrinkled her nose. "It was too hot here."

Ricky laughed. "That's not exactly a good excuse."

"It was hot *and* humid?" They both laughed.

"Plus I was just never comfortable with running along the road by my house," she added. "It's so narrow and twisty."

Ricky nodded.

"But obviously I wasn't that devoted to it if I gave it up so easily," she said.

"I don't know. If I had to move somewhere that I couldn't surf, suppose I'd have to adapt as well."

"Hmm..."

Ricky looked at the clock. "I'd better get in the shower and then head over to the shop. Me and some guys are going out tonight…if you want to join us."

"I have to work, but thanks for the offer."

"All right. I'll see you later."

After Ricky left, Elana got onto his computer and scoured the on-line classifieds. She was really hoping to find a similar situation to the cottage, where she had her own space for dirt cheap, but that was obviously a rare treasure. She looked at the ads requesting roommates and responded to a couple of them. She later wondered if maybe she could just offer to pay Ricky rent since they seemed to get along well so far. He worked days and she worked nights, so they wouldn't be in each other's way too much. And her plan was to go home eventually; she just had to wait it out longer.

Elana found herself thinking about Kyle and Victoria. Would Adelaide ever be able to convince him to marry Victoria? Elana guessed probably not in a million years. In the end she figured she just needed to let some time pass and then she could slip quietly back into Seattle and no one but her family would have to know.

At work that night, Elana immediately found Jack to tell him that she wouldn't be leaving in two weeks after all and was shocked when his face fell.

"What's wrong?" she asked. "I thought you would be thrilled to not have to replace me."

"Problem is I already replaced you," he said.

"What?"

"I hired someone yesterday, and she starts shadowing today. In fact I was going to have her shadow you."

"But couldn't you tell her that the position is no longer available?" Elana asked in desperation.

"That wouldn't be very professional of me. If you want, I could see if she would be willing to split the hours with you."

Elana frowned. She was barely getting by with the full hours. But it was that or nothing for the time being. "Only if she can afford to do that. You're right.

It's not very professional of me to give notice and then change my mind. I'll work on finding something else as soon as possible."

"I'm so sorry, Elana," said Jack.

"Don't worry about it. Things just haven't exactly gone according to plan. I'll figure it out though."

Elana got started on her prep work and was soon joined by Nikki, the new server. She was a sweet girl, a couple years younger than her. Elana did her best not to take any frustrations out on her, but she couldn't remember the last time she had wanted her shift to end so badly.

Elana was relieved to find Ricky was still out when she got back to the house that night. She was in no mood to make nice with anyone. She cracked open the bottle of wine she had picked up on the way home and carried it and a glass tumbler into her room. Ricky clearly wasn't much of a wine drinker, but she wasn't feeling particularly picky at the moment.

Light from the full moon was streaming through her window, so she left the light off and sat on the bed with her back against the wall. She took a nice long sip and tried to remember her original reason for leaving Seattle.

She had told herself it was because there were too many bad memories. That it would be better for everyone if she wasn't around. Then last week her mother accused her of burying her head in the sand, and Kyle had said she was trying to be a martyr. She'd vehemently denied it and figured they just didn't understand what she was going through. But now she realized they had both been right. She had been living in a self-imposed exile thanks to her guilt and her reluctance to deal with it.

But now that she was ready to go home and deal with it properly, she couldn't get off the island. And to add insult to injury, she was left here with next to no job and no real place to live.

She took another drink.

What if she did go back and Adelaide found out? What could she do to her? She considered the night Adelaide showed up in the hotel room. Elana was sure it was only a taste of what that woman could do.

She refilled the glass, feeling pretty buzzed from the first one.

Screw Adelaide, she thought in her alcohol-induced bravery. Elana was going home. She picked up her glass and moved out to the computer in the living room. She guessed the ticket from Kyle was still good even though she had the hotel clerk throw away the print-out, but she bought another one. She didn't want Kyle to know she had used his. She was going home all on her own.

With the second glass finished, Elana crawled into bed. She vaguely heard Ricky pulling into the driveway as sleep overtook her.

Elana woke up to a pounding headache the next morning, confused how only two glasses could have caused it. But when she looked at the near-empty bottle next to her bed, she realized she had poured those glasses generously.

She also found the itinerary printout next to the bottle and groaned. Had she really gone through with that?

It was already past ten, which meant Ricky had long since left for the shop. She walked out into the kitchen for some water and thought about the ticket she had bought. She was scared, but strangely exhilarated. Not just from going home, but at the idea of sticking it to Adelaide. Not that Adelaide was going to know Elana was sticking it to her, at least Elana hoped not.

After some coffee and breakfast, Elana was back in the bedroom digging through her suitcases. She'd already found her running shoes and a shirt; she just needed some shorts.

"Aha!" she cried as she whipped them out. Her conversation yesterday with Ricky had put running to the forefront of her mind, and it made her realize how much she missed it. Until her current lapse, she had managed to continue running throughout the trials and attributed keeping most of her sanity to it.

The laces were tied, the iPod was strapped on, and Elana found herself with no more excuses. Well, except for the hot and humid part, but she decided that was just her being a wimp.

It took her body a while to remember what running felt like, but once she found her stride again, Elana's mind was free to wander, hashing through everything from her decision to leave Seattle to Kyle finding her on the island until the day she found Adelaide in her room.

She was terrified of Adelaide finding out she was going back to Seattle, but if she kept up her end of the deal in leaving Kyle alone, then maybe it wouldn't be as scary. She wondered what would happen if she ran into Kyle or he discovered she was in Seattle. Her heart raced at the idea of seeing him again. But how long would it take Kyle to give up on her? Had he already? He had not made any other attempts since the day he sent her the tickets, and even though she knew it was for the best, it still hurt like hell.

Elana didn't necessarily feel like anything was resolved by the time she got back to the house, but it still felt good to have mulled it all over.

She was about to jump in the shower, but

decided to check her phone first and was surprised to find she had two missed calls while out running.

The first was from one of the classifieds she had responded to, looking for a roommate. It was from a girl around her age who lived right in Hanalei, within walking distance of the restaurant. Elana would be able to save money on gas and hopefully maintenance on the jeep.

The second was from the Kalypso Bar and Grill. They were hiring again and wanted her to come in for an interview.

Just when things had been looking so dire on the island, Elana now found herself with a potential job and a place to live. She had already bought her ticket, but would it be so bad to change her mind? Maybe she could use it towards a round trip ticket and just go visit her parents.

Elana took her shower and got ready to go into work. She had been able to pick up another shift even though she was normally off on Saturday nights. She managed to focus on the task at hand, but in the back of her mind she was trying to decide what to do. Should she go home or continue to make a life here? She knew she was at a crossroads.

But by the time she got back to the house that night, Elana knew what she wanted most. She wanted to go home.

The next day she called Kalypso and the other girl back to tell them thanks, but no thanks. She hoped that she wasn't making a big mistake by turning down these offers that had practically jumped in her lap.

After she got off the phone she went into the kitchen, where Ricky was eating a sandwich and reading an auto magazine.

"Hey," he said when she walked in.

"Hi." She sat down across from him. "I have decided to move back to Seattle."

The sadness on his face surprised her.

"You are?" he asked. "When?"

"In a little about weeks," she answered.

His eyes went big, and he made an "o" with his mouth, but no sound came out.

"It was actually my original plan when I had to leave the cottage," she explained. "But then something happened and I thought I was going to have to stay here. But I've decided to go home anyway."

"I'll be sad to see you go. You're one of my best customers," he teased.

Elana smiled.

"I want you to have my jeep," she told him. "You're welcome to either sell it or part it out, but it's yours."

Ricky shook his head. "I can't take that."

"Yes, you can and you will. I've already signed the title over to you. I know you've been giving me a break whenever you could. This is the least I can do to repay you. I'm not going to pay to ship it home, so what else am I going to do with it?"

"You could always try selling it yourself."

"Ricky, just take the damn thing."

"Okay, okay," he said. "I'll make sure she finds a good home."

"Thank you."

That night at work Elana posted a sign on the communication board offering to take shifts for anyone and listed the four days she had off before her last day. By the end of the night all but one were filled.

The extra money she would make those nights was a bonus, but really she was just looking for something to keep her busy until it was time to leave. During the days she was spending a lot of time at

Ricky's shop, helping out with organizing paperwork and answering the phone.

"Are you sure you want to go home?" Ricky asked. "My shop has never been so clean and organized."

Elana smiled. Maybe being stuck on the island wouldn't be such a bad life, but she was ready to give Seattle another shot. If things didn't work out the way she was hoping, she just might consider coming back.

She was also getting in more runs and found herself going farther and enjoying it again. She spent most of that time thinking about her plan for when she got home. And in the back of her mind was always Kyle. She kept wondering what if. What if she ran into him? But with almost three million people in the Seattle area, it shouldn't be too hard to disappear.

The hardest part was not telling her parents. They had been so excited about her coming home and then so disappointed when she changed her plans. She still worried something might happen to keep her from going so she didn't want to put them through that again. They would be just as ecstatic when she showed up on their doorstep in a few days.

The night before her flight Elana was a mess. She couldn't sleep and kept wandering the house, looking for anything she might have forgotten.

"It's not like you even spread out that much," Ricky said as he raised his feet so she could look under the couch.

Elana got up and plopped on the couch next to him. "I know. I just want to be sure."

"And if by some chance you do forget something, it's not like I can't just ship it to you."

"But it's so expensive to ship anything to the mainland."

"I think I can handle it. Everything you own

can fit into those two suitcases. It's not like you would be forgetting a couch. Or a jeep," he added.

"I'm just so nervous about going home."

"Nervous? What do you have to be nervous about? You should be excited."

She hadn't explained about the whole Adelaide situation. She didn't know how to.

"I am excited. I'm also nervous because I've been away for a while. You never know how things have changed. You know what they say, 'you can never go home.'"

"I always thought that was bullshit," said Ricky. "If you can't go home, then it was never really home in the first place."

Elana sighed. "Perhaps you're right. I should try going to sleep again."

"Just sit here and watch TV with me. It might help distract you. Have you ever seen this show?"

"I don't think so."

"It about these people who buy other people's storage lockers in an auction, and then you get to watch them go through other people's crap," he explained. "It's really entertaining."

"I suppose I could sit here for a bit longer." It occurred to Elana that Ricky was going to miss having her around. She really wished some great woman out there would hurry up and figure out what a catch Ricky was.

Elana woke early the next day, even though she didn't have to leave until closer to noon.

Ricky was out surfing, so she made a pot of coffee and waited for him to get home. She had wanted to take a shuttle to the airport, but Ricky insisted on driving her, even though it meant closing the shop for a good part of the day.

The minutes ticked by excruciatingly slowly, but finally they were loading her bags into the back of Ricky's truck. For as many times as Elana had cursed it, she was a little sad to be leaving her jeep behind as they pulled out of the driveway. She found herself soaking in the lush green scenery as they made their way south. It wasn't long before it became more arid, and then she was watching the waves hit the beach whenever they had glimpses of the shore.

"I realize I may have picked a bad time to be headed home," she said.

"Why is that?" asked Ricky.

"The weather is probably just starting to turn gray. It might be a bit of a culture shock after all the warm beautiful sun."

"Well, that warm Kauai sun will still be here waiting if you should change your mind."

Elana smiled at him.

At the airport, Ricky pulled up to the front and climbed out to help her with the bags.

"Thank you so much for everything," she told him. "I can't even begin to tell you how much I have appreciated all that you have done for me."

"It was my pleasure, Elana." He hugged her. "So that guy Kyle..."

Elana frowned. "What about him?"

"He's definitely not your boyfriend now."

"No. Why?"

Ricky answered by kissing her. It didn't last long, but there was no doubt it was a kiss.

"I'm sorry. I was going to hate myself if I let you go without doing that. But I wasn't about to kiss another man's girl either."

Elana stood there with her fingers on her lips not sure what she was feeling. She supposed she should be feeling violated, but she knew there was no malice behind it.

She stretched up and kissed his cheek. "You're a real sweetheart, Ricky. I hope you know that."

Ricky grinned. "You too, Elana."

She gave him one last hug, and he squeezed her before getting back into his truck and driving off.

Elana took her bags to the agriculture inspection station and then to the ticket counter. Once checked in and through security, she found a seat by the window at the airport bar and grill and ordered some lunch and one last Mai Tai.

When the bill was paid, she walked across to the sundries shop and picked out a magazine to keep her company for the almost six-hour flight home. She couldn't believe that in less than seven hours she would be touching down in Seattle. It was going to be late by the time she made it to her parents' house. She hoped they didn't mind. Who was she kidding? Of course they wouldn't mind.

Elana found her gate just as the plane she would be flying home was pulling up to the jet way. Her heart was pounding. It all seemed so real now.

An attendant opened the door, and it wasn't long before people were disembarking the plane. Elana couldn't believe her eyes when Kyle walked through the door.

Ten

SHE JUST STOOD there, staring at him, wondering if he was a figment of her imagination. But then he caught sight of her, and his whole face lit up with happiness and surprise.

Kyle walked over to her and dropped his bag so he could wrap his arms around her, and Elana felt ready to cry. She'd forgotten how good he smelled, how good he *felt.*

"Kyle!" she said as she broke their embrace. "What are you doing here?"

"I'm here to make sure that you get on that plane tomorrow."

She looked confused.

"The plane ticket I sent you at the hotel. I bought two seats."

"Oh," she said, biting her lip. "I threw that away."

"Why doesn't that surprise me?" he said with a frown. "But then what are *you* doing here? How'd you know I would be here?"

"I didn't. I was—I'm flying home. I bought my own ticket."

"Were you just planning on surprising me?" he asked with a smile.

"No. I was hoping you wouldn't find out."

"Why would you not want me to know?"

She lowered her gaze, unsure how to answer. But Kyle lifted her chin and looked into her eyes.

"Elana, I know my mother came to see you. She doesn't know that I do, but I found out."

"I'm so sorry," she told him.

Kyle caressed her cheek with his thumb. "Don't apologize. I can only imagine the things she said to you."

"She threatened to cut you off if I didn't stay away."

Kyle laughed. "That threat is meaningless. I don't care about the money."

"That's easy to say now. You've never been without it."

"That sounds like something my mother would say."

Elana blushed.

"Oh, Elana," Kyle sighed. He leaned down and kissed her with such longing that Elana forgot about everyone around them. She wrapped her arms around him and wished that she could stay in this moment forever, with his beautiful soft lips pressed against hers.

"What do you say we get out of here?" Kyle asked when they finally came up for air.

"But I have a flight to catch," she said.

"You have a flight to catch tomorrow as well."

"But I've already checked my bags. They don't take too kindly to people checking their bags and then not getting on the plane."

Kyle furrowed his brow. "Well, I'm not letting you out of my sight, so let me go see what I can do. Wait here."

"What? Kyle..."

But he was already working his way to the attendant.

She tapped her boarding pass on her chin, wondering what Kyle could possibly have up his sleeve.

Just as they were getting ready to board Elana's flight, Kyle came striding back.

"They're digging out your bags now. We're supposed to meet them in baggage claim to collect them. Make sure you have your boarding pass and ID."

Elana's jaw dropped.

"I tried to get us both on this flight," he said, "but it was full, so we will just have to hold out for tomorrow."

"How did you manage that?" she asked.

"I told them that you weren't supposed to be flying unaccompanied for personal reasons and there had been a misunderstanding."

Elana punched him. "You made me out to be some mental case?"

He caught her arm and pulled her in close to him. "I did what I had to to keep you close to me."

Elana couldn't help but smile. "You always get what you want, don't you?"

"Yes." Kyle grinned back. "And I want you."

His words sent a warm sensation down her spine.

"Now let's go get your bags and figure out where we're staying tonight." Kyle took her hand and led her towards baggage claim.

Elana collected her bags while Kyle got on his phone and found them a room for the night.

"They have a room for us at the Marriott Resort," Kyle told her when she returned, "but it won't be ready for another hour or so."

"The Marriott Resort? You couldn't have found

anything a little less posh?" she asked. "We're only staying for one night."

"They're close and they have a room. What else could I ask for? We can go have an early dinner at the restaurant there while we wait."

A taxi dropped them off at the Marriott, and they left the bags with the bellhop before walking into Dukes.

"I never imagined it would be this easy to find you," Kyle said while the hostess checked on a table for them. "I was starting to worry that a day wouldn't be long enough to figure out where you had gone to."

"I still don't understand how this is all happening. I was sure I was imagining you when you walked off the plane."

The hostess returned and led them to a table.

"What would you have done if I had left yesterday?" she asked.

There was a twinkle in his eye. "I would have known."

"How?"

"I'm sure I would have found someone in Hanalei who knew where you had gone to. But what I want to know is when you decided to come home, and why you wouldn't answer my calls."

Elana explained Adelaide's appearance in the room and what she said about Kyle just having some fun before his walk down the aisle.

"And did you believe her?" Kyle asked.

"Not really. But by the end, she had me worried that you would resent me for no longer being able to live the life you've become accustomed to."

"I told you the money isn't who I am."

"I know, but have you ever been without it?" Kyle started to say something, but Elana cut him off.

"And yes, those are your mother's words, but what if she's right"

"All right," he said. "You have a point. I can't really know what I haven't experienced. But I think you're forgetting something."

"What's that?" she asked.

"I have a career of my own. A very successful one in fact. I can lead a pretty comfortable life without my family's fortune."

"Oh," said Elana. She knew that Kyle owned his own architectural firm, but had not really taken that into account.

"So you believe my mother and call me," Kyle prompted.

"Yes, she insisted I make the call right there with her standing over me. She even told me I would regret it if I told you she was there. She's the one who ended the call, not me."

Kyle nodded.

"I—I was a mess after that. When I saw your missed calls and messages, I just deleted them all. I figured you were angry or hurt or both, and you had every right to be. I just couldn't bring myself to listen to it all."

Kyle sighed as he took her hand and kissed it. "I'm so sorry."

"No, I'm sorry for not trusting you."

"Where did you go after you left the hotel? Where have you been staying this whole time?"

"I went and stayed with Ricky. He had an extra room and offered it when he found out I was…well, homeless."

Kyle arched an eyebrow. "You're telling me you've been living with another guy this whole time?"

He said it in jest, but Elana detected a hint of jealousy in his voice.

"Yes, and he even kissed me good-bye this morning." It had sounded funnier in her mind, but the look on Kyle's face told her he didn't think so.

"He what?"

"I shouldn't have said anything; he didn't mean anything by it."

"Then why did he kiss you?"

"He said he would hate himself if he didn't take the chance. He had even asked if you were my boyfriend, because he didn't want to kiss another man's girl. I swear it was nothing. I didn't even kiss him back."

The corners of Kyle's mouth twitched. "I guess I can't really blame the guy for trying."

"I have no idea what you mean by that."

Kyle didn't have a chance to respond when the server showed up to take their orders.

"And at what point did you decide to come home anyway," Kyle asked when she left.

"I believe it was Thursday night after I found out they had already replaced me at work. I thought if I could sneak home quietly, then everyone would still be happy."

"I wouldn't have been," said Kyle.

Elana stared into his eyes. "I know. But I hoped that in time you would move on."

He stared back. "Did you really?"

"No. Not really. Secretly I hoped I would run into you and we would figure something out."

"And you did run into me," he said. "And we will figure something out."

"Now your turn," she said. "When did you decide you weren't going to give up?"

"Elana, I decided after our first night together that I wasn't going to give up."

She blushed.

"But I assume you are referring to why I am here now," he said.

"Yes."

"Let me back up a bit first. Do you remember at the hospital when my phone kept going off, and I said I needed to deal with something?"

Elana nodded. "Yes. I'm guessing something to do with Victoria."

"It was. She was threatening to tell my mother about us. I was doing my best to diffuse the situation, but I wasn't sure how successful I was. That's also when I found out she was sleeping with Stephan."

"I'm so sorry, Kyle," Elana said. "I didn't think I was the person you needed to hear it from. I had a feeling you were going to find out eventually."

"How did you know about it?"

"I figured it out when she came to see me at the restaurant."

"It was Stephan who finally came clean," said Kyle. "Apparently he was tired of Victoria's bullshit as well."

"Are you guys still friends?" she asked.

"I don't know. We haven't spoken since that day. I won't say never, but it will take a lot to ever trust him again."

Elana took his hand and squeezed it.

"Fast forward to the night you called me," he continued. "I was hurt and angry and after you hung up—or rather my mother, as I now know, I didn't know what to think. But the more I went over it, the more I wondered if my mother had a hand in it. Especially when I remembered our conversation from earlier that day. You told me you had nowhere left to go but home. You even sounded excited about it. I knew then that Victoria had told my mother. I made some calls and found out that she had taken the plane to come out here. That was when I decided that I needed to come out and get you personally."

"Wait, your family has their own plane?"

"Yes, but that's not important right now."

Elana made a mental note to come back to that later.

"If you had listened to any of my messages, you would have known that I was onto my mother and had a plan. But when you never called me back, I suspected you had ignored them, because that seemed like something you would do in the heat of the moment."

It shocked Elana how well Kyle knew her. She was also a little embarrassed that it was so true.

"I take it you haven't said anything to your parents," Kyle said.

"No. My mother was so disappointed when I told her I wasn't coming home after all. I was worried something else may get in the way, so I decided to not say anything."

"I'm sure they will be excited to see you." Again there was that twinkle in his eye.

"Is there something you're not telling me?" Elana asked.

Kyle furrowed his brow. "I don't know what you're talking about."

The food arrived, and she let him off the hook.

"What are we going to do about your mother?" Elana wondered.

Kyle smiled at her. "I don't know yet, but we'll get through it together. I'm not afraid of her, and you shouldn't be either."

Elana's eyebrows went up. "You do remember what she did to me less than two years ago, right?"

"And you overcame that, didn't you?"

She straightened up a bit in her chair. "Yeah, I

guess you're right." She took a bite of her salad and swallowed. "Can we go back to the fact that your family has their own plane?"

"Technically it's the company plane. It's nothing really."

"Why do you fly commercial then?"

Kyle set his fork down and wiped his mouth with the napkin. "I've been distancing myself from my family's fortune for some time now. I stopped using the plane for my personal travels a long time ago. When I started my own firm, I even chose to lease from a building that wasn't owned by my family."

Elana felt like she was seeing a whole other side to Kyle. "You really don't care about the money, do you?"

He laughed. "That's what I've been trying to tell you this whole time. Don't get me wrong; I do enjoy the finer things, but I think I prefer them when I've put in some of my own blood, sweat, and tears. My mother has been losing her grasp on me for some time. She just refuses to accept it."

Elana shook her head. "I love you, Kyle."

He grinned. "Good. Because I love you as well."

She smiled as she took another bite. But then her brow creased.

"Something wrong?" Kyle asked.

Her head shook. "No, not really. Actually, can I ask—do you mind if I ask how you and Victoria met? I know you guys were together during the trials."

"What? Who told you that?"

"I remember seeing her sitting in the courtroom with your family."

"Oh." Kyle took a deep breath. "She and Jarod were together."

Elana's fork made a clanking sound as it hit the

plate. "She was *Jarod's* girlfriend?"

"Yes," Kyle muttered, not meeting her eye.

"You were engaged to your dead brother's girlfriend."

He grimaced. "This isn't really something I want to go into."

Elana found herself imagining them comforting each other. And then one thing leading to another....

"You're right," she said.

"It was doomed from the beginning," Kyle told her. "For so many reasons."

Elana nodded. Instead she thought of everything Kyle had done to be with her. To prove that he loved her.

The server came by with their check.

"Let's go see if our room is ready," said Kyle.

The bags had already been sent to the room by the time they swung by the front desk.

Kyle unlocked the door and let Elana in first. As soon as the door shut Kyle was pulling Elana into his arms, and she was tearing his clothes off as quickly as she could. They had some lost time to make up for.

They never left the room again until they checked out the next morning just before ten. They took a taxi back to the airport, and Elana had to run her bags through the agriculture inspection yet again.

"You know, I could have been home by now," Elana teased as they stood in the security line.

Kyle pressed his mouth close to his ear. "But then I wouldn't have been able to have you all to myself last night," he whispered.

She blushed and felt a charge go through her belly. Last night was pretty incredible. And she knew it wouldn't be the last.

They were finally boarding the plane and taking their seats.

"I've never flown first class before," she commented.

"Well, enjoy it while you can, baby," Kyle told her. "Because if my mother has her way, we'll be lucky if we can afford the cargo hold next time."

Elana playfully punched him. "You are not funny." But she giggled and he kissed her.

"You don't know how much I've missed that giggle."

Elana had her magazine and the first class passengers were provided with complimentary digital video players, but she and Kyle never needed them. They spent the entire plane ride just talking. They told stories from their childhood about crazy aunts or uncles, and compared notes about time spent at the UW.

With every piece of information Elana gleamed from Kyle, she felt she was falling even more in love with him.

By the time the plane made its approach into Sea-Tac, Elana was giddy. She was home. Kyle took her hand and didn't let go until they were off the plane and she went to use the restroom.

Kyle was on the phone when Elana came out of the restroom.

"Sounds good. We'll see you soon." And he hung up.

"Who was that?" she asked.

"You'll see. Let's go get the bags. We have somewhere to be."

"We do?" She was confused. "Where are going?"

He smiled. "I told you, you'll see."

Eleven

ONCE ELANA'S BAGS were collected, they headed out to airport parking, where Kyle had left his car for the night. He walked up to the trunk of his dark gray Infiniti G37 Coupe, dropped the bags, and scratched his head.

"Something wrong?" Elana asked.

"We might have a problem getting your luggage home."

Elana stood next to him as he popped open the trunk.

"Holy shit, that's a small trunk."

"I don't use it very often. It fits my blueprints, and that's mostly all I ever needed it for."

"What are we going to do?" Elana asked.

"Don't worry. We'll make this work," he assured her.

Kyle opened the passenger door and got to work squeezing her suitcases into the back seat. The front seats had to be pushed up, but in the end he made them fit.

Once inside, Elana scanned the interior. "This is a pretty sweet car," she said, "even if it is a bit short on cargo space."

He grinned. "Thanks. I like it. I might even let

you drive it some time."

"So are you going to tell me where we are going?" she asked when Kyle drove out onto the freeway.

"I'm sure you'll figure it out soon enough."

He followed the freeway when it turned into I-405 and drove up into Bellevue, where he took the WA-520 exit heading east.

She suspected she knew where they were heading, but it wasn't until they were on Avondale that she spoke up.

"We're going to my parent's house, aren't we?"

"I figured that would be the first place you would want to go after landing."

"But I'm still not sure how my parents are going to feel about you."

He took her hand. "We'll figure it out, remember?"

Elana nodded, but she was incredibly nervous.

They pulled in front of the Tanner house, and Elana found herself shaking. She was excited to see her parents, but she wasn't entirely sure that Kyle being here was a good idea.

Kyle wrangled out the suitcases, refusing to let Elana take one of them.

"Go say hello to your parents," he said. "I've got these."

She walked up to the door, and before she even made it to the first step, the front door swung open and her mom and dad rushed out to greet her.

"You're here!" Her mother cried as she enveloped her. "I can't believe you're finally here!"

Elana watched over her mother's shoulder as her dad went down and grabbed one of the bags from

Kyle. They even shook hands.

"Mr. Tanner," Kyle said.

"Kyle, good to see you again."

Elana pulled away from her mother, completely flabbergasted.

"What? But how?"

"Why don't you come inside, dear?" Renee said. "We'll explain everything."

The four of them walked into the foyer, and Elana's father set the bag down and gave Elana a big bear hug. "It's so good to have you home, kiddo."

Elana felt the tears building up, and she knew she was powerless to stop them. Her mother came over and wrapped her arms around both of them. It wasn't long before she was crying as well.

"I can't believe my baby is home," Renee said. She released them and walked over to where Kyle was standing and gave him a hug as well. "Thank you so much for bringing her home."

"My pleasure," Kyle replied.

Elana stepped back from her dad and wiped her face on her sleeve. "You guys need to tell me what is going on."

"Let's move into the kitchen where we can sit down." Renee led them into the other room. "Are you guys hungry? I have leftovers I'd be happy to heat up."

"We ate on the plane, Mom. But thank you."

"How about something to drink then? You must be dehydrated from the flight."

"Water would be great," said Kyle.

Renee poured a couple glasses of water and brought them over to the breakfast table where they were all seated.

"So Kyle here shows up on our doorstep about two weeks ago," Renee starts, "and I have to admit I was tempted to slam the door in his face."

Kyle laughed. "But fortunately she listened to what I had to say, and it turns out we all wanted the same thing."

"To bring you home," Elana's dad chimed in.

"Was this before or after I called you to say I wasn't coming home?" Elana asked.

"After," her mother answered. "It was that evening. Kyle told us he was worried his mother had spooked you and that he had a plan to go out there and fetch you himself."

"Sounded good to us," her father added.

"And your mother and I have been working on something else as well," Kyle told her.

Elana looked at her mother.

"Kyle and I have lined up three interviews for you next week. We knew you would be eager to get back on your feet. I knew what positions would interest you the most, and Kyle here had the connections to get you in the door."

Elana narrowed her eyes at Kyle.

"It's just interviews," he said, holding up his hands. "I swear I have no say as to whether you get hired or not."

"Wow," Elana said, "I—I don't know what to say."

There was an envelope sitting in the middle of the table and Renee slid it towards Elana.

"You will probably want a vehicle to help you get around, so I thought this might help with a down payment." Renee said as Elana opened it and found a couple thousand dollars in it.

"What is this?" she asked.

"It's the cash you've been sending us," her dad said. "Every last penny of it."

"But this was supposed to be for you. To pay you back for helping me out."

"Sweetie, you're our daughter," he said. "Of course we were going to help you out. You never needed to pay us back."

"But what about your retirement and the equity loan you had to take out?" Elana exclaimed.

"So we have to push back retirement a couple years," her mother said. "Big deal. And don't you worry about that loan. It's really not that much of a hardship. I think you blew things way out of proportion."

Elana sat at that table, surrounded by people who loved her more than she had ever realized, and started crying again.

"I'm so sorry," she said.

Kyle put his arm around her and kissed the top of her head.

"Honey, what do you have to be sorry about?" he mother asked.

"I really was just making things harder than they had to be, wasn't I?"

Her dad spoke up. "You were dealing with things the best way that you could. The important thing is that you're home and everything is going to be right again."

She smiled at all of them.

"We've also been working on getting some of your things unboxed and putting your room together," her father added. "Why don't you go show Kyle around?"

She nodded as Kyle stood up and took her hand.

She led Kyle up the stairs and to her bedroom. She opened the door, and so much emotion swept over her that she had to plop onto the bed before she got dizzy. Kyle sat on the edge and stroked her hair.

"How are you doing?" he asked.

"I'm great," she said. "I'm home." She looked up into his eyes. "And I'm with you. I can't believe it."

Kyle lay down next to her and kissed her lips as he placed his hand on her stomach.

She smiled when he sat back up. "I can't believe my parents just told me to show you to my room."

He laughed. "I think they knew you needed a moment to absorb it all."

Elana got up onto her elbows. "I don't know how to thank you," she said.

He touched her nose. "For what?"

"For everything. For bringing me home. For making me happy again."

"You would have gotten there eventually. You'd even bought your own ticket after you said you weren't leaving the island."

"But it all started with you," she told him. "If it weren't for you, I would still be there, wallowing in my misery and guilt."

"Don't forget that you saved me too."

She sat all the way up. "What do you mean?"

"I was stuck in a dead-end relationship that I was too chicken to pull the plug on. Even if you wouldn't have me, I knew I had to get out of it. Plus you helped bring some 'other' things to light."

"I guess we found each other, didn't we?"

Kyle cupped her chin. "Yes, we did." He leaned forward and nipped at her bottom lip. Elana leaned forward to kiss, but Kyle teased her by pulling back. Elana grinned and grabbed his shirt, pulling him into her. She leaned back onto the bed, bringing Kyle down with her, and he threw a leg over her.

She was just wondering if it would be inappropriate to make love to him right then on her bed, when she heard a knock on the door, and they both shot back up.

"Um, come in," she called out, and her dad walked in.

"I brought your suitcases up," he said.

"Thanks, Dad."

"Your mother was wondering if you wanted anything else from the kitchen before she cleans up for the night."

Elana looked at her watch. It was already after midnight.

"No, but I'll be down to say goodnight in a minute."

Her father nodded and left. She turned back to Kyle, who tucked a stray hair behind her ear.

"I think I'm going to head out," he said, causing her to frown. "You have some catching up to do with your parents, so I'm going to hang back for the weekend. But I want you to call me and tell me how your interviews go. Your mom has all the details."

She hugged him. "I don't want you to go."

"I know." He rubbed her back. "But we have all the days before us. It's going to be great, Elana. I promise."

They stood up and she walked him to the door and kissed him goodnight. She waited at the door as he walked to his car where he turned and waved before getting in and driving off.

Elana stayed up chatting with her parents for way too long. When she finally crawled into bed, she couldn't believe how exhausted she was. But it was a happy and content exhaustion.

The weekend proved to be very busy. On Saturday her parents took her into Bellevue to go car shopping, and she drove home the proud owner of a pre-owned Honda Civic. It wasn't anything fancy, but it was in great condition, had low miles, and even came with a limited warranty. Quite the step up from the jeep she had left behind on the island.

Her first interview was on Monday, so Sunday was spent hammering out Elana's resume with the help of her mother. Her three interviews were lined up for the next three days, and she couldn't wait to get them over with.

Before going to bed, Elana went through her closet, trying to decide on the perfect outfit. It had been so long since she had worn anything fancier than a pair of black pants and a clean t-shirt.

"Knock, knock." Renee walked in with two glasses of wine and found Elana in a dark A-line skirt and one-button blazer. She handed one of the glasses to Elana. "I had a feeling you might be suffering from wardrobe drama. And that you might like something to help you relax."

Elana took a sip. "Thanks. This is exactly what I needed." She set the glass down on the dresser and did a turn for her mother. "What do you think of this one?"

"I like that one, but I think the white camisole is a little boring. You should wear something with a little more color. What about that bright blue one?"

"I don't know. Do you think it's too bright?" Elana asked.

"Not at all. And it really brings out your dark features."

"It's settled then." Elana went into her bathroom to change into her sleepwear. When she came back, out she picked up her glass of wine and sat on the bed next to her mother.

"I'm so happy to have you back," Renee told her.

Elana leaned her head on her mom's shoulder. "Me too. I really missed you guys."

They both took a sip.

"So. Kyle Barnett, huh?"

Elana sat up and smiled as she swirled her wine glass. "Yep. Kyle Barnett."

"He seems to really care about you," said Renee.

Elana looked at her. "He loves me, Mom."

"And you love him?"

Elana nodded, and Renee put her arm around her daughter. "I just don't want to see you get hurt."

"I know. But he's a pretty great guy."

"He seems like it. And he's not too hard on the eyes either."

Elana laughed. "No, he is not."

They finished off the wine, and Renee left so that Elana could get some sleep.

The next morning Elana was sitting at the breakfast table trying to choke down some breakfast when Kyle called her cell. She answered it, excited to hear his voice again.

"Hey you!"

"Good morning," he replied. "Have you left for your interview yet?"

"No. Soon though."

"Are you nervous?" he asked.

"Yes. I can't eat, but I'm trying to force myself so that my stomach doesn't start growling halfway through."

He chuckled. "That's probably a good plan."

"I miss you," she said.

"I miss you too. Where is the interview today?"

"It's in Bellevue."

"Why don't you stop by my office when you're

done?" he said.

"Ooh! I get to see where you work?"

"If you would like to."

"I would love to."

"Great. It's in the Expedia Building on 4th street. Just go up to the 10th floor and look for my name."

"I can't wait," she said. "See you soon."

"Good luck, Elana. I know you'll do great."

"Thanks."

"And one more thing," he said.

"What's that?"

"I love you."

She grinned. "I love you too."

They hung up, and Elana finished getting ready.

The interview lasted an hour and a half, and Elana felt pretty good about it. When it was over, she walked over to Kyle's building, and took the elevator up to the tenth floor as he had instructed, and found Barnett Designs at the end of the hall. Upon entering she found a small but well-decorated waiting area and a desk where a young Vietnamese girl was sitting.

She smiled upon Elana's entrance. "Hello. How can I help you?"

"Um, hi. I'm here to see Kyle."

"Are you Elana?"

"Yes."

"He's been expecting you. Right this way." The girl stood up and led Elana past a modest conference room to a door at the end of the short hall. She knocked on the door and opened it for Elana.

Kyle was on the phone, but he smiled and waved her in. The receptionist closed the door behind Elana. Elana sucked in her breath at the sight of Kyle in dark dress slacks and a button-down striped shirt.

He jotted a note on a tablet by his computer. "I will get started on that right away. I'll be in touch soon." He hung up the phone and walked around the desk to Elana.

"Wow, you look incredible," he said.

"Thanks. I could say the same about you."

"I've never seen you in heels before." He leaned in close, "And good god, I could take you over my desk right now in that skirt."

Elana could feel her cheeks flushing, and Kyle grinned at her reaction. He took a step back.

"How did your interview go?" he asked.

"Really well, I think. They asked me to come in again on Thursday and meet with some other managers."

"That's a good sign."

She nodded and started walking around his office. He had several framed design plans and sketches on the wall.

"Are these yours?" she asked.

He nodded as he came over and stood next to her.

"These are incredible, Kyle. I had no idea."

"Thanks. So far it's mostly high-end home designs and a few one-story retail and office space buildings. But next week I pitch my first multi-story commercial building. I'm pretty excited."

Elana looked up and saw him grinning like a schoolboy and couldn't help but smile back.

"Can you stay for lunch?" he asked. "Or do you have somewhere else you need to be?"

She leaned against his desk. "Nope. I'm free for the rest of the day. Although my mom wanted me to invite you to dinner at our house tonight."

Kyle placed his hands on her hips and gave her

a quick kiss. "I can do that." And then he kissed her longer. "I don't know how much longer I can resist you in those heels though," he muttered between kisses.

"Aren't you afraid your receptionist will hear us?" she whispered back.

Kyle reached for the phone behind her.

"Michelle?"

"Yes, Mr. Barnett?"

"Could you do me a favor and run out and grab some lunch for Miss Tanner and I?"

"Of course. What would you like?"

Elana watched the wheels spinning in his head.

"Why don't you run to Chipotle and grab two burrito bowls?" he replied.

"Chicken or vegetarian?" Michelle asked.

"Chicken?" Kyle mouthed to Elana who nodded. "Two chickens. And don't forget to order something for yourself."

"I'll get on it, sir."

"And go ahead and lock up and put the 'out to lunch' sign up," he added.

"Of course."

The line went dead and Kyle moved to lock his office door.

"Chipotle is always crowded," he said when he returned to where Elana was still propped against the desk. "She'll be gone a while." A devilish grin spread across his face as a hand slid up her thigh and under the skirt. "You're not wearing any pantyhose."

"I can't stand those things," she said breathlessly.

"That's okay. Neither can I," he groaned and hooked a thumb along her panties and pulled them down.

Elana pulled Kyle's face close to hers and

thrust her tongue into his mouth. Then she moved her hands to his belt and began undoing his pants. Kyle grabbed her bottom and lifted it up onto the desk. He pushed her skirt higher so that she could spread her legs wider, letting him move in even closer to her.

While one hand was shoving down Kyle's boxer briefs, Elana moved the other up around his neck and moved her mouth over to his ear.

"Fuck me, now," she moaned.

Kyle scooted her ass to the very edge of the desk and thrust into her. Both hands braced her back to keep her from sliding away as he continued to pound into her. Elana now had both arms wrapped around his neck, keeping him close to her. It wasn't the most comfortable position, but the excitement was compounded by the fact that there were no blinds on the window behind Kyle's desk. Elana had never felt so dangerous.

She wrapped her legs around his midsection and dug her heels into his back, causing one shoe to fall to the floor with the other just barely hanging on.

Elana's moans increased in volume as she got closer to the point of no return, and Kyle responded by pumping even harder. Suddenly Elana was screaming, and Kyle's hand moved to cover her mouth. It only intensified her climax, knowing that she shouldn't be making any noise right now. Needing to release that energy somehow, she bit down on his hand, but it didn't slow him down. Her heels dug even harder into him and he exploded into her.

Elana leaned back on her elbows, careful not to knock anything off of the desk. Kyle placed his palms on either side of her hips for support.

"Wow," he said. "I—wow."

She giggled as he just grinned at her.

"Sorry about your hand," she said.

He looked at it. "The skin's not broken. I'll survive. Sorry I had to do that. Michelle's not here, but there are other tenants and I'm not sure how sound proof the walls are."

"You mean you don't have sex on your desk all the time?"

"This was definitely a first for me."

"Mmm...well, perhaps it won't be the last," she murmured.

"You're going to get me all excited again."

"We can't have that now, can we? Plus, I'm sure Michelle will be back with our lunch soon."

"Next time, then."

"Next time."

Elana stayed for lunch and then headed home so that Kyle could get some actual work done. The whole drive back she kept grinning every time she thought about what had happened in his office. She'd never done anything like that, and she had loved every second of it.

Kyle showed up for dinner that night right on time with a bottle of wine and two bouquets of flowers—one for Renee and one for Elana. Kyle was a charmer, there was no doubt about that. But Elana loved knowing that his charm wasn't only skin deep. He genuinely cared for people and, best of all, he was as hopelessly in love with her as she was with him.

It was late when Elana finally walked Kyle out to his car.

"Are you sure you don't want to spend the night? I'm sure my parents wouldn't mind. At this point I don't think you could do any wrong in their eyes."

Kyle kissed her cheek. "I don't think I could keep you from screaming if I were to share a bed with you."

Elana blushed.

"But why don't you come spend the night with me tomorrow? Your next two interviews are in Seattle, aren't they?"

She nodded.

"I could afford to take a half day tomorrow," he said, "maybe do some work from home. Call me when you're done."

"All right."

It was a long kiss goodnight, but Elana eventually made her way back up the path, waving to Kyle as he drove off.

Elana's next interview was much later in the day, so she didn't get to Kyle's apartment until early afternoon. Kyle met her at the lobby and accompanied her up to his two-bedroom apartment.

"This place is incredible," she exclaimed as he gave her the tour. "Although I have to admit I was expecting something bigger."

"It's over a thousand square feet! Is that not big enough for you?"

"No, no, it's not that. I guess I just pictured you living in some massive multi-storied condo high above the city."

"It was only supposed to be temporary."

Elana was confused. Then she wondered why she hadn't remembered until now.

"You lived here with Victoria," she said.

"My lease is up next month. I've already told them I won't be renewing it. I'd rather be closer to Bellevue anyway."

"What did she do? Victoria, I mean."

"She was a model. Mainly local print work. Most of her shoots were here downtown."

"Of course she was a model."

Kyle frowned. "What is that supposed to mean?"

"I'm just not surprised that you dated a model."

"I think you just insulted me."

"Sorry. It's probably my self-consciousness coming through, but I have to wonder how you go from a model to, well, me."

"You're joking, right?"

Elana just cocked her head and looked at him.

"I'd like to reiterate that you are insulting me as well as my intelligence. And have you looked in a mirror lately?"

Elana's brow wrinkled.

"If you had wanted to be a model, I am sure you would have no problem. But I'm glad that you aren't. Models are high maintenance and moody. They are worried about being bloated for their shoot the next day. It's quite difficult to live with." He took her face in his hands. "You, on the other hand, are incredibly easy going and adventurous and tough as nails."

A smile started to appear on her face.

"And you are as smart as you are sexy. I can't think of anyone I would rather be with." He kissed her in that way that wiped away whatever doubts may have crept into her mind. "I love you, Elana. Don't ever forget that."

"And I love you too," she whispered. "But there's something I don't understand," she said, taking a step back.

"And what is that?"

"Why does your mother overwhelmingly approve of Victoria? What makes her so special?"

"You know her father is Witt Lansing, right?"

"No. Should I?" Elana asked.

"Sorry, I forgot we don't always...know the

same people."

"I'm guessing he's rich then."

"Sort of. He's a very well-connected person. Friends with some very influential people. I think my mother may have seen our union as a merging of sorts."

"If Victoria's family is so wealthy, then why was she after your money?"

"I wondered the same thing, so I did some digging. Turns out her family is only wealthy on paper right now. They have some big assets, but for the past few years, Witt has been cash strapped. I think he may have put his daughter on a financial diet and she didn't like it."

"I find it ironic that your mother hates me because she thinks I'm after the family fortune, but adores Victoria who really is after the money."

"Unfortunately, Victoria still has the connections that make my mother willing to overlook that flaw."

"Incredible," Elana muttered.

"Let's not worry about it. It doesn't change anything."

He pulled her into the kitchen and poured them both a glass of wine.

"Are you up for being my sous chef tonight?" Kyle asked as he started pulling ingredients out of the fridge.

"Are you telling me you cook as well?" Elana said as she jumped up onto the counter. "Better watch yourself or I might just have to marry you," she teased.

Kyle winked at her. "Be careful what you wish for."

Elana's eyes went wide as she took an awkward sip of her wine.

Kyle broke out in laughter. "The look on your

face right now is priceless." He walked over and started to kiss her, but she tried to push him away and he caught her hand.

"You are not funny," she said.

"You're right. I'm hilarious."

Elana was trying hard not to smile, but it wasn't working.

"Go ahead, giggle. I want to hear you giggle."

"No."

"I know how to make you giggle."

"No!" she repeated even louder, but it didn't stop Kyle from tickling her, and the giggles broke free.

"Stop," she gasped. "Stop!"

He laughed as he stopped and simply rested his hands on her hips. He twitched his fingers and she flinched.

"It would be so easy right now," he said.

"Don't," she begged.

"I should. But I won't. We've got a meal to prepare." He stepped away and went back to the items he had pulled out.

She slid off the counter and stood next to him. "What exactly is on the menu tonight?"

"I thought we could have pan-seared salmon in a red wine sauce with some grilled asparagus."

"Now you're just showing off."

"Is it working?"

She kissed his cheek. "Yes, it is."

"Here, why don't you wash these and trim the ends while I get started on the sauce." He handed her the bag of asparagus, and she took it over to the sink.

She was just putting them onto the cutting board when the buzzer by the front door went off.

Kyle washed his hands and dried them on the towel before walking over to answer it.

"Hello?"

"Kyle, dear, it's your mother."

Elana froze. Kyle looked at her before responding.

"What do you want, Mother?"

"Well, I'm here to see you, of course."

"You really should have called first."

"Kyle James, just buzz me in."

And he did.

"I see where you get your demanding ways from," Elana said rather dryly.

"Sorry," he mumbled and braced his hand against the wall.

"Do you want me to go hide?" she asked.

"No. We may as well get this over with." Kyle unlocked the door and went to stand by Elana. "We're in this together, right?"

She gave him the best reassuring smile she could muster, but the truth was she was terrified. Her last meeting with Adelaide Barnett didn't exactly go so well.

They heard footsteps coming down the hall, and Elana held her breath. Kyle put his arm around her and gave a squeeze.

The door opened and Adelaide walked in with a smile on her face. But the second she saw Elana, the smile disappeared. She paused for a moment, and Elana expected fire to erupt from her nostrils the way they were flaring. Adelaide pushed the door shut behind her and took a step towards them.

Twelve

"WELL, WELL, WELL. What do we have here?" She peeled off her leather gloves and slapped them down on the kitchen counter. "I see that you did not heed my warnings, Miss Tanner."

"You had no right to tell her to stay away," Kyle said.

Adelaide glared at Elana, and it was all she could do not to cower.

"Elana, *dear*, do you mind giving my son and I some privacy so that we can chat?"

"Anything you have to say to me you can say in front of Elana," Kyle told her.

"It's okay, Kyle," Elana said. "I don't mind."

"Are you sure?"

Elana nodded. "I'll be in the bedroom."

Kyle kissed her forehead, and Elana thought she saw Adelaide blanch.

She walked through the living area and slid open the barn-style door to the bedroom, closing it behind her before sitting on the bed. Their voices carried into the room, but most of it was mumbled.

"I'm doing this for your own good," said Adelaide, but Elana couldn't make out Kyle's response.

"If that's the choice you want to make, then so be it!" Adelaide screamed. Elana could now hear every word.

"Yes, it is!" Kyle yelled back. "And it's the best decision I've ever made!"

"You are dead to me, Kyle! I wish she had run over you instead of Jarod! He would never have fallen for this bull shit!"

Elana gasped. The door slammed and she jumped. She cautiously stood up and slid the door open. She peeked out and saw Kyle sitting on the sofa with his head in his hands. Elana sat next to him and put her arm around his shoulders. He stood up and walked over to grab their jackets.

"I don't feel much like cooking anymore. Let's go out to dinner."

Elana stood up. "Do you want me to put the stuff back in the fridge first?"

"Nah, just leave it. Let's get out of here."

He helped her into her jacket and they walked out.

Kyle took her hand as they stepped out onto the pavement, and walked silently across the street to the Purple Café and Wine Bar. Elana was a little relieved when Kyle let go of it once they were seated. He had been gripping pretty hard the whole time.

Still not a word was said while they looked over their menus and Elana was worried. A server showed up to take their drink order.

"I'd like a glass of scotch please," Kyle said and Elana worried about him.

"And for you, miss?"

"Huh? Oh, I'll just have water."

"Are you really going to make me drink alone?" Kyle asked.

Elana wasn't sure what to say. She had a feeling Kyle was looking to get lit, and she didn't want to join him.

"Fine, I'll have a glass of Syrah."

"Go ahead and bring a whole bottle," Kyle said.

Elana's heart sank.

"I'm not going to drink a whole bottle," she told Kyle when the server had left.

"Don't worry, I'll help you."

"That's what I'm worried about."

Kyle looked up from his menu, but then looked back down at it without responding.

"Talk to me, Kyle," she begged.

"What's there to talk about? I know you heard what she said. I'm pretty sure the neighbors heard what she said."

"Do you regret me coming back to Seattle?" she asked.

"What? No." He put his menu down. "Why would you say that?"

"She is your mother, Kyle. She carried you in her womb for nine months."

"No, she didn't."

"What?"

"After having Jarod," he said, "she was worried how much damage a second baby might do to her body, so she had a surrogate for me."

Elana's jaw dropped.

"That's probably why she always preferred Jarod." He went back to reading his menu.

Elana felt like crying. She wanted to tell Kyle that wasn't true, that of course his mother loved both her children the same, but even Elana didn't buy it.

Kyle put his menu down again and reached across the table to take both of Elana's hands.

"Yes, my mother has asked me to choose between her and you. And I chose you without hesitation."

"I just wish that you didn't have to choose."

He looked into her eyes and mustered a half smile. "And that is what makes you a better person than her and why it was so easy to choose."

Kyle's words were intended to make Elana feel better about the whole situation and at first it did. He was withdrawn through most of dinner but for one exception.

From where she was sitting, Elana had a perfect view of the bottom of Rainier Tower, which sat on the base of an inverted pyramid.

Kyle noticed her gaze and asked what she was looking at.

"Just the Rainier Tower. I can remember driving or walking by it as a kid and always wondering if it was going to fall over onto us."

Kyle's face lit up. "Yes, it was an engineer's nightmare, but an architect's dream."

"Do you know who designed it?" she asked. Kyle was talking to her and she wanted to keep it going.

"Of course. It was Minoru Yamasaki. He was another UW alum. Did you know he also designed the original World Trade Towers in New York?"

"I did not." She looked up at the tower again. "Is it really all that safe in an earthquake?"

"Believe it or not, it is one of Seattle's safest buildings."

Elana smiled. "Then I will sleep better tonight knowing it won't fall on us anytime soon."

Kyle took her hand and returned her smile.

It was nice while it lasted.

In the end they didn't finish the bottle of wine, and the restaurant bagged it for them to take home. Elana was quietly thankful that Kyle decided against ordering any more alcohol. They walked back to the apartment and Kyle unlocked the door, hung his jacket up, and walked to the kitchen to begin throwing away the now spoiled fish, but Elana remained by the door.

"Maybe I should just go back to my parents' house tonight," she said.

Kyle spun around. "What? Why?"

"You just seem really distant right now. I thought maybe you would rather have some alone time."

Kyle came back to where she was standing and brushed her hair back. "But I don't want you to go."

"Are you sure?"

Kyle answered by kissing her slowly. "I need you here with me tonight," he said, and pulled her back into the bedroom. He stopped at the foot of the bed and started to undress Elana. His hands making contact with her bare flesh sent currents through her body, but she knew this moment was only a band-aid.

"Kyle, don't you think we should talk about what happened today?"

"I don't want to talk anymore," he said between kisses. "The only thing I want to do tonight is make love to you."

"But—"

He put a finger to her lips. "Not right now."

Elana suddenly realized just how vulnerable Kyle was. He had grown up in the shadow of his brother for so long. And even with that shadow gone, his mother now withheld her affection simply because he had fallen in love with the wrong girl. Adelaide had all but abandoned her only son.

Elana grabbed Kyle's face and kissed him as

hard and as passionately as she could. She loved Kyle. And she would never abandon him.

"I love you, Kyle."

"I know."

Afterwards they continued to lie in bed tangled together. It was still too early for sleep, but neither wanted to leave the comfort of each other's arms.

"What time is your interview tomorrow?" Kyle asked.

"It's at nine. It's the Amazon one."

"Mmm." He ran his fingers though her hair. "Do you want to come spend the night here again tomorrow?"

"I should probably go see my parents. Plus I have that second interview again in Bellevue on Thursday." She could sense his disappointment. She adjusted her position so that she could look into his face. "But I could come see you again afterwards." She swirled her fingers on his chest. "Maybe have a repeat performance."

A smile spread across his face. "As enticing as that is, I have to be on-site out in Sammamish."

"Oh." Elana frowned. "Well, maybe you could stop by on your way back. Or better yet, spend the night."

"I'll see if I can swing it."

Suddenly he was pushing back the sheet. "I just remembered some work that I meant to finish earlier today." Kyle climbed out of bed and threw on some lounge pants. He kissed Elana on the cheek and walked out to the other bedroom he used as his home office.

Elana pulled the sheet tighter around her and heaved a sigh. She just wished Kyle would talk to her. Then maybe she would know how she could help to make it better.

Elana lay in bed for a while, but eventually climbed out as well and grabbed Kyle's t-shirt from the foot of the bed to throw on. She walked out to the kitchen for a glass of water and was soon joined by Kyle.

"You look pretty damn hot in my shirt," he said as he came up behind and wrapped his arms around her.

Elana set the glass down and turned around. "Are you all done with whatever it was you had to do?"

He shrugged. "Done enough. Why?" he asked with a sly grin. "Are you ready for more?"

Elana stopped the hand that was beginning to work its way under the shirt.

"Actually I was hoping you would talk to me now."

Kyle's head fell against her shoulder. He straightened up and said, "I told you I didn't want to talk." He tried again to lift the hem of the shirt and again Elana stopped him.

"No more sex until you talk to me."

Kyle sighed and backed away until he was leaning against the kitchen island. Elana waited patiently for him to speak, but when he finally did, they were not the words she had been hoping to hear.

"I'm going to bed. Come join me when you're ready." And he walked away.

Kyle could have slapped her and it would have hurt less. She finished her glass of water and then went back into the bedroom where she tore off Kyle's shirt and proceeded to get dressed.

He sat up in bed. "What are you doing?"

"I'm going home."

"What?" He moved to the end of the bed and grabbed her wrist. "Don't go. I want you to stay."

"You're always telling me I need to open up to you and now you won't do the same for me."

He let go of her wrist. "What the fuck am I supposed to talk about?"

"I don't know, but you are shutting me out right now, so it is clearly bothering you."

"Of course it's bothering me!" he said. "Wouldn't it bother you if your mother said she wished you were dead?"

Elana sat down on the bed, half dressed. "Yes, it would. Do you think maybe this is just your mother overreacting because things didn't go as she planned?"

"I don't know. Maybe."

"We knew that she wouldn't be happy when she found out about us." Elana took his hand. "But you told me we were going to figure it out together."

He squeezed her back. "I know. I expected her to cut me off from the money, but I didn't realize she would practically disown me."

"Do you think," Elana started, "do you think it might help if we took a break and gave her more time?"

"No." He squeezed her hand even harder. "This is her choice. I won't lose you because of her."

Elana climbed all the way up onto the bed and straddled him. "No, Kyle, you won't lose me." She took his face in both her hands and gently pressed her lips against his. "You won't lose me."

Elana's interview with Amazon didn't go as well as she had planned. They ended up asking a lot of questions about her time in court and why exactly did she move to Hawaii for a year. She answered them as best she could, but by the end she just felt uncomfortable with the whole thing. Thursday's interview went just as well as her first on Monday, and on Friday morning they called to offer a job. The first person she called with the good news was Kyle.

"How is your day going?" she asked when he answered.

"Pretty good," he said. "Even better now that you've called. Why? How is your day going?"

"I'm so happy you asked, because my day is fantastic."

Kyle laughed. "And why is that?"

"Because I got offered a job today."

"You did? That's fantastic. Did you accept it?"

"I did. I thought about telling them I need to think about it, but jobs are hard to come by these days, so I told them yes."

"Where will you be working?" he asked.

"I will be working in the legal department at PACCAR in Bellevue."

"That's not too far from my building."

"No, it is not," she said.

"I think I see many lunch dates in my near future."

Elana laughed. "If you're lucky."

"Hmm... speaking of lunch, would you be up for meeting me at Seastar for lunch today?"

"You mean instead of your office?"

"I have something I want to show you."

"Okay," she said slowly. "Sure, I can meet you there. What time?"

"How does 12:30 sound?"

"Sounds good. I will see you then."

Elana managed to find street parking close to the restaurant and rushed up to the entrance. She had forgotten how bad traffic could be so early on a Friday and was running late.

Kyle greeted her as soon as she walked in the

door.

"I'm so sorry!" she said, and planted a kiss on his cheek.

"It's fine. I have a table already." He took her hand and led her to a table where another gentleman was seated. Elana immediately recognized him as Kyle's father.

Thirteen

SHE PAUSED FOR a moment, and Kyle turned around.

"It's okay," he whispered, "I promise."

Elana reluctantly nodded and continued to follow him.

Charles Barnett stood up when Kyle and Elana reached the table and extended his hand to Elana.

"Elana, I would like to formally introduce you to my father," said Kyle.

She took his hand and shook it. "It's a pleasure to meet you, Mr. Barnett."

He smiled the same warm smile that she often saw grace Kyle's face. "Please, call me Chuck," he said.

The three of them sat down at the table and were soon joined by the server. Elana perused the menu quickly while the other two placed their orders.

"I will have the chicken salad, please," she said.

The server took their menus and left. Elana nervously sipped her water and waited for someone to speak.

"Kyle here tells me you were offered a job with PACCAR," said Chuck.

"Yes," she replied. "Just this morning."

"Congratulations."

"Thank you, sir." It was shocking how polite and warm Kyle's father was. Elana had always envisioned him to simply be a male version of Adelaide.

"I have to say I'm glad that I am finally meeting you. Kyle has told me so much about you."

"Oh, really?" She glanced over at Kyle, who blushed for the first time since she had known him.

"Yes, he has," Chuck continued, "and it is clear that you make him very happy."

This time they both blushed.

Elana looked at Kyle again. "I can honestly say he has done the same for me."

"I understand that my wife paid you two a visit the other night."

Elana nodded, unsure what to say.

"I apologize for her actions that evening. Although," Chuck looked sideways at Kyle, "a warning may have been nice."

"Really, Dad," Kyle cut in, "You think that would have made things any better?"

"Well, it couldn't have made them worse."

Kyle shook his head. Clearly he didn't agree.

"I do believe that my Addie may be overreacting a bit, but she tends to do that when her loved ones are involved."

Elana spoke up. "If I may be blunt, sir, Adelaide has done anything but show her son love in the time that I have been with him."

Both men looked at her. Kyle's expression was one of shock while Chuck's was more mild amusement.

"Kyle mentioned your honesty."

"I'm sorry."

"No, it's quite all right. Addie said some horrible things that night that I'd hope she will soon regret."

"I understand her cutting him off if she was so worried I was a gold digger," said Elana, "but why the hateful words?"

Kyle spoke up. "Because it turns out she couldn't cut me off."

"What do you mean?" she asked.

"Kyle's trust fund was set up by his grandfather, my father," Chuck explained. "Addie has no control over it."

"Oh, so you're not penniless after all?" Elana joked.

Kyle laughed. "No. I won't have to live in a cardboard box after all."

Concern crossed Chuck's face as he looked between the two of them.

"Sorry, Dad. Inside joke."

"Oh," said Chuck. "There is something else regarding the trust fund though."

"Yes," agreed Kyle. "The best part. Remember when I said that the money from the settlement didn't affect me personally?" Elana nodded. "Turns out I was mistaken."

"The money that you have been paying towards the settlement award was set up to go directly in Kyle's trust fund," Chuck explained. "The fund had been intended for both Jarod and Kyle, and Addie and I had thought it best to go into there."

"So this whole time I've been paying," Elana pointed to Kyle, "*you*?"

"Yes," he answered. "And seeing how we are together now, it seems silly for you to continue paying me."

"Oh." Elana's face screwed up as she processed

it all.

"What we are saying," Chuck explained, "is that Kyle and I have spoken with our lawyer, and the payments will cease, effective immediately."

"Are you sure?" Elana asked.

Kyle looked at her in amazement. "Are you crazy? Of course we're sure. Elana, you never should have owed us anything in the first place."

"I know, but somehow this feels wrong. Like I got away with something." She placed a hand over Kyle's. "Just because I'm with you doesn't mean I shouldn't pay up my debts, justified or not. Maybe the money should just be diverted elsewhere."

"Elana, dear," Chuck started. "You will not be paying another penny to this family in any shape or form. I have to admit, this is not the reaction I was expecting. I thought you would be happier."

"I am," she said. "I just hope that you don't think this has anything to do with why I am with Kyle. I never expected this."

"I don't," replied Chuck, "but I do have one thing to ask."

"Yes?"

"When my wife is ready to have a relationship with her son again, I ask that you don't stand in her way."

"Dad—" Kyle objected, but Elana cut him off.

"It's all right, Kyle. I don't mind. Sir, regardless of what your wife may feel towards me, I would never come between Kyle and his mother. This decision to not be a part of Kyle's life is hers and hers alone."

Chuck nodded. Elana was pretty sure she just received his seal of approval. Kyle's phone started ringing.

"I'm really sorry, but I need to take this. If

you'll excuse me." Kyle stood up and moved over to the waiting area.

"Sir, can I ask you something of a more personal nature?" Elana asked Chuck.

"I can't promise I will answer, but you are welcome to ask."

"Is it true that Adelaide had a surrogate for Kyle because she was worried about her figure?"

A long deep sigh escaped from Chuck. "Is that what Kyle told you?"

"Yes. Is it not true?"

"I knew that story would come back to bite her in the ass."

"I'm sorry?"

"Kyle was conceived with a surrogate, and that is the story that Addie told everyone. I hadn't realized it had reached his ears."

"But it wasn't the case?"

"No," said Chuck. "About a year after Jarod was born Addie was diagnosed with uterine cancer. They caught it early enough, but in the end she was so scarred there was no way she could ever carry a child again."

"Oh my god, that's horrible. But why not tell people the truth?" Elana asked.

"Because she thought it would make her seem weak. That there was something she couldn't do. In her mind, it sounded better to tell people that she had made the choice not to carry him."

"Kyle deserves to know the truth."

"You're right, but it is something she needs to tell him in person." Chuck eyed Kyle, who was making his way back to the table. "I'd appreciate it if you didn't say anything to him."

"Of course."

"I'm really sorry, Dad," Kyle said when he

returned, "but something has come up and I need to be somewhere." He opened his wallet and started to pull out cash, but Chuck stopped him.

"Don't even think about it. I've got this."

"Well, thank you for lunch then." Kyle turned to Elana. "I think I might need your help with something. Do you mind coming with me?"

"Of course." Elana couldn't imagine what he might need her help with. She stood up and took Chuck's hand. "Thank you for lunch as well, and it was great getting to meet you. I hope we can talk more in the future."

Chuck smiled. "Of that I have no doubt. Take care."

Elana and Kyle left the restaurant and started walking towards his building.

"What do you need my help with?" she asked.

"You'll see."

"Is it a work thing?"

"No."

"Kyle!"

"You'll see."

Elana decided to just enjoy the walk hand in hand with him. But then she was even more confused when they continued past his building.

"Where are we going?"

He was grinning like a schoolboy again. "I said, you'll see."

After a couple more blocks they ended up at the Bravern complex.

"Are you taking me shopping?" she asked.

"Nope. Not today, at least."

Kyle led her past the high-end shops that included the likes of Jimmy Choo and Neiman Marcus, until they were in a lobby where a professionally dressed woman was waiting for them.

"Mr. Barnett. I'm glad you were able to make it on such short notice."

"Elana, this is Roslyn," Kyle explained. "She's the real estate agent who has been helping me look for a new apartment. Roslyn, this is my girlfriend, Elana Tanner."

Roslyn shook Elana's hand. "It's a pleasure to meet you, Miss Tanner. If you two will follow me, we will go up and take a look at the apartment."

They followed Roslyn into an elevator that would take them to the luxury apartments built above the shopping complex.

"You wanted to show me your new apartment?" Elana asked.

"I wanted your opinion on a potential new apartment."

"Oh. That makes me feel special, actually."

Kyle touched her nose. "You are special."

They stepped off the elevator at the fifteenth floor and Roslyn unlocked the door of one of the apartments.

Elana did her best to keep her jaw off the floor as they toured it. There was a master bedroom with a walk-in closet, five piece master bath and private balcony, plus another bedroom that she was sure Kyle would use as his home office again. The whole apartment was bright with high ceilings and large windows that had perfect views of not only downtown Bellevue, but of the skyline of Seattle across Lake Washington, vistas that could also be seen from the additional balcony off the living area.

After giving them the tour, Roslyn stepped back to give them some privacy.

Kyle pulled her out onto the balcony off the master bedroom.

"Well, what do you think?" he asked.

"It's gorgeous, Kyle."

"Really, do you think you could see yourself spending time here?"

"I suppose it wouldn't be so bad."

"Because I was hoping you would move into it with me."

"Here? You want me to move in with you *here*?"

He laughed. "Yes, here."

Elana shook her head. "Oh, Kyle. I could never live here."

His face fell. "Why not?"

"This place is too much. I could never feel comfortable living here."

"Sure you would, because it would be our place together."

"I wouldn't be able to afford my share of this," she said. "New job or not."

"Ah!" he exclaimed. "I have a counter offer. You let me worry about the rent, and you could take care of the utilities." When she didn't answer, he continued. "Just think, it's close to your parents, and you could even walk into work." But still she said nothing.

"What are you thinking right now?" he asked.

"Kyle, honey," she said softly, "if you want this apartment so badly, then you should get it."

"But you just told me you didn't want to live here."

"I know."

"Wait, are you saying that you don't want to move in with me?" he asked.

"It's not that I don't want to, Kyle. It's just so soon and I only got back a week ago."

"I understand," he said. "You're right. I did

243

kind of spring this on you."

"So are you going to get the apartment then?" she asked.

"No. You're right. It is probably a bit over the top. C'mon, let's go tell Rosalyn I'm going to pass on this one."

They rejoined the realtor and exited the apartment.

On Saturday night Elana finally convinced Kyle to spend the night at her parents' house, and together they enjoyed a game night with some neighbors.

"I can't remember the last time I had that much fun," Kyle said when they crawled into bed well after midnight.

Elana laughed. "Alcohol improves any game."

"No, I'm pretty sure it was the game. What was it called again?"

"Cards Against Humanity. It was pretty raunchy, wasn't it?"

"I still can't believe some of the things that came out of your mother's mouth. Or yours for that matter."

Elana giggled. "Don't let our angelic demeanor fool you."

"Angelic, my ass," Kyle said, and Elana giggled again. He pushed back her hair. "I love that sound."

"You're crazy," she told him.

"You're probably right."

Elana laid her head on his chest and Kyle slid his hand under her top to caress her back.

"You know we've spent more nights in the same bed than apart since you've come back to Seattle," he said.

"Yes."

"Are you sure you're not ready to move in with me?"

Elana sighed.

"I'm not trying to push," he quickly explained. "I'm just trying to wrap my head around this. I feel like you want to spend just as much time together as I do. The minutes always creep by when we're not together."

She searched for his free hand and intertwined her fingers in his. "I do. I mean, it is the same for me. But I'm scared that living together could change that."

"What would change?"

"I don't know, but it always does. You've lived with someone before. You must know what I'm talking about."

"Yes, but you're not Victoria. And I promise you I'm not Benjamin."

"I know," she mumbled. "I just need more time. Let me at least feel more stable with a job before we make any plans."

"Agreed." He was quiet for a minute and then spoke again. "I still have to find a new place. Will you help me choose one that you think you could see yourself living in one day?"

"Yes, that I can do for you."

"There is one more thing I was hoping you could do for me," he said.

"Let's hear it."

"I have to attend an event next Saturday. And I would love for you to be there with me."

"What kind of event?" she asked with caution.

"It's a charity auction at Benaroya Hall."

Elana groaned.

"Please," he begged. "It's an annual event I attend, and I really want you there with me."

Elana decided that getting all dolled up with Kyle might not be such a bad thing. "Yes. I will go with you."

"Thank you, Elana. You don't know how much I appreciate it."

"I suppose I'll need to be in a dress," she said.

"Er, yes, it is a formal event. Black tie and all. If you need help shopping for a dress, I would be more than happy to go with you."

Elana knew that by 'help', Kyle meant buy it for her.

"Don't worry about it. I've got it." She planned to talk to her mom about it the next day. "Now go to sleep, Kyle. You're exhausting me."

He chuckled. "As you wish."

"Mmm," she smiled. "I like the sound of that."

Monday morning Elana was putting on the finishing touches of her makeup when her phone rang.

"Do you want me to get that?" Kyle called from the kitchen.

"Yes, please!"

Moments later he was bringing the phone into her. "I think it's PACCAR," he said quietly.

Elana frowned as she took the phone. "This is Elana."

"Ms. Tanner, this is Gina from Human Resources at PACCAR."

"Yes?"

"I wanted to let you know that unfortunately the position we have offered you has been absorbed into another job and I'm afraid we are going to have to rescind our original offer."

"Oh. Well, is there another position that I could perhaps apply for?" Elana asked.

"Not at this time, but we wish you luck in your

future employment endeavors. Good day, Ms. Tanner."

Elana ended the call and sat on the edge of the tub, feeling deflated.

Kyle came in. "What's the matter?"

"I don't have a job," she mumbled.

"What do you mean? Aren't you supposed to be going in this morning for orientation?"

"I was. But they just told me the position has disappeared and they won't be hiring me after all."

Kyle exhaled loudly. "God damn it," he swore.

Elana looked up, surprised. "It's not your fault," she said.

"No. But I can guess who was behind it." He ran his fingers through his dark hair. "My mother has close ties to a couple of the board members. But I never imagined she would ask them to pull any strings in her favor."

She looked up at Kyle, fighting the desire to cry. "What am I supposed to do then? Find a company where your mother doesn't have a connection to someone in power? There aren't many in this area, are there?" Her voice started going up in pitch. "That leaves me right back where I was in Hanalei. Working somewhere I don't really want to be."

Kyle knelt down in front of her. "We'll figure something out. Maybe we just need to wait it out a bit longer and let her cool off."

"How long?" She asked. "My first car payment is due next month, and I have no money. Pretty soon I won't even be able to put gas in the damn thing." She was starting to whine. And she didn't really care. "Your mother warned me what would happen if I came back. I should have listened to her!"

"Hey," Kyle said, and took her face in his hands. "It's going to be all right. Don't worry about the money."

Elana's eyes went big. "No," she said, shaking her head. "I won't take your money."

"Stop being so stubborn. We're in this together; let me help you out. It's only temporary."

She stared into his eyes. This wasn't charity. It was him honestly wanting to take care of her. "Fine," she resigned. "But I can only imagine what Adelaide would think if she found out."

Kyle smiled. "And since when did we care what my mother thought?"

Elana meekly smiled back.

Kyle stood up. "Now go put on something more comfortable. I'm taking you to the zoo."

"The zoo?"

"Yes. How can anyone possibly feel down when they see all the adorable animals?"

"But what about your work? You still have a job."

He shrugged. "I don't have any appointments until the afternoon."

"I love you," she said.

He kissed her cheek and started to undo his tie. "You should."

Elana just rolled her eyes.

Kyle had an early morning pitch in Portland on Friday morning, so Elana spent Thursday evening at her parent's house while he made the drive down the night before. She had gone to bed early, but found herself unable to fall asleep. Just after eleven she decided to go downstairs to use the computer. If she was going to be awake, she might as well be useful and do some more job searching.

Coming down the stairs, she could hear her parents' voices from the kitchen and paused, worried that she was interrupting something.

"And when did they say it had to be paid?" her father said.

"The end of the month," her mother answered, "so basically two weeks."

"I don't understand. Did something happened to our credit? Should we be worried about identity theft?"

"No, I checked the credit reports. We're fine."

Elana walked in. "What's going on?"

Her parents rushed to pile the papers they had spread over the table. Elana could see the bank logo at the top of several of them.

"Oh, nothing," her mother said. "Just paying bills. You know how much fun that can be."

"This late at night?" Elana asked.

"I just remembered some things were due at the last minute."

Elana looked from her mom to her dad who were both trying to front a smile. She wasn't buying any of it.

"Then why is dad so worried about your credit?"

Their smiles faltered, and then her dad heaved a great sigh.

"The bank is calling in on our home equity loan," he said.

"Mark!"

"Our daughter's not an idiot, Renee. She knows something's wrong."

"What do you mean they're calling on the loan?" Elana asked.

"We have until the end of the month to pay off the loan," Renee said.

"But why? I don't understand."

Mark shrugged. "Neither do we." They just called today and said they had been going over various accounts and decided they could no longer extend the credit to us."

Elana sat down at the table, shaking her head. "How strange." Then her eyes went big. "Oh my god!"

"What is it, sweetie?" asked Renee.

"Adelaide Barnett!"

"What's she got to do with this?"

"Don't you see? She's behind this."

"Surely she wouldn't...." Renee trailed off.

"Of course she would! She tried attacking me by keeping me from getting that job. When that didn't work, she decided to try something bigger." Elana stood up. "I have to go call Kyle. This is too much!"

Mark stopped her. "Don't call Kyle, sweetie. Let's not bring him into this."

"But we can't let her get away with this!" said Elana.

"We don't know for sure that Adelaide is behind this," Mark said. "And if she is, this is exactly what she wants. Let us deal with this. You don't need to worry. We'll figure it out."

Elana looked again at her parents, not sure what to say.

"Go back to bed, Elana," her mother said. "Your father's right. There's no need to bring Kyle into this. We'll be fine."

Elana slowly nodded and went back up to her bed, but it was still a long time before she fell asleep. She wondered how long she would be able to keep this from Kyle.

"Elana, babe," Kyle called from the living room, "are you almost ready? The car will be here any minute."

Elana stepped out of the bedroom, trying to get the side zipper up on her gold silk charmeuse halter gown.

"Will you help me with this?" she asked. "I'm afraid I'm going to get my skin stuck in it. And what car? Why do we need a car?"

She had been fidgeting with the zipper, and when Kyle still hadn't responded, she looked up to see him standing by the couch in his perfectly tailored tuxedo with a slack jaw.

"What?" She was worried that she had made a poor choice on the dress. "Is there something wrong?"

Kyle slowly closed his mouth and shook his head. "No. Nothing's wrong." He walked over and carefully zipped up her dress. "You look incredible." He kissed her shoulder when he was finished.

"What do we need a car for?" she repeated. "I thought it was at Benaroya Hall. Isn't that only two blocks from here?"

Kyle made his way to the door to grab their coats. "Even two blocks is a bit much in that dress. And this is not an event that you *walk* to."

Elana took a deep breath. "I can do this," she muttered to herself.

The car arrived, and Elana and Kyle were dropped off in front of the home of the Seattle Symphony. They entered the hall and stood in line for the check-in table.

Kyle was immediately greeted by several colleagues. Most were just in passing, but a few paused to make conversation.

"Jennings," Kyle said as he took the hand of one such gentleman. "Good to see you again."

"Haven't seen you at the Athletic Club in a while."

"I've had a lot on my plate lately."

"I heard you got the newest UW Medical Building bid. Congratulations!"

Elana looked up at Kyle proudly.

"Jennings, I would like to introduce you to my date, Elana."

Elana bristled a bit at the term *date* instead of *girlfriend*.

"Elana, this is Roger Jennings. He and my father go way back."

Elana held out her hand. "It's a pleasure to meet you Mr. Jennings."

"And you as well." Jennings smiled as he shook her hand, but Elana caught the inquisitive look in his eye and realized he probably knew about Kyle's former engagement to Victoria. *Recently* former. "Well, I'd best go find my wife before she spends all my money." Kyle laughed with him. "Join me for a game of squash soon," he said as he walked off.

Elana was about to ask why Kyle introduced her as simply his date when she caught the banner over the stage and gasped.

"You have got to be kidding me!" she hissed as she punched Kyle.

"Ow! What was that for?"

"The Reese *Barnett* Guild? Seriously?"

Fourteen

"DID YOU REALLY think I wouldn't notice your name all over this event?" she asked.

"No, I was just worried you wouldn't come with me if you knew."

"Of course I wouldn't have come! I'm assuming your mother is here somewhere."

"Yes, she is the president after all."

Elana was on the brink of tears.

"Please don't cry, Elana. It's fine. She won't make a scene here. There are too many people around."

She drew a deep breath and tried to regain her composure while they stepped up to the booth to get their table assignment and provide a credit card for faster checkout. It took her a second to realize there was a complication.

"I'm sorry, sir, but this event is invite only."

Kyle raised his eyebrows. "I have an invite, and Elana Tanner is my guest for the evening."

"Yes, I have you, but I have your guest listed as Victoria Lansing, and she has already checked in."

Elana froze.

"She what?" Kyle seethed.

"She already checked in, sir. Twenty minutes

ago."

Elana tugged on his sleeve. "Maybe I should just go home," she said quietly.

"No." He turned back to the attendant. "Well, there has been a mistake, because Miss Tanner here is my guest."

"But sir, I have clear instructions not to—"

Kyle leaned down close and spoke quietly, but harshly. "Do you realize who you are talking to?" Elana had never seen Kyle throw his clout around before. "Do you *realize* that my name is at the top of your little list?"

The man shrunk back. "Yes," he squeaked. "It's just that Mrs. Barnett—"

"What exactly did my mother tell you?"

Just then a women with an earpiece came up behind the man and whispered something in his ear. The attendant nodded.

"I apologize, Mr. Barnett. Here are your bid numbers. You are seated at table five. We will have someone get an extra setting on it right away."

Kyle stood up, looking satisfied, but it was all Elana could do to keep from running out of there that instant.

"Wait, are we sitting at the same table as your mother?" Elana asked in horror as they meandered over to table five.

"Yes, but she won't be there much. She spends most of these events mingling."

"This is a mistake Kyle. Why would you bring me here?"

"It'll be fine. I promise."

Elana wasn't so sure, but before she could say anything, they were interrupted by another associate of Kyle's. He continued to introduce her as his date, and she knew exactly what they were thinking. *Wow, dating so soon after Victoria!* Elana didn't know how she was going to make it through the evening.

And then they ran into Victoria herself. Kyle was perusing the silent auction items when she appeared across the table from him wearing some gaudy red number.

"Elana! So nice to see you again!" Victoria exclaimed. The words were benign, but they were dripping with venom.

"Victoria," Kyle said reprovingly.

"I love your dress, Elana. Badgley Mischka, am I correct?"

Elana gave a slight nod.

"A gift from Kyle, I presume," Victoria said with narrowed eyes.

"No," Elana answered. "I—I bought it myself."

"Interesting."

"What do you want, Victoria?" Kyle asked through a strained smile. Elana caught more than one person looking at them with curiosity.

Victoria walked around the table and adjusted Kyle's lapel. "Can't a girl just say hi?"

"Don't make a scene," he whispered.

"Oh honey, I wouldn't dream of doing that. This is your mother's night, and I wouldn't want to make her mad at me." Victoria sneered at Elana, who turned beet red. "See you at the table," she said, and walked away.

Elana put her hands on Kyle's chest. "Please, can we go home?"

He gripped her shoulders and gave what was probably mean to be a reassuring squeeze. "I can't. Not yet. How would it look if I walked out right now? We can't let Victoria get to us."

"Too late," she muttered.

Kyle lifted her chin. "Hey! You're tough. You

can handle this."

Elana's heart sank. Kyle was asking a lot of her. But she nodded and he kissed her cheek.

They continued down the line of tables, and Kyle was stopped by a middle-aged woman. Rather than face another awkward introduction, Elana kept moving along. She stopped in front of the bid sheet for an African safari that was already up to three thousand dollars.

"Were you thinking of bidding?"

Elana looked up and saw a handsome gentleman about her father's age standing next to her.

"Oh, not today, I'm afraid," she told him.

"You should," he said. "I won it last year, just got back last month, in fact."

She smiled at him. "How was it?"

"It was incredible! Hard to believe they let you get that close to wildlife."

Elana was about to respond when Victoria reappeared out of nowhere and hooked an arm through Elana's.

"Victoria, how are you?" Elana's companion asked.

"I'm wonderful, Doctor Prichard. I see you've met my friend Elana."

Elana was terrified. She had no idea what Victoria was up to, but it couldn't be good.

"We were just talking about the African trip," he said.

Victoria ignored his comment. "You remember Elana Tanner, don't you?"

Elana tried to move away from Victoria, but she tightened her grip on Elana's arm.

Dr. Prichard cocked his head. "The name sounds familiar. Do you work with the Barnetts?"

Instead of answering, Elana looked over her

shoulder, desperately wishing Kyle would come rescue her, but he was still engaged in his conversation with the woman who had stopped him a couple tables back.

"Oh, no" Victoria said with a light laugh. "Elana Tanner is the driver that struck Jarod."

Dr. Prichard's eyes went wide as he made the connection. Elana just wanted the ground to open up and swallow her whole.

"Um, yes, if you'll excuse me, um, it was nice meeting you, Miss, um...." And he walked away.

Elana gave one last hard jerk, and Victoria released her arm.

"What the hell do you think you're doing?" Elana hissed at her. "You promised Kyle you wouldn't make a scene."

Any sweetness Victoria had faked for Dr. Prichard was gone.

"Then he's as much a fool as you are for believing me," said Victoria. "Did you really think you could steal Kyle away from me without paying the price?"

"Hard to steal something that you had already lost," Elana shot back.

Victoria gave Elana a little shove, just enough to send her off balance and knock into another guest who was standing nearby. Kyle rushed over and Victoria slinked off into the crowd.

"I'm so sorry," Elana told the guest.

"Elana," said Kyle, "what's going on?"

"I just tripped on my dress," she lied.

"Sorry about that," Kyle said to the guest as they stepped away.

"Where's the restroom?" Elana asked.

Kyle pointed her in the right direction, and when Elana entered the ladies room, she found Adelaide among the other women fixing their makeup.

Adelaide's eyes quietly followed Elana through the mirror to the stall.

Elana didn't actually have to go to the bathroom. She had just wanted a moment's peace, and it turned out she had gone to the wrong place. She now stood in the stall and waited for the bathroom to clear out. When she thought the coast was clear, she stepped out and found one person had in fact remained.

"I see they don't know how to follow the simplest of directions up front," said Adelaide.

Elana looked at her but said nothing as she walked up to the sink and began washing her hands. She dried them and started to walk towards the door, but Adelaide stood in her way.

"Why are you still here?" Adelaide asked.

"Because Kyle wants me here," Elana told her, placing her hands on her hips. Though she still didn't understand *why* Kyle wanted her here.

"That's not what I mean. Why are you still with Kyle? You've got what you wanted."

"What are you talking about?" asked Elana.

"I'm talking about the settlement money. The money you *owe* us," said Adelaide.

"Oh," said Elana. Of course Chuck was going to tell his wife. "I never asked anyone to do that."

"And now there's talk of cutting you a check for everything you had paid up to this point. The whole lawsuit will have been for nothing!"

"Check? I don't know anything about a check."

"You expect me to believe that?" Adelaide asked. "This was your plan the whole time, wasn't it? Well, bravo."

"I never had any plan!" said Elana.

But Adelaide ignored her.

"I'm sure the second Kyle showed up on that island, you saw an opportunity."

Elana, shaking with anger, and maybe a hint of fear, took a step forward, and was now only inches from Adelaide who pursed her lips, daring Elana to challenge her.

"I don't know how to get it through that thick skull of yours, but Kyle chose me. And the only, *only* reason I am here is because I love him. I never asked him to cancel the payments, and no one ever said anything about cutting me a check."

Adelaide's nostrils were flaring, but before she could say anything else, Elana continued.

"But if it will make you feel better, write the check out to my parents, seeing as how the bank just called in on their loan.

"I have no idea what you could be referring to," said Adelaide, looking off to one side.

She stood there looking so smug, Elana found herself doing something she had been wanting to do since their first face to face encounter in the Princeville hotel room. She slapped Adelaide Barnett. The timing was unfortunate however, because just as her hand made contact with Adelaide's face, two women walked in. They gasped. Elana saw the anger in Adelaide's face mixed with restraint, and knew the only reason she wasn't clawing out Elana's eyes right now was because there were witnesses.

Elana ran out of the bathroom, pushing past the two women. Who was she kidding? Hell, who was Kyle kidding? She needed to find him now.

He was standing by their table, laughing with yet another gentleman, this time closer in age to Kyle, and a woman.

"There you are!" Kyle said when Elana reached them. He started to introduce them, but Elana cut him off.

"I can't stay here any longer. I'm sorry, but I

just can't. You can stay if you want, but I need to leave."

Kyle took her arm and gently pulled her out of earshot. "They're about to serve dinner, and then I promise we will leave."

"I'm leaving now."

"How would that look if you leave me?"

"I don't care how it looks!" Elana said, much louder than she had intended.

"Keep your voice down," he whispered.

Elana looked up into Kyle's eyes as her own began to fill with tears. She thought about telling him that she had just slapped his mother, but she wasn't sure that would change anything. Because, again, how would that look? He was going to be hearing about it soon enough. The two women were probably already gossiping about how Kyle Barnett's *date* had just slapped Adelaide.

She slowly pulled her arm away from his hand and backed away. Elana shook her head as she turned around and made for the door.

Outside she ran across Third Avenue and up the block to the entrance of Kyle's building. Once there she realized that she had no key to get into it. She didn't have anything. They had checked their coats and her cell phone was in the purse still sitting on the table. Elana covered her face with her hands, and the tears finally spilled over. She leaned against the wall and was about to slide down it when she remembered the dress. Elana had only been half lying when she told Victoria she had bought it; it was a rental.

Elana shivered in the cold and tried to decide what to do. She contemplated taking a cab all the way to Redmond and asking her parents to foot the bill. But then she would have to explain everything to them.

"Elana!"

She looked down the block to see Kyle running up, carrying her coat and clutch. When he caught up to her, he wrapped the coat around her shoulders and unlocked the door.

"Let's get you upstairs," he said.

"What about the Gala?" Elana said acidly as she walked into the lobby.

"I'm sorry." He put an arm around her shoulder, but Elana shook it off.

"I said I was sorry," he repeated.

"I heard you," Elana snapped and entered the elevator.

Neither spoke again until they were back in the apartment.

"I need to call the driver and let him know we won't need to be picked up," said Kyle as he grabbed the phone.

Elana went back into the bedroom to change into jeans and a t-shirt and started gathering up her personal items.

"What are you doing?" Kyle asked from the doorway. "Was tonight really that bad?"

Elana continued stuffing her bag without looking up. "Tonight, Kyle, was a culmination of everything I had feared when you first asked me to come back with you."

"What are you talking about?"

She looked up at him now. "I'm talking about your mother, your wealth. Hell, even your ex-fiancée made an appearance."

"My wealth? I thought this was about you being uncomfortable at the event."

"Of course I was uncomfortable! You dragged me to an event hosted by your mother who hates me, and when I wanted to leave, all you could say was, 'what would people think'! Because you're right. What *would* people think if a Barnett left a Barnett function too early? And then you couldn't even introduce me as your girlfriend, because what would people think of Kyle Barnett not only having a girlfriend so soon after breaking off his engagement, but to be dating the same person that killed his brother. Face it, we were doomed from the start."

Kyle moved to where she stood. "I'm sorry. I should have prepared you better. But I was afraid if I told you, you wouldn't come and I wanted you there with me."

"Of course I wouldn't have come, because it was a bad idea, as tonight proved." She sighed and zipped up the bag. "I never should have let you convince me to leave Hawaii."

"How can you say that?" Kyle whispered.

"Because it's true," she sobbed. "Because we were kidding ourselves if we thought I could fit in here. Because your mother was right. I am ripping this family apart."

"That's insane! How are you ripping this family apart?"

"By taking not just one, but both of her sons away from her."

"You can't let her get to you."

"Too late. And it's not just me anymore either."

"What do you mean?"

Elana took a deep breath before continuing. "My parents didn't want me to tell you, but your mother convinced the bank to call in on their equity loan. The one they took out to pay for my legal fees."

"I had no idea," said Kyle.

"I know. But it just proves that your mother's reach is longer than I could have ever imagined."

She slung the bag on her should and she walked out of the bedroom with Kyle following.

"So you're just going to run away again, aren't you?" said Kyle.

Elana's whole body froze.

"Because we both know that's what you do well. As soon as things get difficult, Elana Tanner runs away."

"Call you mother and tell her she won," Elana said without turning around. "Maybe you can still repair your relationship."

"You said you wouldn't leave me!" Kyle called out in desperation as she opened the front door.

"And you said we were in this together, yet tonight you threw me under the bus for your name." And Elana closed the door behind her.

It had been an hour since Elana had walked out the door when Kyle's buzzer went off. He walked over to it, praying with every fiber in his being that it was her.

"Elana?" he asked hopefully.

"Elana—what? No, this is your mother."

"I don't want to talk to you right now," he said.

"Dammit, Kyle, let me in!"

He reluctantly buzzed her in and propped open the door. He walked over to the couch and sank into it.

Adelaide stormed in and positioned herself squarely in front of him.

"What the hell happened to you tonight?" she yelled.

Kyle's eyes didn't move from the spot on the floor. "She's gone."

"What are you talking about?"

"Elana left me."

"Well if she was willing to leave on tonight of all nights, then good riddance."

Kyle raised his head. "How dare you!"

Adelaide was aghast. "How dare *me*?"

He stood up and was in her face. "She left me because of you. You were the one who made this evening unbearable for her. You're the one who tried to keep her out when *you* knew what this night meant to me. Elana had no idea."

Adelaide frowned. "Why wouldn't you tell her?"

He shook his head. "It doesn't matter. Now I want you to leave. I don't ever want to see you again."

"You're upset right now. You don't mean that."

"Yes, I do!" He was practically yelling now. "Elana was the best thing that ever happened to me, and you did everything in your power to drive her away. And apparently that wasn't enough, because then you had to go after her parents with the whole loan thing!"

Adelaide's lips went tight. Her silence only confirmed that she had been behind it all.

"If I get her back, the only way we could ever be happy is if you are out of the picture."

"Do you even know what that woman did to me tonight?"

Kyle raised an eyebrow at her.

"She slapped me! In front of people!"

"I'm sure it was no less than you deserved."

Shock swept over Adelaide's face. But Kyle wasn't finished.

"You're the one who wished I was dead. Well, let's do us both a favor and pretend it's true."

He stormed off into his bedroom, slamming the door shut behind him.

Elana pulled into the driveway and tried to fix her face before going in. It was still early, which meant she would probably have to face her parents. She hadn't been able to come up with a good lie for why she was coming home so early and decided they were going to figure it out anyway, so she might as well start with the truth.

When she walked into the house, she was surprised to find her mom in the living with a bottle of wine and two glasses.

"Hey," Elana mumbled.

"I sent your father to the movies. I had a feeling you'd be home soon."

Elana sat down next to Renee, who began filling the glasses.

"How did you know?" she asked

"I was watching the news and they happened to mention an event at the Benaroya Hall for the Reese Barnett Guild. All I could think was, 'that asshole'."

Elana started crying again. "It was horrible, Mom."

Renee put her arm around her daughter. "I can only imagine, sweetie."

Elana filled her in on the details.

"How could I have been so stupid?" she asked when she had finished.

"You weren't stupid, honey. You were in love."

"But I thought he was in love with me as well."

"He does love you," said Renee. "It's just that…well, I don't know. I have no idea what the hell he was thinking tonight."

"He was thinking about his image and not much else." Elana took a huge swig of wine and focused on the comfort of it. "I give up, though."

"Give up on what?" her mother asked.

"On love. I give up on my hopes of ever finding the real thing."

Her mother was stern. "Don't you dare say

that."

"And why shouldn't I?" Elana demanded.

"Do you honestly think I never loved anyone else before you father?"

"Well no, but—"

"And do you think it didn't hurt when those relationships ended?"

"No," Elana said slowly.

"In fact, they hurt like hell! But if you never experience the pain, how will you know when you've found the good stuff?"

"I suppose you're right."

"Of course I'm right!" Renee was on a roll now. "I'm your mother, dammit."

Elana couldn't help but smile.

"Even your father and I had some rough patches along the way."

"How do you know when a rough patch is the end though?" Elana asked.

"I don't know, sweetie. I guess when it doesn't feel worth fighting for anymore."

Elana finished her wine and set the glass on the coffee table.

"Thanks, Mom. As always. That was just what I needed."

Renee squeezed her daughter's shoulder. "Anytime, dear."

Elana kissed her on the cheek and stood up. "I'm going to head up to bed. I'm beat."

"Of course. See you in the morning."

Renee gently knocked on Elana's bedroom door the next morning and popped her head in.

"I made some breakfast, if you want to come down and join us."

"I'm not hungry right now," Elana said.

"You have to eat something, sweetie."

"I know. I will, I promise. I'm just not hungry right now."

Renee left the door ajar and headed back downstairs.

The doorbell rang, and Elana climbed out of bed to look out her window. She wasn't surprised to see Kyle's Lexus parked in front of the house. Elana walked to her door and listened through the crack as her father answered the door.

Kyle was the first to speak. "Good morning, Mr. Tanner. I was hoping I could talk to Elana."

"I'm afraid now is not a good time, Kyle," her father answered.

"I realize that, but I thought if I could just explain—"

Her father must have done something to cut him off. And then Mark spoke.

"I think it would be best if you didn't come by here anymore."

There was a pause.

"I understand," said Kyle. "Will you at least tell her that I love her?"

If her father responded, Elana couldn't hear it.

The door closed, and Elana went back to her window to watch Kyle walk back to his car. He was about to climb in when he looked up and caught sight of Elana. He just stared at her, looking lost, before finally getting into his car and driving off.

Elana crawled back into bed and began sobbing again.

Elana spent most of the week in bed, and by Thursday she decided it was time to stop feeling sorry for herself. With more effort than it should have required, Elana dragged herself out of bed and strapped on her running shoes. It was time to clear her head.

There was a black sedan parked outside the Tanner home when Elana returned from her run. Her pace slowed down while a gentleman climbed out of the driver's seat and walked around to the rear passenger door. Adelaide Barnett stepped out, and Elana groaned inwardly.

"Elana," said Adelaide, "I was hoping I could have a word with you."

Elana frowned, but nodded and led Adelaide inside.

"Can I get you something to drink?" she asked when she had closed the door behind them.

Adelaide did a once over of the house, but her impression of it remained unreadable. "No, I'm fine. Thank you for asking."

Elana sat on the stairs. She was too exhausted to try and keep up any appearances. "So what is it that you wanted to talk to me about, Mrs. Barnett?"

"Do you know who Reese Barnett is?" Adelaide asked.

"Reese?" Elana furrowed her brow, trying to think where she knew the name. "Oh, wasn't that the guild that did the auction?"

"The Reese Barnett Guild, yes."

"I don't know. One of Kyle's grandfathers, I assume." Elana was confused. Why the hell would Adelaide drive all this way just to give her a lesson on the family tree?

"Reese was Kyle's cousin. More accurately, his second cousin, and they were incredibly close."

Elana paid attention. She noticed Adelaide's use of the past tense.

"Reese's own father, Kyle's first cousin, was away on business quite frequently, and Kyle filled the void. He would take Reese to the ball games, the zoo, you name it. And he spoiled the hell out of that child every Christmas and birthday."

Elana closed her eyes. She knew where this was going.

"Then five years ago, only two weeks after his ninth birthday, Reese was diagnosed with acute lymphoblastic leukemia. He never made it to his tenth birthday."

Elana opened her eyes and wiped the tear that had run down her cheek. She noticed that even Adelaide's eyes were watering.

"A month later," Adelaide continued, "Kyle founded the Reese Barnett Guild with the proceeds benefiting ALL research."

"But I thought you were the president," Elana said.

"I am. Kyle was just getting his firm started and we decided I would take the helm. Most people assumed that it was my project, and Kyle preferred it that way."

"Does Victoria know this?" Elana couldn't help but ask.

"I'm not sure, but I don't think so."

Elana remembered Victoria's comment about this being Adelaide's night. "No, I don't think she does either."

"Kyle had never missed the Gala, which is held on Reese's birthday, or passed up the opportunity to present the check to The Children's Hospital at the end of the night. Until this year."

Elana closed her eyes again and felt sick to her stomach. Then they flew open. "But wait, you tried to have me banned from the event."

Adelaide sighed. "Yes. I knew Kyle would not miss it, and I thought that perhaps it would drive a wedge if you couldn't be there but he insisted on staying. I forgot just how persuasive my son could be."

"But then he did leave anyway. Because of me."

Adelaide nodded. "When you left, I thought that I had succeeded. But when he followed you, I knew I had underestimated just how much he cared about you. After the event I went to his apartment to give you both a piece of my mind. But I was shocked to discover that you were gone and Kyle was a mess."

Elana sat there feeling guilty, but then she looked up at Adelaide, feeling just as confused as when the woman had arrived.

"I still don't understand why you are telling me this. You've won. You made my life miserable as promised and I have left Kyle. Why are you here?"

"Because I was wrong."

Elana's eyes went big. Granted, she didn't know Adelaide that well, but Elana was fairly certain that those words didn't pass the woman's lip very often.

"I never believed that my son could truly be in love with you. But since you walked out Saturday night, Kyle has been miserable, and it is reflecting in his work. He is refusing to see clients, and I have received word that if he doesn't start meeting with the UW Medical developers soon, they are going to cut him from the project."

Elana gasped. "But he worked so hard on that. He was so proud!"

"I know. But he doesn't seem to care at this point."

"And why do you care now, Adelaide? You were the one who said you wished he had died instead of Jarod."

Adelaide sighed again. "I regret saying those words. I was rather...upset at that moment. But I honestly thought that by withholding my affection he might decide to let you go."

Elana was quiet as she considered everything Adelaide had just confided in her.

"I'm not saying that you and I will ever be chummy," Adelaide said. "But I am willing to accept you in Kyle's life if that is what truly makes him happy."

Elana knew this was as close to a peace offering as she was going to get from Adelaide. "Thank you," she said softly.

"And now if you'll excuse me, I have other appointments to attend to."

"Of course."

Adelaide prepared to walk out the front door and then turned back around. "And Ms. Tanner, I have called my colleague at PACCAR. If you are still interested in the job, then it is yours. Turns out they have been hard-pressed to find a candidate they liked as much you. Apparently you are an exemplary employee. You should be receiving a phone call later today. Let me know if you don't. You can also tell your parents as well that the little 'glitch' with the bank loan has been resolved."

Elana nodded. "Thank you," she said again. Adelaide was about to step out the door when Elana remembered something else.

"Kyle thinks you had a surrogate because you were worried about your figure," she called out.

Elana saw a hint of emotion cross Adelaide's face, but her voice was even. "I was not aware of that."

"He thinks that's why you loved Jarod more than him."

Adelaide's eyes softened with sadness. "Thank you for telling me." And she left.

Elana sat on the step for a moment longer and

then she suddenly jumped up and ran the stairs to get in the shower and dressed. There was somewhere she had to be.

Elana walked into Kyle's firm and was greeted by Michelle, who appeared shocked to see her.

"Is Kyle in?" Elana asked.

"Yes, but he has asked to not be disturbed," she answered.

"I'm sure he won't mind," Elana replied and started walking down the hall.

She opened the door to Kyle's office, where she found Kyle standing in front of the window. Just staring.

"I told you I didn't want to be disturbed," he snapped over his shoulder.

"I promise I won't be long."

Kyle spun around. "Elana!"

Her heart dropped. Adelaide wasn't kidding when she'd said he was a mess. He looked broken.

He started to walk towards her but then stopped.

"Your father said I wasn't welcome anymore."

"I know," she said. "Your mother came to see me. This morning."

"I'm so sorry," he started.

"No, it's okay. It was good, actually."

"It was?"

Elana took a step forward, lessening the gap between them. "Yes. She told me about Reese." She took another step and was able to reach out and grab his hand. "Why didn't *you* tell me?"

"I tried on Sunday, but your dad said you didn't want to talk to me."

"But why didn't you tell me before?"

"I don't know." Kyle took her other hand and

pulled her closer into him. "I was worried you wouldn't go if you knew my mother was going to be there. And then it just got to be too late. And once we were there, the gala didn't seem the right setting to share something that personal."

Elana sighed. "If we're in this together, you need to share these things with me."

Kyle pressed his forehead to hers. "I know."

"Do you promise to not keep me in the dark next time?"

Kyle's eyes brightened. "Does this mean there will be a next time?"

She smiled. "Only if you promise to stop shutting me out just because you worry how I will handle it."

"I promise, Elana." Kyle kissed her, and she felt the hole in her heart begin to heal.

She pulled away. "And I promise to trust you when you ask me to be there for you."

"I love you, Elana Tanner."

"And I love you, Kyle Barnett."

Epilogue

ELANA WOKE TO the sun peeking through the curtains of her bedroom window. She rolled over and was disappointed to find the other side of the bed empty. She and Kyle were putting in a lot of overtime lately, and she had been looking forward to a leisurely Saturday morning in bed with him.

A clang echoed from the kitchen below, and Elana figured it was Kyle already starting on the prep for their party that night. It had been six months since moving into the townhouse they had purchased together, and they were finally throwing a housewarming party for all their friends and family. Even Adelaide was planning to make an appearance.

Reluctantly climbing out of bed, Elana grabbed Kyle's t-shirt from the floor and threw it on. She walked downstairs into the kitchen and found Kyle making pancakes.

"Good morning," she called out and Kyle jumped.

"What are you doing out of bed?" he asked.

Elana frowned. "I could ask you the same thing. How is anyone supposed to sleep through all the racket you're making down here?"

"I was going to bring you breakfast in bed. It

was supposed to be a surprise."

"Well, we can eat here instead," she said.

"Please, just go back upstairs," he begged. "I'll be there in a minute."

She was confused, but curious. "Fine. But be quick. I'm hungry now that I can smell how delicious they are."

"I will. Now scoot." He smacked her bottom as she started to walk away. She let out a little yelp and hurried up the stairs, grinning.

She sat on the bed and rested her chin on her knees, wondering what the big deal was with serving her breakfast in bed. But Kyle kept his word and arrived shortly after carrying a tray full of warm breakfast goodies garnished with a plumeria blossom. He placed the tray on top of the comforter and sat on the bed next to her.

"On the menu this morning we have banana pancakes drizzled with coconut syrup," he announced.

Elana got excited as she sensed the theme. The only other time she'd had coconut syrup was in Hawaii. She picked up the cup of coffee and inhaled its aroma.

"Kona coffee," she sighed.

"There is even milk if you should feel the need to tarnish it."

Elana laughed, remembering the first time she served Kyle a cup of coffee that desperately needed it.

"Were you feeling nostalgic for Kauai this morning?" she asked.

"I was," he answered, "and for good reason."

"And why is that?"

"Because exactly one year ago today I ran into you at the Bar Acuda."

Elana screwed up her face. "That wasn't exactly a pleasant night."

"True. But it was the night that I found you, and that has made all the difference." He pushed a silver butter dish towards her plate.

"What's this?" she asked.

"Lift the lid."

She did and instead of butter, Elana found a diamond ring in the dish. She was speechless as her heart began to race wildly.

Kyle picked up the ring and took her hand. "Elana Tanner, would you do me the honor of marrying me?"

Elana's right hand clasped over her mouth. She couldn't believe this was happening. Then she removed it to speak. "Are you sure?"

Kyle was dumbstruck. "What?"

"Are you sure you want to spend the rest of your life with me?"

Kyle laughed. "Of course I'm sure. I put this all together, didn't I? The question is, are you ready to spend the rest of your life with me?"

Elana nodded enthusiastically. "Yes, Kyle! I'm ready to spend every day with you! Yes, I will marry you!"

The ring was slipped onto her finger and she kissed him. Lips still locked, he pushed her back onto the bed, careful not to knock over the tray.

"Wait," she interrupted, "what about the party tonight?"

He started kissing on her earlobe. "What about it? There's still plenty of time to get ready."

"But should we tell people?"

Kyle pushed up to look her in the face. "I have to admit that this whole time I was hoping to be able to turn it into a surprise engagement party."

She grinned. "You little devil!"

He smiled back.

"Do you think we should prepare your mother first? Might not be wise to spring this on her in the middle of everything."

He went back to leaving a trail of kisses on her neck. "We should probably call our parents first. But I don't want to think about it right now." He lifted up her shirt and started kissing her abdomen. "Right now I just want to make love to my fiancée."

"Mmm," she muttered enjoying the warmth of his lips on her flesh. "I like how that sounds."

He came back up and kissed her mouth. "And I *really* can't wait to make love to my wife."

"Sounds even better," she gushed. Then she laughed. "And to think exactly one year ago you were calling me a murderer."

Kyle frowned. "Regrettable words on my part. Turns out you were just a thief."

Now she frowned. "How so?"

"Because you stole my heart."

She giggled. "Well, then, I guess that makes two of us."

Acknowledgments

First off, I want to thank my fabulous friends Andrea and Tama for their input and especially for being my biggest cheerleaders. You ladies rock!

I also have to thank my amazing sister for her slave labor on the art work. Well, I don't have to, but I want to because I love you and I think you're pretty awesome!

And last, but certainly not least, I need to thank my wonderful husband for putting up with me through it all; the late nights, the neglected house and home. But you never (rarely) complained. Even before I decided I was going to be a writer, but knowing that I enjoyed writing, you bought me Stephen King's *On Writing* for my birthday all those years ago. I don't think you realized the chain reaction you were starting. And thank you for finally taking me to Hawaii, the trip that sparked this whole story. I love you and look forward to so many more adventures together.

Don't Miss

Love & Lies

A Romantic Suspense Series
by Alex Strong

CrossFire: Book 1

Now Way Out: Book 2

Ghost Lies: Book 3

Available on Amazon, Barnes & Noble, and
other on-line book retailers

Stay in Touch
AlexStrongWrites.com
Facebook.com/AlexStrongWrites
@TheAlex_Strong